Praise for

THE DRAGON LAIRD

4 ½ Stars
"This was a wonderful adult fairy tale and I could not put it down. I sat up until the wee hours of the morning in order to reach an astonishing ending, which left me eager for the sequel. Deborah Lynne has penned a captivating tale which can be enjoyed by romance and fantasy genre fans alike".

-- B Small, PNR

"This was an extremely enjoyable read. The mystic elements were well woven and kept me turning the page. Dylan and Rhiannon are wonderfully likable characters, and the author makes you really care about their fate and the union of the two. Also, I must say, Deborah does extremely well at love scenes. Hot and tense and totally in the moment. Definitely a book that lovers of wizards and dragons and love stories should put on their list of "To be read"

--Christi Jewell, romancejunkies.com

"An action-packed tale with ageless themes of good and evil -- and of course, love. Ms. Lynne doesn't just write about romantic love (though there's plenty of steamy romance!) her story also explores family love and loyalty. Thanks for the fun read!! It was so engrossing, I read it in one session."

--M.K. Rothwell

Novellas by DEBORAH LYNNE

The Dragon Sorcerer

THE DRAGON LAIRD

A fantasy romance by

DEBORAH LYNNE

♡
Echelon Embrace

Echelon Press
Crowley, Texas

Echelon Press
P.O. Box 1084
Crowley, TX 76036

Echelon Embrace
First paperback printing: June 2003

This is a work of fiction. Names, characters, places, and incidents are either the product of the author's imagination or are used fictitiously. Any resemblance to actual events, places, organizations, or persons, living or dead, is entirely coincidental.

Copyright © 2003 by Deborah Taylor
Cover Illustration Copyright © 2003 by Stacey L. King

Trade paperback ISBN 1-59080-233-0

All rights reserved. No part of this book may be used or reproduced in any form without permission, except as provided by the U.S. Copyright Law. For information, please address Echelon Press™, P.O. Box 1084, Crowley, TX 76036.

Published by arrangement with the author.

The name Echelon Embrace and its logo are trademarks of Echelon Press.

Printed and bound in the United States of America.

www.echelonpress.com

Acknowledgements

Thank you to Christie Brown and Yvonne Grapes, for all their support with the long hours of brainstorming, reading, and critiquing.

To Karen Syed, a long time friend and author.

But mostly to my husband David, who believed in me and gave me my inspiration.

Also to my two beautiful daughters Hope and Heather, who shared their mother with pen, paper, and a bit of magic weaving.

Thank you to all my readers for giving me your support.

Dedication

To my mother Eileen Yoakam. She always told me I could do anything I set my mind to. Love you, Mom.

Part of the royalties from this book will go to breast cancer research so our mothers will live longer, happier, lives.

Prologue

Scottish Highlands, Western Coast

"Sweet Virgin Mary." Dearg crossed himself as he cowered in the dark of the enchanted forest.

"Quiet, you fool, 'afore a harpy descends upon us," urged his companion, Ethan as he glanced around nervously. "Laird Dylan requested meat for his table, so let us be about the hunt, then leave this cursed place."

Dearg tilted his head back and stared up at the malevolent shadows of twisted tree limbs. No light penetrated the unholy darkness that deepened with each step. Suddenly a flicker of movement passed his vision.

Grabbing Ethan's arm, he pulled him to a stop. "What be that?" So powerful was his dread, he feared his legs would not hold him. They waited, their anxious gazes bored into grotesquely twisted mass of trees. Through the dancing leaves, the shadows flickered briefly on a huge mass moving toward them.

"There it be again."

"I see it," Ethan confirmed.

"I do not like this." Dearg's heart stopped in a moment of terror. His blood ran cold with fear.

He could take no more of these woods or their unseen forces! He turned to run, or crawl on trembling knees if he must, back to the great hall.

"Look, Dearg! 'Tis a dark cloud of smoke," Ethan whispered loudly, his voice shaking with fear.

Dearg's stride faltered as he turned to look where Ethan pointed. A great cloud of thick haze moved toward them with rapid speed. He heard the roar of trees and bushes being consumed. The very ground thundered with power.

Dearg sucked in a paralyzing gasp. "By the sword, 'tis dragon's breath. If it reaches us, we will be swallowed up and never found." He turned to flee and found Ethan had abandoned him to run ahead.

"Dragon's breath! Run, man!" Ethan yelled over his shoulder.

Dearg tried to make his legs move, but they felt leaden, as if they had grown roots. He screamed and forced his frozen legs to follow as the heat of fear crawled up his spine. His gaze fastened on Ethan, always keeping him in sight. Branches grabbed out at Dearg as he ran, trying to keep him from escaping. He jumped a rotten log then glanced toward his friend only to watch Ethan drop from sight, with one shrill, blood-stopping scream echoing round him.

Dearg rushed to where Ethan had disappeared. A huge pit yawned where the earth had fallen away, leaving only bared roots and rocks. "Ethan!"

His friend's cries came filled with pain and terror, but glancing back at the approaching black cloud, Dearg left the man to his fate. He took off, running into the darkness, his trembling legs barely carrying him. He prayed the forest would not devour him as panic fueled his need for life.

Chapter One

The tall, dark, wraith-like figure stood at the edge of the enchanted forest in the glowing pre-dawn. A large cloak and hood concealed his features and true form. He leaned over to adjust a bone-handled dagger in his deer-hide boots, then tugged on the leather straps laced to his knees. Heavy fog moved from the trees at his right to whisper around his form. He pulled an arrow from his quiver, notching it before moving to let the dark woods swallow him.

Not since his youth had Dylan Conner McGregor given thought to any religion, especially the ancient ones like the Druid, with its faeries and dragons. He believed in bow, blade, and the strength of his arm.

He was a warrior, a Laird. Magic and spells were for bard songs and old ones' tales. He came often to the enchanted forest, for the game proved plentiful as few entered. Now two of his men were missing.

They had been hunting in these woods some four days before. His clan, a superstitious lot, had claimed dragons ate the men. And of course, there was the bloody curse. He snarled. Since the day he was born, he'd been under its darkness. All foul deeds were laid at his door, his soul blackened, and his wants shunned, yet he carried the load as any man of honor to see his people safe, if even from himself.

He moved with purpose, pushing aside snarled vines,

jumping unearthed roots. Fog swirled around the forest floor, filling every low spot and creating a deceptive calm.

Above the trees, the sky brightened. Though he had started his search before dawn, the morning sun had caught up with him. With the greater light, he spotted a partially hidden animal trail off to his right. He crouched down and pushed the bushes to one side, examining closer the bare ground. Stag tracks marked the trail, but there were also human footprints. "So. I am not alone."

He glanced sharply around the forest for signs of life. It could not be Dearg or Ethan. The prints were too slender.

So—who? Puzzled, he followed the trail to a secluded pool where he stepped from the darkness into the light of heaven.

This place leapt from the very bard's tale of fairies and magic he could not disbelieve. Lilies and violets grew along the pool's edge. Ivy and ferns climbed up the rock face, worn smooth by water pouring from the lip to the pool below. The hypnotic cadence of water filled the glade with a mild, sensual music.

Streaks of gold ran diagonally through the rock, showering the area in sparkles of light as the sun peeked from between branches to touch the precious metal, a leaf, a flower, only to wink and touch something else. A soft mist hugged every tree root, every fern, and danced upon the water.

The voice of a siren came riding upon the wind, filling his mind. Softly at first, then stronger as she neared. Dylan stepped off the path to stand behind a large tree surrounded with berry bushes, waiting for the bearer to step forward.

His heart raced with the hunter spirit. Anticipation filled his every breath. He pulled his hood down farther to hide his face from the growing light. He kept his gaze fixed to the path and soon was rewarded as the holder of the sweet voice moved toward the pool.

Dylan drew in a breath. She was a vision. A golden light surrounded her as she danced and twirled on naked toes. A white chemise showed beneath her green kirtle. A flower wreath crowned hair that hung past her hips in fiery curls. Silk ribbons were woven among the flowers and fell to tangle along her back.

He digested her beauty and stared, spellbound. She moved with grace, as if floating on clouds. As she neared, the forest filled with exuberant life.

She bent under a bowed branch, seeking something among the patch of flowers, then she stood, twisting a white lily under her nose. Her voice permeated his mind until he heard nothing else. Her dress swayed with every twirl. She threw her head back, beseeching the sun's warmth, and held her arms wide, beckoning. She danced to the tune of mist and enchantment until she stood at the pool's lip.

Would she let the water kiss her warm flesh? His body hardened with the mental image of his hands caressing her soft pale body.

Driven by forces he knew well, he moved forward, but stopped by grabbing a branch. He feared she would disappear if she saw him.

A dozen butterflies took to the air as she passed, fluttering around her head and ankles like little faeries. They flew from one lacy-petaled flower to the other, careful not to get their dainty feet wet on the drops of moisture at the ends of each leaf. Some landed in the woman's fiery hair. He thought them drawn to the brilliant color as he was. Here stood a forest faery to steal his soul.

When she reached to remove her dress, pulling it over her

head, his body tightened with anticipation. Her chemise followed to glide over her shoulders, clinging to the tips of her breasts but a moment before sliding to the ground in a pool around her fragile ankles.

She thrust her fingers through her thick hair, lifting it off her neck, then let it fall. He felt her every move as if he were the one caressing her.

She closed her eyes, running long slender fingers down her throat and over a golden chain that caged a smooth white stone lying between her firm breasts. She moaned her enjoyment and rolled her head to one side. Her fingers continued down to a slim waist, which flared into womanly curved hips.

A powerful need welled up inside as he tried to believe what his eyes beheld. He wanted to make her his, here among the sweet violets. Stunned by his reaction to her, his knuckles whitened on the branch. He stifled a groan. He was not a callow youth, one who had not seen his first battle or taken his first woman; yet, she affected him so.

Unable to turn away, he watched her swing around and glance toward him. Her facial bones were delicately carved, her mouth full and ripe. Her eyes tore his soul from his body. If he had not believed in magic before, here it was in human form.

Her depthless emerald eyes reflected the forest. They shone with a wide-eyed innocence, yet showed intelligence and independence of spirit. Had she seen him? She seemed to look right through him. When she turned back to the pool, he realized she had not unearthed his hiding place among the shadows.

Still unhurried, she removed her flowered wreath and gracefully stepped into the water. The mist around the pool moved to enfold her like a lover. She sank into the water and out of sight, the vapor closing her in its protective shell.

When she did not reappear, he stepped out from his dark haven. Dylan drew back his hood. She was gone and he had nothing of her. Then the breeze caught one of the ribbons from her discarded wreath of wild violets, buttercups, and sprigs of lavender. He walked over to her clothes and picked up the wreath. A few strands of her fiery hair hung intertwined among the flowers.

Looking from the flowers that had crowned her head to the quiet pool, he whispered, "Whoever you be, know this, you have stolen my soul and one day I will have you."

With a sigh of regret, he moved back. He had to continue the search for his men, but he would carry her wreath with him.

Rhiannon emerged from the cool water to dress. She loved coming to this secluded pool in the mornings to bathe and had stayed longer than normal. However, something about this morning had been different. A feeling only, of being watched by a warm gaze, but having glanced around, she had seen no one. Few came to this forest. It held too much mystery and enchantment for the unwary traveler.

She felt safe in these woods, as if she belonged. No harm ever befell her here. Bending over, she twisted her hair to remove some of the water, then threw its wet length over her shoulder, giving it no mind. She dressed and stretched her hands overhead before bending down for her flower wreath. A quick scan of the area showed it missing. The uneasy feeling invaded her again, but she shrugged it off with mild annoyance. Perhaps an animal carried it away, or faeries found it to their liking.

She shook her head. She hadn't the time to worry over it.

Today she visited a friend who lived among these crooked trees and fallen leaves. Some called Dela a hag or witch, but to Rhiannon she was the grandmother she never had. Dela had the gift of sight, whether future, past, or present, and the gift of healing.

Rhiannon followed a well-worn path only she could see, for after she moved on, the ferns concealed her passing. A hint of wood smoke filled her senses as she walked around a shrub and stepped over a moss-covered log.

There, hidden among the overgrown ivy, she spotted the small wood cabin. Smoke curled from the rock and clay chimney. An alluring light glowed from the only window. Rhiannon walked up to the aged-wood door and knocked. She heard the clatter of things being moved and waited for an invitation.

"I have been expecting you," came a woman's voice from within.

Rhiannon pushed the creaky ancient door open and peeked around its worn edge to find its owner. "You are sure 'tis all right, Good Mother?" She knew the elderly woman was not well.

"Come in, lass. I have something important to tell you."

Rhiannon stepped in and shut the door. A warm fire blazed in a stone hearth off to her right. At the center of the burning heat hung a large cauldron suspended by chains from an iron tripod. A small iron pot hung higher by a swinging iron arm that projected from the hearth's stone wall.

Sweet rushes lay strewn over an earthen floor. Animal skins of every kind covered the walls; red deer, beaver, boar, and badger. The wooden planks above held bundles of drying herbs. A table with two benches huddled against the wall opposite the fire, a bed, and cupboard stood along the back.

Here was a place that felt like home, where she knew peace and comfort.

The old woman's long white hair stood out in stark contrast to the shadows near her bed. She hobbled toward Rhiannon and soon the firelight made her visible.

A knobby-jointed hand held the oak staff with which she supported her bowed back. Dark woolen clothing draped her thin body. Lines like spider webs fanned out from the corners of her mouth and eyes and across her forehead.

Dela had often claimed the eyes were a doorway to the soul. Rhiannon knew this to be true when looking into Dela's golden eyes, so like autumn leaves.

She moved over to help Dela settle down at the table, then planted a kiss on her time-worn cheek. "Has the light revealed something to you?" Rhiannon sat, biting at her finger while she waited for an answer.

"Aye, my child. I was told you would come today. The light has given me a peek of your future."

"My future?" Excitement poured over her and she put her hands down to clutch at her skirt.

Though in her eighty-third year, Dela's eyes remained sharp as a youth's and her voice soothing. The old one took Rhiannon's hands from her lap and clutched them between both of hers. Her intense tawny stare held Rhiannon's gaze.

"Listen well, young one, for the knowledge I give you may save your life. You are about to embark on a great adventure, as well as find from whence you came."

Rhiannon would have interrupted, but Dela tilted her head forward in warning to wait. "Among enemies, a warrior who carries the dragon's mark will be the half you seek in destroying evil."

Frowning, Rhiannon could restrain her question no longer.

"Am I to love an enemy?"

Dela held up a knobby hand to forestall her. "I have taught you not to judge others without weighing their actions. Some enemies may be truer than friends. Do you still have the Moonstone I gave you?"

Rhiannon flattened her hand over her chest; feeling for the cool, smooth stone resting there. "Aye. 'Tis always here, next to my heart."

"'Twill give you protection. 'Twill shine it's brightest and burn like fire when evil is about."

Unable to contain herself, Rhiannon asked, "What will my family think if I side with the enemy?"

"Rhiannon, you are not of their blood. I have told you this many a time 'afore. 'Twas I who brought you and your brother out of these woods and gave you unto their keeping. Your younger sibling has no memories of the forest, or the other time. But it still lives within you."

Rhiannon sighed. A sense of finality settled over her need to belong. Mayhap she was always meant to be outside looking in. "What must I do?"

"You must mate with this dark warrior and combine your strengths, or death and pain will visit us all."

"I cannot do this. I have no knowledge of bedding, and afterwards, I will be an outcast."

Dela crossed her fingers and pressed them on the center of Rhiannon's forehead. Rhiannon closed her eyes as the warmth of the woman's touch burned into her thoughts. "'Tis so important that you follow my words, Rhiannon. Remember what I say, and know I will be with you." The old one's hand fell away, but the feeling of being alone did not return. Rhiannon opened her eyes to face Dela once again, but this time with a purpose of heart.

"You must show the warrior the light, dear one, for darkness has a hold on him. The Light of Goodness is strong in you and bravery runs in your veins. Evil follows close behind and wants to destroy you."

Fear welled inside Rhiannon and must have shone on her face, for Dela smiled encouragingly. "Have no fear, young one. The Light looks after her chosen. Your life's path is written in the stars." She patted Rhiannon's hand. "I can see the questions hanging on your soul, but I cannot tell you more. 'Tis not wise to know too much of one's future."

Doubt clouded Rhiannon's mind. If she failed, Dela said pain and death would befall them. How could she do what was asked of her?

"Child, do not doubt yourself. Doubt comes from the darkness. Draw your strength from the forest. Within its arms comes the light." The witch stood, took a jug from beside the stone hearth, and set it on the table. Two cups rested near at hand. She poured a portion of the warm mead into each. Steam curled from the mug as she handed one to Rhiannon. "Here, drink."

She took a sip. The mead tasted sour with a touch of sweetness, but it warmed her insides, and she drank deeper.

"Now, tell Dela what is on your heart."

Rhiannon set the mug down on the table and ran a finger around its chipped rim, finding the right words to speak. "The McKays have taken my brother Robbie under their wings, and for this I am grateful. *Och*, but I feel like an unwanted relative, so out of place within their dark walls. I serve them, tending their sick and wounded with the knowledge of healing, but I come alive only in this forest."

She thought she caught a knowing glint in the witch's eyes before Dela turned her head.

"Well, I have told you 'afore child, my door is always open."

Rhiannon nodded and Dela rewarded her with a pat on the shoulder.

"Soon your life will change. Mark my word, the passion that yet sleeps within you will burst forth, and you will sit in a place of honor. I admire your spirit to cope with what life has given."

Rhiannon's gaze fell to the steaming amber liquid in her mug. How could she bed with an enemy? It ran against everything inside her. Her sense of loyalty and honor warred with her need to do what she must to save herself and others.

What was to come? She glanced up to see Dela smile and wondered again if the old one could not read minds as well.

"Come, young flower, today you will help me heal the sick. Leave your innocent doubts of the future for tomorrow. All will be as it should be."

Chapter Two

Robbie burst into Rhiannon's bedroom. "I am going," he shouted, grabbing her around the waist and swinging her around.

Even though only fifteen, he stood a half-foot above her. His hair, black with fiery highlights, hung straight and long about his shoulders, curling slightly to the ends. His greenish-brown eyes twinkled with excitement.

She laughed, grabbing his shoulders for balance. "*Och,* lad, you make me dizzy. Hold still and tell me where you are going?"

"I am off to fight the McGregors and bloody my sword."

Rhiannon tightened her lips and shoved his chest to make him set her down. "Nay, you will not. I'll not be losing you to a clan feud that is not even our own."

"You will not say nay. We are McKays. The fight is ours."

"Nay, it was started eons ago 'afore we were born. 'Tis no fight of ours."

"I have waited a long time for this, Rhiannon, and I will be taking the test of manhood as did our father and his father 'afore him," Robbie shouted, a scowl marking his face.

She knew she had spoiled his moment of glory, but it could not be helped. A great fear wrapped around Rhiannon's heart. She might never see him again.

"Where are all those proud men now, I ask you?" Rhiannon stormed her hands on her hips. "Moldering in their graves, they are, leaving us to fend for ourselves. I will not be left alone. Do you hear? You are all I have."

Rhiannon turned her back and squeezed her eyes shut. Her hands twisted the fabric of her dress, and a terror raged through her soul, causing her heart to cramp with pain. He was her whole family. She had known this day would come, but facing it now was inconceivable. She wasn't ready for this and guessed she never would be. What happened to their youth? He was grown and would make his own way, and his choices might take his life.

Robbie took hold of her shoulders and gently turned her, pulling her into his arms. She rested her head on his shoulder and wrapped her arms around him tightly, holding on to something so dear.

"Have no fear, Rhiannon. I'll not be dying like the others. But you knew this day would come." He echoed the thoughts she would not speak aloud. "'Tis something I must do. I have worked for this day all my life. I will go with or without your approval. But as I go to my first battle, I would have your blessing."

Rhiannon knew she had lost. She squeezed him, adding all the emotion swelling in her heart. The thought of him lying on a battlefield alone, his life's blood pouring to the ground, made her sick with dread. "Is there naught I can say to sway your mind then?" A warm tear ran from the corner of her eye. She already knew the answer.

"Nay."

"Then I give you my blessing and pray 'twill keep you safe."

Robbie stepped back to look at her and smiled. "How

could it not? 'Twas you who kept me safe all these years past. 'Twill be you that keeps me safe many years to come. Only now I will protect you as well."

Rhiannon made an effort to smile and swept her hand toward the door. "Away, lad, I have work to do."

"Thank you, Rhiannon," he said as he dashed out the door.

Hot tears trickled down her cold cheeks. She looked again at the gray, stone walls of her room in the north tower. No colorful tapestries warmed their cold damp surface, and her only furnishings were a straw mattress with a wool blanket and a small side table. How fitting that her life was as barren as the room she lived in.

Standing at the window, she glanced down at the torch-lit bailey below, raising her gaze to stare longingly at the moonlit forest beyond the gates. It whispered to her on the night's breeze. *"Soooon, soooon."* The forest warned her of something, but her mind clouded with Robbie and the battle. She shook her head to clear her thoughts, and the night quieted.

Out of long habit, Rhiannon reached for the dainty gold chain around her neck. She rubbed the smooth Moonstone between her fingers. Its familiar touch quieted her fears. She would find a way to keep Robbie safe.

A murky cloud passed over the moon, shutting out the light and casting dark shadows in Teg McDonald's way, but he reached the tomb without mishap. He grasped the iron ring of a stone door marked in intricate Celtic designs and gave a mighty heave. It opened on well-oiled hinges. He stepped inside and pulled the door closed with a swish, leaving himself encased in stone walls and naught but stale air to breathe.

He hated the dark and the forces that lived within it. So why was he, a simple man, forced to do this job? Perhaps, it was his greed, but whatever drew him here, he had no power over it. He slid his hand down one wall to find a torch and with the strike of flint lit it. The illumination showed stairs leading into the bowels of the earth. The smell of rotting flesh came up from the hellhole. He gagged on the stench before descending the stairs.

As he moved deeper into the earth, the eerie darkness closed in behind him. His hand brushed against the damp wall, and he shook off the sticky green slime that layered the cold stone. The squeaking of rats somewhere ahead made him squint to see beyond the darkness. The stairs ended abruptly at an opening to a larger passageway.

A gust of wind loomed up from ahead to lance his face with smells of mildew and putrefied remains. His torch spit and sputtered before flaring brighter. Large rectangular holes holding decomposing corpses gaped in the walls on both sides. Celtic designs marked their passing in the stone at their heads.

Teg spotted something sparkling in one of the holes and moved closer. The emerald and diamond ring would buy him many nights in a bonnie wench's bed. When the ring would not easily slide off the bony finger, he snapped the bone and grabbed the ring without remorse. He smiled and held it to the light, admiring its worth.

A prickling of something sliding around his throat made him reach up and touch his skin. Nothing surrounded his neck, but he found it hard to breathe. He panicked, as the pressure increased, cutting off his air. He dropped the ring and torch, clawing at his throat with desperation.

Then, on a whisper of wind, came a malevolent voice. "You would keep me waiting, while you steal baubles from the dead."

"S-sorry, M-master." Teg struggled. The pressure around

his neck released, and he took gulping breaths of air. Glad for the reprieve, he leaned down to pick up the torch. Spying the ring again, he carefully slipped it into his pocket before standing. He stepped hesitantly forward a little further before entering through an arched doorway to his left.

A large fire burned in a pit against the wall to his right. Shadows of flickering firelight climbed up the walls, like fingers from hell, giving the room an eerie, forbidden atmosphere. A shiver of dread ran the length of his body.

In the illumination, he spotted a figure bent over something on a table. He could not tell what because the Sorcerer had his back turned to him. The man wore the hood and robes of a monk, but a sense of the unholy clung heavily about him.

Here stood evil.

Teg broke out in a sweat, fearing what lurked in the gloom of the Sorcerer's mind. With a certainty, he knew the mage was aware of his presence. While waiting to be addressed, he looked about the room.

A workbench with an assortment of jars and bottles, as well as dried plants for potions sat across the back wall.

A moan came from one corner of the room and he turned toward the sound to see a tortured being chained to the stone wall. He crossed himself as apprehension clenched his stomach. Dozens of cuts covered the human's body. He could not tell if it was male or female because so much flesh was torn away. Its eyes had been burned from its head, leaving only blackened sockets.

A cackle came from the Sorcerer. "You do well to cross yourself in my presence. Have you found the daughter of Meg, Giver of life?"

"Aye, *Maighstir*."

"Gaelic is forbidden. I will not hear it from your lips again. Now tell me where she is hidden."

"She lives at the McKay's stronghold."

A low growl came from the door Teg had just entered. He turned to see the flash of white fangs exposed in a menacing snarl. Teg feared to breathe, for the bitch kept her silver gaze fastened to him and her snarl in place, even as she moved to sit by the Sorcerer's feet. The graceful movement of the black hound told why he had not heard it earlier.

The Sorcerer stroked the hound's head with a gentle caress, a gesture out of character for one so evil.

The mage stepped away from the table to a rack of drying plants, exposing what he was working with. A shallow bowl filled with a thick red liquid sat in the middle of the table. The light from a tall tallow candle set in an iron cup danced off the ruby fluid. Beside the bowl lay a narrow crooked stick and a Celtic ceremonial dagger.

The Sorcerer's voice broke the silence. "Soon, after all these years, I will have the gate and the power of nature will be mine."

The mage turned then to pierce him with his stare. Here stood a savage, unheedful of the laws of God, a demon bound only by his own evil intent. Teg quickly turned away and took a step back.

"You are wise not to look upon me." The Sorcerer said. "Now bring her here. I will have her blood. Moreover, I must keep her from finding the key. For if the two consummate, my plans may fail. Go now and do not disappoint me." The hooded man bent down and stroked the hound again. "For Balin is a faithful bitch, and if I bid her to rip out your throat and feast on your heart she would naught hesitate. Then 'twill be your blood I drink."

The Dragon Laird

* * *

Rhiannon did not have much time. Robbie, as well as most of the clan's men, would meet and march to the battlefield this morning, and she planned to follow. It had been three days since she had agreed to let Robbie have his wish. Not a lot of time to see her plans ready.

A knock on her chamber door interrupted her thoughts. "You may enter."

"'Tis I, Lady." A young, dark-haired chambermaid entered, carrying a tray. "I brought food for your journey. I will set it here—" She indicated the table with a nod, "'Til you are ready."

"You are very helpful, Ora. Tell me, have my cousins left yet to recruit for the battle?"

"Nay, lady, they be breaking their fast yet."

"Good. Thank you. You may go. I shall not be needing you again this day." When the maid did not leave, Rhiannon tilted her head to one side. "Speak."

"'Tis a fair bit of worry I have for your safety, Lady Rhiannon. Will you not change your mind?"

"Do not be afraid for me, Ora. I will be fine." Rhiannon moved to the table and picked up something wrapped in linen. "Take this and wear it."

Ora took the small cloth and unfolded it. She sighed, her small eyes widening and her lips forming an "O". "'Tis a Scottish thistle."

"'Tis magic. 'Twill give me luck on this journey, if worn near the heart of a friend. 'Twill also bring you luck as well."

"Thank you, lady. May the goddess you are named after give you her protection. I will wear it 'til you are home once more."

After the maid left, Rhiannon quickly added the cheese,

bread, and two apples Ora had given her to the small pack she would carry. She also added a bottle of heather wine and strips of linen to bind wounds.

In a small pouch bound at her waist she carried a bone needle, silk, mint, and sheep's fat salve with elder bark and a bit of sorrel.

She had no idea how long the march would be, but she dared not take more. With a swift glance, she looked around before slipping from her room and closing the door.

Rhiannon took care going down the steep stairs. Silence was her main goal, hoping she would not meet anyone on the way out.

Boisterous laughter made her pause a moment at the bottom step. The mirth came from her cousins in the great hall to her right. Her brother would be sitting with them as they broke their fast.

A whisper in her head warned she was on a fool's quest. She glanced uneasily over her shoulder. Was she doing the right thing? Then a greater voice pushed her on with urgency. *Aye, this was meant to be.* Turning to her left, she passed through the kitchen, which lay on the backside of the castle and slipped out the door.

A shiver of relief coursed through her body. No one had stopped her. She took a deep, cleansing breath. Spring's early morning air carried a nip, but she gloried in its freshness.

"Rhiannon McKay, what are you about?"

Startled, she jumped and spun around. Her old nanny came, bearing a cloak over her arm. "I'm going for a walk, Beitris," Rhiannon answered, her heart slowing somewhat. At first, she had thought one of her cousins had found her out, but that was unlikely. Only two people knew her plan: Ora, her trusted maid, and her friend, Fianna.

"'Twould be best not to be forgetting your cloak, or you will come down sick," the woman chided and placed the cloak around her shoulders. "There my child. Now be off with you. Enjoy an hour or two while you can."

"Thank you, Beitris. 'Tis a blessing you are." Rhiannon yanked the edges of her cloak together and headed for her loyal friend's hut in the village. The rest of her things were hidden there.

Fianna's small cottage stood but an arrow shot from the main castle. Rhiannon hoped to catch her alone. She remembered the day they had first bonded as friends. It happened during a foot race one spring when they were fourteen. Both were out in front hoping to win the May crown. When the finish line came in sight Fianna turned to her and said, "I have not the strength left to win. So 'tis yours."

"Nay! Finish with me! I am as winded as you." They both giggled as they reached the finish line where Rhiannon slowed, letting Fianna take the crown. Months later, Fianna married the May king.

Rhiannon smiled at the memory and waved to the blacksmith's wife, Edana, who carried a large bucket of ash. Edana brushed a wisp of blonde hair from her eyes with the back of one hand, leaving a soot mark across her pale cheek as she returned her wave.

The clanging of the sword maker's hammer echoed along with the neighing of horses. The smells of animals, manure, hay, and the iron master's wood fire scented the air.

Smoke curled from the chimney of Fianna's dwelling attesting to the warmth inside. The hide-covered window and wooden door remained closed against the previous night's chill.

The early hour gave Rhiannon a moment's pause. Would she be intruding? Fianna knew she would visit this morning, but her husband, Sheen, would join the fight and mayhap they were spending time in an intimate farewell.

The door swung open before Rhiannon could knock and a young woman with long dark hair and twinkling blue eyes stepped out, only to be caught from behind by the strong arms of her husband. Fianna squealed happily as he twirled her around.

He set her down on her feet and pulled her close. His eyes shone with the smoldering fire of pleasure.

Rhiannon felt her cheeks heat at their by-play and knew she intruded. She envied her friend's happiness and knew no one deserved it more.

"I spoil you, lass," Sheen commented.

"Aye, you do, husband," Fianna cooed, running her fingers down his bearded cheek.

He caught her hand to him. "I would have it no other way." He brought his lips to hers with great force.

Rhiannon looked on wide-eyed, fearing the slight woman would break in half, but noticed her friend giving as good as she got. Sheen put Fianna from him. A large smile curved his lips.

"Lass, if I touch you again I will not be leaving. You ken?"

She laughed. "I ken." Then she sobered. "If I had my way I would keep you with me or I would follow you to the battlefield."

"I know this too, sweet lass, but we have a bairn growing strong within you, and I want my wee laddie safe and warm." Sheen placed his hand over her small rounded belly.

"Promise me you will come home," Fianna pleaded.

"Aye, love. In but three days I will be with you again. I have a lad to name."

"And if it be a lass?"

He laughed then turned to Rhiannon. "My lady, see that Fianna does not work too hard."

"Have no fear, I will send her my maid so the hours will not be lonely 'til your return."

He nodded his thanks then held his wife's gaze once more. "I must take my leave of you now."

"I pray the gods keep you well, husband."

"I love you, Fianna McFie."

"And I, you, Sheen McFie." She watched him walk off toward the castle until he disappeared around the corner of its stone wall.

Rhiannon turned back and saw tears rolling down her friend's pale cheeks. Without hesitation, she pulled Fianna into her arms.

"Cry not, sweet lady. You have the bairn to hold safe. Naught but pleasant thoughts must enter your heart to ease its way."

"I know this, Rhiannon, but of late I am often weepy."

"'Tis normal, I have heard."

Fianna moved to open the door. "Come inside."

"I am sorry to have interrupted your morning. I have to say if Sheen were my man I would stop him from going."

Fianna raised her eyebrows and smiled as they stepped into the one room cabin. "You mean like you stopped Robbie."

"*Och*." Rhiannon burst out laughing, as did Fianna. They closed the door. "Aye, I think men put battle as their first love and women are even with food."

"'Tis pride that comes first to them, Rhiannon. Remember that and always have a care for it. For if 'tis broken, the man has lost everything."

"Married life has made you wise of men. I still have not

figured them out," Rhiannon said, shrugging.

"I am so glad you came. I need to keep my mind busy so images of Sheen and battle do not fill it."

Rhiannon sighed and took Fianna's hand. "Forgive my rudeness, but I have naught the time to chat. I am in need of the things I hid here. Do you still have them?"

"Aye." Rhiannon followed Fianna. "They lie under the bed. Do you still plan on going through with this?"

"Aye."

"You are a strange one, Rhiannon. What will happen when you are found out? For 'tis certain you will be."

"I cannot think on that. 'Tis as if some unseen force guides my way."

Fianna shook her head. "I will pray for you, as I do my husband. I wish I could follow you. While you dress, let me fix us something warm to drink."

Rhiannon watched Fianna turn to put a black pot on the fire and pour a bucket of water into its depths, then set a jug of mead near the flames to warm.

She wondered again if she were doing the right thing. But only a belief that she followed her fate filled her thoughts. Reaching under the bed, Rhiannon pulled out a woolen bag and set it on the bed. She undressed first by removing her kirtle, then her chemise, standing naked in the small room. "I pray your husband has not forgotten something and decides to come home."

The other woman turned with a smile. "Aye. Let me tie the door rope to give some security. I fear the shock of seeing you naked would kill him."

Fianna moved toward the door as Rhiannon took a strip of the linen she brought for bandages and bound her breasts. If she was to look and act like a boy, she could not have an upper curve to her chest. While the strip did not flatten her well, it was enough. She was thankful the gray shirt would hang loosely.

"Are these Robbie's clothes?" Fianna asked, having locked the door and was now testing the mead for warmth.

"Nay. He would know 'twas me when he saw the clothes. I bought them from a goat-herder a few days ago. The lad did not ask any questions when I handed him a silver piece. He pulled his shirt and kilt off right there and handed them to me." She had warmed with embarrassment, yet took the clothes and hid them away in her woolsack.

Rhiannon wrinkled her nose at the stench of stale body odor. Hopefully, it would keep people from getting too close to see through her disguise. The kilt hung large, so she tied a rope belt around the plaid to keep it on her hips. The clothes on, she moved to her hair. She hung her head upside down and her hair swept to the floor.

She braided the heavy mass all the way to the end and tied it off with a ribbon. Then she stuffed the fat braid down the back of her shirt and covered her head with a large cap. That done, she walked to the fireplace and ran her hands over the soot covered edges.

"Rhiannon, what are you doing? Your hands will be black."

"I need to conceal my features somehow." So saying, she smeared the ash over her face, arms, and into her hair. Now the smell of charred wood mixed with that of the body sweat clinging to the unwashed clothes.

"I swear all those potions you mix have worn your sense away," Fianna said. "You look like a hermit and smell like a fouled stable yard."

"Aye. I do." She laughed, fastening a small sword on the

belt around her waist and slipping a dagger into her boot. "Now, naught to do but sit awhile and wait."

"Please do so over yonder 'afore you make me lose what little I have eaten." Fianna pointed to a spot far from where she worked, a cloth covering her nose and mouth.

As Rhiannon moved off, she said, "I would guess from your reaction no one will bother me." Smiling, she wiggled down in the corner of the room and leaned her head back against the wall. Having had little sleep the night before, she closed her eyes and waited for Fianna to bring her a mug of warm mead, but weariness carried her to sleep, and she dreamed.

She stood by the quiet pool in the forest. Her eyes closed as the mist swirled around her. She belonged here. Then on the air, a voice like fluttering leaves whispered. The voice was too far off to hear clearly. She opened her eyes, waiting intensely for the voice to speak again. The forest was trying to tell her something. Then the words came again and she heard the whisper.

"My goddess, Rhiannon, come. I am the key."

The key?

The clouds of mist rolled back to reveal a path, leading to a small clearing where the sun concentrated all its blinding light and radiant heat.

Rhiannon gasped and shielded her eyes. Crowned with sunbeams sat a strong warrior upon a golden war-horse. The man's black hair hung long with small braids on each side of his face. He was wrapped in a plaid of fiery crimson and held the legendary emerald Singing Sword unsheathed and ready to ward off any attack.

The warrior sat straight and proud, easily commanding the spirited steed beneath him. The pair's very presence demanded respect. Yet when he turned his hard steel blue eyes upon her, they softened with affection and shone with intense sexual heat. He reached out his hand.

"Mo luaidh coille sithiche, Mi feith o chionn fhada thu—My beloved forest faery, I have waited long for you."

The ancient Gaelic rolled off his lips, and caressed her soul. She shivered with pleasure and knew his warmth. She would love this man.

"Come! You are mine!"

"Aye." Even without touching, she knew him. She offered her hand and he pulled her up into his arms. "'Tis fate," he whispered along her neck, then kissed her. But before the kiss ended, blackness swallowed him up. Stone walls surrounded her. An evil presence became a barrier between them. She shivered and wrapped her arms around herself for protection from the cold and loneliness. An unseen force held her trapped by walls of smoke. Her warrior called to her, and she fought the darkness with a cry.

"Rhiannon, Rhiannon." She awoke with a start, looking up into Fianna's face. "I let you sleep as long as possible, but your cousins are now outside recruiting fighters. Here, drink this." She shoved a mug of steaming mead into her hands. "You must hurry if you are to join them."

"Aye, and thank you for waking me." Rhiannon swallowed the warm brew. The dream, always disturbing, affected her more so each time it came. The first time had come after the telling of her future by Dela. Normally the dream's end left her empty and cold, but this time an evil presence filled that place inside and it frightened her.

As she stood, a horrible smell invaded her nose. "I fear I have fouled your house with my stench. This goat-herder feared water and lye soap."

"You do smell." Fianna smiled, wrinkling her nose. "I am betting you will not last the three days there and back without washing."

Stepping to the small hut's only window, Rhiannon peeked out from under the animal skin covering. The length of the shadows told her morning had passed to early noon.

She searched the gathering crowd of peasants and fighters, spying her male cousins and her beloved brother not more then twenty paces from the door. Her time had come to join them.

"I need bid you farewell," she said, handing the empty mug back to her friend.

"Do not be silly. Farewell seems so final. This is but a short parting, so I will say, may the gods guard your path."

"Thank you." She went to hug Fianna then remembered her filth and stepped away. "I will not hug you, but will you take my hand?" For some reason, Rhiannon had the feeling her life would be forever changed by what she did here, but she would accept her fate what ever came.

"Aye," Fianna answered grabbing her hand in a strong clasp. "May the gods bring you happiness."

"And may the gods protect you and yours too, my friend," Rhiannon said before stepping outside to be surrounded by men of all sizes and class.

As the men milled around, waiting for the order to move out, some pawed through their packs, others adjusted their swords or tartans, and hugged their women.

Rhiannon secretly watched her brother scan the crowd. She knew he waited for her to come send him off with a hug. He would be heartbroken when she did not, but when they reached the field of battle she would reveal herself so he would know he was not alone. She would stand with him in all things. He must know this. But every time he looked toward the castle, the knife of guilt jabbed in a little farther.

The horn blared, calling all to follow Laird McKay to an uncertain future. As the clan rode horseback or hiked through the moors on their way to the battlefield, she feared talking to anyone. Discovery lurked at every turn.

She had grown up tending the wounds and ministering to the sickness of these very people and feared someone might recognize her. Rhiannon had not thought much about the McGregors until Robbie wanted to join the fight. Both clans had feuded for a hundred years.

She remembered stories from her youth about the McGregors stealing crying babies from their beds and filling their bellies with their innards. Now older, she knew they were stories to make children behave. However there were still many legends and superstitions whispered about Laird Dylan McGregor.

It was said he stood cursed and without wife because no earthly woman would have him. If the stories were correct, even his father had not given him welcome for fear of an evil curse.

Now she wondered about the man who ruled alone, for she knew the sting of loneliness. Yet, she still had Robbie, Dela and Fianna to make her life easier. To have no one would surely make the mind crack. Had that happened to this Laird? Mayhap she would see for herself on the marrow.

The day wore on and the shadows grew long as evening fell. Her feet hurt and her shoulder ached from the pack's weight, but nothing could cloud the wonder of the sights around her.

A mist rose out of the marsh, hugging both sides of the road to swirl around the men's feet. When the evening sun hit it, a rainbow arched across their path. She slowed a moment, watching man after man walk beneath the arc, unmindful of its beauty. Though her trip would end in a bloody battle, she could not help but smile as she drank in the rolling green hills of Scotland. For that she got an elbow in the ribs.

Turning, she glared at the man walking beside her. She had helped deliver Nel's child last week.

"You are a bit too excited. This must be your first battle," he said.

Before she could answer, Evans, one of the keep guards, on her opposite side, joined in. "Nel, you leave the young lad alone now and hush your mouth. We are getting close to the battlefield."

"I say 'tis not right to be smiling about the day of dying. 'Twill bring us bad luck. That be my last words on the matter."

Nel was right. Men would die tomorrow morning. Husbands, fathers, lovers, cousins, friends, sons, and—brothers. Her steps faltered.

It was too late for second thoughts, and she could not leave her brother alone. She would do what she must.

They reached the battlefield just before sunset and set up camp. The hillside twinkled with many campfires created for warmth and protection.

Rhiannon stood back from the small fire that Nel, Evans, and a newcomer had built, yet close enough to be safe. Seeing others bring out food, and drink, she glanced around for a comfortable place to sit so she could eat as well.

The cold night breeze blew up her kilt and again she wished she had her long kilted skirt. She did not understand how men went without clothes covering their male parts from the cold. Her seat ached from the icy wind.

She chose a log to sit on and pulled out a strip of dried mutton to chew. Her nervous stomach protested. She forcefully swallowed, knowing her body needed the nourishment. Glancing toward the hill on the far side of the field, she saw the lights of the McGregor's fires and wondered what tomorrow would hold.

Unfamiliar warmth tingled across her chest like spider legs. She frowned and unconsciously placed her hand over her breasts. Warmth radiated from her Moonstone. Dela had said it would grow warm when evil neared. She shook as fear, stark and vivid, knotted her insides. She scanned the camp but saw nothing out of the ordinary. Knowing dark forces stood near made her skin prickle. She had to find her brother.

Rhiannon shoved her food back into the pack and made her way through the crowded camp, glancing right and left. As she hurried along, the Moonstone cooled.

On instinct, she glanced back the way she had come, scanning the trees at the edge of camp. Somewhere beyond, evil waited. She could feel its suffocating force and shivered. How had it found her? Or was there another reason for it to be here?

Turning back, she searched every fire-lit face for the one, she held dear; Rhiannon spotted the tall form of her brother seated with her two cousins a stone's throw away. She advanced close enough to hear what they spoke of, but kept in the shadows.

"What festers in you, lad?" Laird Geoffrey McKay asked. "Tomorrow you take your rightful place among the clan."

Robbie raised his head to look at Geoffrey. "'Tis not like Rhiannon to not see me off. Something must be wrong."

"She is naught but a woman, Rob. Who can know their ways? Put it from your mind." Geoffrey turned to his brother. "Tristan, pour the lad some good Scottish whiskey."

Tristan smiled as he threw the animal-skin bag at Robbie.

"Just raise the bag to your lips and take a deep drink. 'Twill warm your innards."

Rhiannon watched Robbie drink from the skin, then hand it back to Tristan. Her brother squeezed his eyes shut and blew out a breath. She smiled, sure the whiskey made a path of fire down his throat, but he had been given whiskey at an early age for colic and knew the burn of it. Robbie returned to his frowning, and she knew he worried about her.

It was time to ease his concerns. While her cousins conversed, she walked up behind Robbie and bent to whisper in his ear. "Come away quietly. I have news from Rhiannon."

She could feel his gaze bore into her back as she moved into the shadows. He quickly jumped up to follow, closing the distance in two quick strides. Then he grabbed her arm, turning her around. "Tell me what you know or I shall shake it from you."

Rhiannon saw they stood far enough away so no one could hear and whispered, "Did you not ken I would see you safe, Robbie."

He frowned.

She smiled, knowing her disguise a good one if she could fool her brother. "Do you not recognize your own sister?"

She watched enlightenment fill his face, as he looked her over with shock. "I swear Rhiannon, are you daft?

"Hold your voice down," she said, glancing quickly around before looking back at him.

"By the gods! You're wearing men's clothing, you've smeared yourself with filth and smell like you came from the swine yard."

She gave a cheeky smile. "*Och*, do not *Fesh* yourself, Robbie. 'Tis naught a good bar of lye can not fix."

A frown marred the curve of his brow. "There will be

blood letting tomorrow. How will I pass my test if I worry over you?"

"Do not fear for me. I can fend for myself. Besides, I had not a choice. I have always been with you in all your learning. Did you think this would be different?"

When he did not respond, she grabbed his hand, then quickly let go in case someone looked on. "Robbie, I will stay away from the fighting, but I would be close if you have need of me. I fear there is evil about." Again, she looked toward the woods.

He lowered his head with a shake. "You have always been different. Dela did right in naming you after our goddess."

Swinging her gaze back, she said, "Now go to your rest and be at peace. I will see you become a man on the morrow. You do your family proud. I love you, brother." She could barely see through the tears clouding her vision. She knew she could not reach out to him, and he must have realized it as well. He had stepped forward then stopped. The need to touch reflected in his eyes. She held his gaze as he held hers and in a blink of time, all their shared memories converged to strengthen an already unbreakable bond. She knew he too felt it.

"And I you, sister."

"Sleep well. May the gods go with you."

"And may the gods protect your way as well."

She sensed his gaze following her as she went back to her fire. Her clansmen were already asleep. Tired, she sat down on the ground and leaned her head back against the log. With the rising sun, so many would die. May the gods have mercy on them all!

Chapter Three

Rhiannon woke with a start to the sound of clanging claymores and battle-axes. She glanced at the brightening sky from where she lay on her back, but the sun had yet to show its face. Rolling over, then sitting up, she reached out to the warmth of the fire someone had kept burning through the night.

Fear folded in on her. When the sun showed its full face today, her brother would follow the clan to battle.

She glanced toward the opposite hill. Movement from the McGregors told her they readied themselves as well. Rhiannon stood and found her body stiff, yet astonishingly rejuvenated as her thoughts raced with morbid anticipation.

"'Tis surprised I am to see you sleep so long, lad."

She turned to face the speaker. "Morning, Nel."

He grunted. "I remember my first battle. I could not sleep at all."

"I have always slept sound." Dela had told her it was because she was pure of heart.

The man grunted again and continued to run a sharpening stone down his blade, with long even strokes. Evan sat slumped over, his eyes closed. Rhiannon thought him asleep until he raised his head and crossed himself in prayer.

Nel set down his sword and took a small vial from his pocket. He poured its contents into the palm of his hand, then dipped a finger and smeared four blue lines of paint down his cheek and into his beard, then four lines across his forehead. War paint. She had seen it many times on the men she had sewn up after battle.

"Is there a meaning behind the paint?" She had always wondered about its significance. "I have noticed many draw on their faces and chests.

"Aye, there is. The lines on my cheek are my four wee ones at home." A smile filled his face. "And the four lines on my brow be for the bairns yet to come and the joy in seeing them beget." Nel elbowed Evan, and they both laughed.

"Aye," Evan painted a cross on his forehead. "I will be seeing to that myself in a fortnight when I take my vows with Doreen. I vow she will be giving birth but nine months later."

Rhiannon pictured Doreen and knew she worshipped Evan. She stuck to him like honey and saw to his every need. They would make a good marriage.

Rhiannon looked again, to where her brother camped and saw Sheen talking to him as they walked over to Robbie's horse. The older man clapped Robbie on his shoulder then turned and climbed on his own steed.

"What do we fight for?" Rhiannon asked, turning back to the two Highlanders.

The men raised their eyebrows in surprise, before Nel answered. "For land. Our Laird wishes to have the northern forest."

Shock ate through her with sharp teeth. "The McKay wants to take the forbidden forest?"

The forest had been in the McGregor hands for hundreds of years. The king of the faeries had given the forest to Meg, Giver of Life. When she went to live with the faeries, Meg gave the keeping of the forest to Laird McGregor and so it passed to the eldest son down through the years.

"Why would Geoffrey want the forest so badly that he would go to battle?"

"Hmmm, why does any Highlander fight? To hold what is his," Nel pointed out. "Meg, the Giver of Life, was a McKay. So the land should be ours."

"Aye, 'tis true, lad," Evan added.

There had to be more to it. The McGregors had held the land for several centuries or more. Somehow, Geoffrey found wealth to be had. Knowing him as she did, it was the only thing that made sense.

The sun began its climb, over the ridge of the far mountain. Rhiannon turned to the blaze of light, heart heavy with the knowledge that the rising marked the end of life for many. She glanced back toward the valley, facing their enemy, as did others for the sun indicated the battle was at hand. From the darkness of death, the Highlander would go to the light of glory.

Silence hung heavily as all waited. A line of men formed with sword and axe at their side. What was each man thinking? She liked to imagine they remembered a time spent with a loved one. She heard prayers raised to the heavens as the ball of fire pushed its way from the earth.

Time seemed to stand still. A sheer black fright swept through her as fearful images passed through her mind. Apprehension gnawed away at her confidence to keep her brother safe. She knew their cause ill fated. The forces of nature would stand with the McGregors.

She pulled her blade from her pack but kept her gaze glued to her brother's form. If she had to give her life this day, it would be for her brother's safety.

Robbie proudly sat on his horse between their cousins, Geoffrey and Tristan. He held a new blade, one given to him in a celebration of honor two days before.

The horses smelled the fear and tension in the air, for they danced nervously. One mount even reared, pawing the air.

"Ever be ready?" The McKay yelled, pulling up his anxious mount. "The sun rises."

Rhiannon watched the yellowish-orange top of the sun throw its fiery fingers up into the dark violet and red sky. The sun pulled free from the earth's hold, and the battle cry rang out clear and cold.

"For the McKays. *Luceo Leis Beannachd!* I shine with blessings!"

The ground thundered as hundreds of screaming men raced down the hill, carrying spikes, shields, battle-axes, and claymores. The sun's rays reflected off the raised steel blades, showering the area with beams of light.

Rhiannon stood, amazed, and shaken as two large waves of men, the McKay green and the McGregor red, converged with clashes of steel and cries of agony and pain.

The force of the clash was so great some men flipped into the air. Horses screamed as blades sliced through their flesh. Charging animals trampled men under their feet, shattering bones and smashing skulls.

The screams of the dying sang as loud as the clang of blades. She lost sight of Robbie in the mayhem until his horse reared. Then the animal stumbled and went down, carrying Robbie into a sea of blades.

Rhiannon screamed, feeling as though her heart had been cut from her chest. She moved forward on unsteady feet until she spotted his tall form, standing. His horse lay bloody from an axe to the throat, but Robbie still fought hand to hand. His blade swung to strike the man who had brought down his mount, only to turn toward another man to protect his back.

She walked woodenly toward him through a living nightmare. Blood splattered her face, and a horse bumped into her shoulder, causing her to stumble. Rhiannon righted herself and realized she had gotten too close to the fighting while trying to keep her brother in sight.

Robbie had his sword raised to deflect a blow when the crowd parted, and she saw a blade pierce his thigh from behind. His cry of pain mingled with hers.

"*Feuch!* I come brother!"

Rhiannon started to run to him and slipped on the bloody grass and mud. The smell of wet earth filled her nose as she lost her sword and landed hard on her side. Her body slid, coming to rest a few feet from Nel. His eyes were open in the stare of death. His head had been torn from his body, but the painted lines representing his children still stood out on his face.

She raised her hand and found his blood on her palm. The metallic smell nearly suffocated her. Wiping her hand on her kilt, she discovered blood smeared on her legs and deer-hide boots. Tears clouded her vision and gorge surged in her throat. Her stomach emptied what little she had eaten.

Rhiannon turned to get up, only to be grabbed from behind. Evan clutched her shirt, his face twisting in pain. One of his arms had been severed. He moaned in agony. "Help me, lad."

Torn for a moment between this man's need and the search for her brother, she hesitated. Despite her desperation, she knew her heart would not allow her to leave Evan without giving aid.

Rhiannon grabbed a bandage from her pack and tied off the stump of his arm. Taking a handful of dried herbs, she pushed them into the wound to stop the bleeding. She had not the time to clean and sew it up. She would tend to that later. "Forgive me. I must seek out my brother. This will see you for a while. Soon you will need someone to wash the wound and sew the flesh shut. Understand me?"

With his jaw clenched and eyes dilated in pain, he nodded.

She stood and the sun blinded her. Shading her eyes to view the battlefield, she felt the bottom fall out of her world. The McGregors held the advantage with many men still standing. Her clansmen's bodies covered the ground with only a few McGregors. How could she hope to find her brother among so many?

When she spotted Sheen nearby, a cry tore from her heart. He lay still as death, another body draped over his. Blood caked his head and hair.

"Sheen. Please God, not Sheen too. He has a wee one on the way." *Fianna could not lose him.* Rhiannon placed her hand on his neck and found the beat of his heart. She sighed her thanks, then rolled the corpse off him. She wrapped his head with bandages and found nothing else wrong. The wound had most likely taken his senses for a time. He would wake with a pounding head.

She moved toward the spot where Robbie's horse lay. She felt drawn in and consumed like air to fire, yet saw nothing of her brother. The urgency of her search compelled her to move into the thick of the fighting.

A large shadow fell over her. She gasped and turned to face a brute. He stood nearly two feet above her, and wore the red plaid of the McGregor clan.

His eyes held the look of a wild berserker. Blood and gore matted his hair and clothes. She knew the battle fever held him and saw her death within his gaze. He raised his bloody sword then swung it in a downward arc.

Rhiannon jumped out of the way just as the sword missed severing her head. His blade sank into the mud, giving her time to grab a sword lying nearby and raise it in defense.

He swung again, and she met his swing with one of her own. Their blades clanged together, echoing in an eerily silent valley.

The giant's strength made her stumble, and her shoulder throbbed in pain. No match for this brute of a man, she knew she would die this day. Her blood would mingle with that of her brother.

With the next blow, Rhiannon's sword flew from her hand, flipping end over end and vibrating as it sank tip first into the earth. She lay defenseless on the ground, staring up at the monster before her.

As he raised his sword over his head, she watched the killing blow come down in slow motion. Her heart sounded loud in her ears as images of her brother and Dela passed before her. She shut her eyes, closing out the sight of the sword impaling her chest. But the blow never landed.

The clash and scrape of steel against steel made her quickly open her eyes. Another sword had appeared out of nowhere to stop the deathblow.

"You will not kill him, brother. The battle is won. He is a prisoner."

Rhiannon moved her gaze up the speaker's sword to his large clutched hand and an arm as thick as a young oak. He had broad shoulders and stood half a foot taller than the man beside him.

He turned to face her, and she gasped. The man was half god, half devil. Black paint covered an entire side of his face and dried blood marked his cheek and hair. His expression was a mask of stone. Surprise and fear siphoned the blood from her brain, leaving her lightheaded.

"Hold your meal, lad. You will not meet your death this day."

Through the roaring din of her heart, she heard his words. *He had spared her life. Why?*

His head held a manly crown of black hair that fell against the *V* of his open shirt. His eyes of deep sapphire blue glowed with a savage inner fire. His entire presence spoke of strength and power.

She could do nothing but stare at him. Fear clouded her brain, but she had the feeling she knew the rugged man before her. As if something snapped, she suddenly remembered her brother. She must go to him. She needed to bind his wounds.

Dylan bent down, looking into the most beautiful green eyes he had ever seen on a boy. "Do you ken, lad? You will march with us and work at the McGregor's hearth. Because you have fought bravely, I grant you life."

"I will be no man's slave!"

Dylan heard the cool ring of authority and wondered to whom the lad belonged. He watched in stunned amazement as the boy drew a small dagger from his boot. Before it could be put to use, Dylan sprang and easily knocked the dagger to the ground with a well-placed kick to the hand.

The lad screamed and grabbed at his wrist. Dylan took hold of the youth's arm and jerked him around so that they came face to face. "I admire your spirit, lad, but is it not better to live as a servant with the hope of freedom than to die a victim of this damnable battle? If you had drawn my blood, 'twould surely have been mixed with your own."

He could not imagine why the McKays would let a child that appeared no more than thirteen, fight in a man's battle. The youth's arm was as thin as a twig and could be broken with a simple twist. The top of the lad's head came no further than his armpits. What advantage would casting a child into a man's battle hold for the McKays? The idea repulsed him.

How the lad held his own against his berserker brother, he did not know. Yet, the fire in the lad's eyes told him he held a determined spirit that ran deep.

The young man lifted his chin and glared with the green fire of his eyes. "I will not go with you 'til I find my brother."

Dylan shook his head. He was too tired to deal with this child. "Oh, lad, you're going to be a bit of trouble. I have no time for this." He turned to his brother. "Owain, if you have calmed, put the lad with the others. We need to care for the wounded and start the journey home."

Dylan watched as Owain swung the youth over his shoulder as if he weighed less then a stick. He smiled as the lad's kicking connected with his brother's hard stomach, causing Owain to grunt.

The day had seen victory, and soon he would be home with new servants and hopefully, in time, a chest full of gold for the return of the McKay's men.

Standing with the other prisoners waiting to move out, she heard a cry of agony cut through the breeze. "Rhiannon!"

Her heart leaped as she turned to see her brother leaning across a borrowed horse, on the far hill where they had camped. The distance was too far to make out his features clearly but he raised his hand in salute. So much was said in that simple gesture. He was telling her he was well and had escaped. He knew of her plight and would come for her.

Everything compelled her to answer back, yet she knew she could not. Her eyes hurt with suppressed tears, and she closed them tightly to hold his image in her heart. When the air stilled, she opened her eyes to meet the intense, probing gaze of the blue-eyed McGregor. She faced him, unwilling to be the first to look away. She would share nothing with him.

He turned to speak with the Highlanders beside him and sent two after Robbie. Glancing back to the far hill, she found him gone and sighed in relief. They would not catch him.

Feeling the heat of the McGregor's gaze on her again, she shivered. Robbie would fare better than she. Even waiting in fear of what the McGregor would do to her, she would not trade places with Robbie. He was safe.

It was a hard day's march. Night had fallen before they reached the McGregor's castle. Rhiannon sat on the cold ground with the other prisoners just outside the main hall's front doors. She was feeling the ache of her encounter with the giant Highlander, but her heart was eased. Just moments ago, the two men the McGregor sent after Robbie had returned empty-handed.

A sharp command cut through her thoughts. "The Laird will see you now," their guard said, pushing them toward the castle door. The McKays struggled to stand, some needing help. They were herded into the great hall before the head table. The McGregor Laird sat in the chair of honor at one end. He took no notice of them now, while filling his belly.

The castle had the same gray stone walls as the McKay's, but that was where the similarity ended. The Laird of this castle was wealthy beyond measure. Beautifully sewn tapestries covered the walls. The wooden benches and chairs at the tables had fur coverings. Two hearths, one on the right wall and one on the left, were large enough for Rhiannon to walk into without bumping her head. The roaring fire's heat from each reached her even as she stood at the door.

Torches hung from the walls, but she found the iron wheel hanging by a rope from the rafter most interesting. It had tallow candles, mayhap ten in count, placed around the outer ring. The great hall glowed with light.

Glancing around at the McGregors in the room, Rhiannon saw many gazes travel to her kinsmen, but mostly her captors laughed and talked, ignoring the captives. Rarely did the great hall at the McKays have so many people in it. Nor had she seen such obvious signs of ease and comfort at one time. The Laird must be a good man, yet glancing at him; she noticed no one stood with him. In a crowd of people, he sat alone as if a line had been drawn that no one crossed. *Fear of the curse.*

When he turned toward her, she gasped. The man who had saved her from losing her head! The paint and blood had been washed away, leaving the most handsome man she had ever seen. His black hair hung long and straight, and his deeply piercing blue eyes met and held those of every prisoner.

When his gaze touched hers, the breath left her body. It was as if her soul somehow connected with his. This must be the man Dela had spoken of, the enemy who would be hers. She wondered how he would affect her life. She could not look away, but he broke the gaze first, as he continued his inspection of the prisoners. A guard to her right yelled, startling her from her thoughts. "Kneel 'afore your Laird."

Rhiannon watched the members of her clan kneel one by one. Some of the men were bleeding, and most of them were muddy and defeated. A new shaking took over as anger filled her.

Her thoughts turned to the women without husbands, children without fathers, and sisters far from their brothers. When all kneeled but her, she knew she would not and stiffened her spine. She would not see this humiliation. She stood up for all that died that day.

The guard advanced, pulling his sword free. "Kneel or I

shall cut you down where you stand."

Never taking her gaze from the Laird, she spoke clearly, "My knees are stiff from the mud and blood. They will not bend."

She knew they saw through her lie from the expressions of surprise, to open irritation, and even apprehension. The warrior sneered and moved to strike her.

There was a stirring among the people kneeling on either side of her. The spirit was returning to them and though unarmed they would protect her.

The McGregor's eyes narrowed. Their dangerous sparkle pierced her soul. She knew he saw the peril of more bloodshed and barked a command before the blade met her flesh, "Hold!"

The guard stayed his hand and turned toward his Laird. The blue fire in the McGregor's eyes severed her failing courage, yet she could not find the strength to bend her knees.

"Lad, speak truth, why do you not kneel, knowing you will be struck down if you do not?" The Laird asked.

Before she could hold her tongue, words bubbled forth. "The McKays have been humbled enough. We have lost this day's fight and have yet to bury our dead. We concede to your victory, for battle is honorable. But we will not toss our already wounded pride and honor upon the floor to be trampled."

A few gasps echoed in the hall from those standing about, followed by a deathly quiet. Even the hounds that sat around the Laird's feet raised their heads from their bowls.

All waited to see what Dylan McGregor would do. He held her gaze for a long time, making her uncomfortable. Again, she felt him piercing through her disguise to touch her very soul. He wanted something from her. What, she did not know.

"You speak well, lad. You have courage to speak truth. For this, we will leave you your honor."

He turned to the Highlander who had commanded them to kneel. "Put a task to each man, then find them a warm place to lay their heads and someone to bind their wounds. They may start work on the morrow. The lad will serve me."

She gasped and curled her toes in worry, but gave no other outward sign of her terror. Had he guessed she was a lass and not a lad? Would he take her maidenhead before the night was through? It was his right as victor. The Laird still had his dark gaze locked on her, and she had no wish to give her fears away. She had a part to play.

As each McKay passed, they slapped her on the shoulders to show their pride. Several slaps almost sent her to the floor, but she accepted each with pleasure.

The McGregor went about filling his trencher, but she knew he missed none of the exchange. Then, with all her kinsmen gone, she stood alone.

Dylan McGregor's handsome face and body moved with a predator's grace. The hair that hung around his shoulders shined like black onyx in the candlelight. His clean-shaven chin stood out strong. Deep blue eyes, the color of the sea were set with thick black brows. The muscles in his arms twisted and bunched as he used his hands to cut through a piece of meat. His straight white teeth tore into the flesh, causing the meat's juice to run down his fingers. The smell of roasted chicken made Rhiannon's stomach gurgle. She had not eaten since the night before.

Leaning over the table, The McGregor motioned for a man to come to him, then spoke in low tones. The man nodded.

She was having trouble separating The McGregor from the man in her dream. Dela told her she was to join with her enemy or great evil would befall them all. Being a maid, she had no idea how to go about finding out if he was the one. She had yet to see the mark of the dragon. There must be no doubt before she gave herself to him.

She shook her head. She was more than a little weary, yet she continued to stand and wait. A thirst pulled at her throat. Mayhap this weakness was going to her head. She noticed a large barrel with a drinking scoop near the door and turned toward the water.

"Hold!"

She stopped and turned around to meet the Laird's angry gaze.

"You will not attempt to leave."

"I was not leaving. I but wanted water to ease my thirst."

"You will stand by my chair and wait upon my pleasure."

She wanted to stomp her foot but clenched her hand into a fist instead as she went over to stand close to the table. Ignoring her, he resumed eating. Rhiannon waited a few minutes more, and when it seemed he would not give her a drink, she stepped to the table and took a cup full of liquid. She lifted the cup to her lips.

The scrape of a chair was her only warning, before a strong hand grabbed her wrist, making her spill some of the liquid down her arm. He took the cup from her hand and put it back on the table.

"What are you doing? I thirst," Rhiannon snapped. Would he starve her, too?

"You will not take anything but what I give you. You are a prisoner now and subject to my demands. If you thirst, 'tis I you will ask for drink, and if you hunger, you will wait 'til I give you food. Do you ken?"

So, he wished her to beg. Well, he would soon see she

would not bow to anyone. She raised her chin.

The Laird's brow narrowed and he leaned close. "'Tis by my good grace that you will receive all you need. Do not defy me, lad. For I am law here." Dylan waved his hand in dismissal of the man beside him. "You may take your leave, Orin. I wish to speak to the lad." The man seated at the table nodded and left.

"Do all jump to your command?" Rhiannon asked. Geoffrey often had to hit a person before his orders were followed.

"Aye." He answered as he reclaimed his seat. He kicked out a chair beside him. "Do you think your knees will bend enough to allow you to sit?"

Rhiannon moved over to sit in the chair. Every bone ached with tiredness. She yawned and put her hand to her mouth, then realized what she had done. She closed her mouth and looked at The McGregor. He watched her, and one corner of his mouth lifted, as did an eyebrow. A small smile curved his lips and a sparkle lit his eyes.

Without comment, he handed her his mug. "Drink. A lad seeing his first battle should have good Scottish whiskey. How old are you?"

"Old enough."

"For what? For battle? For women? I think naught. You cannot even grow a beard. Here, eat, you are by far too skinny."

Rhiannon was too hungry to take offense at his words and found the meat fresh and juicy. She had seen how her cousins treated their prisoners. No mercy was allotted them. Her clan had said Dylan McGregor was worse, yet this seemed unfounded. "Why are you being kind?"

"Why should I not be? Have you done something to

warrant punishment?" She shrugged. "Being kind does not make me less of a man. My judgments are swift, but deserving. Do as I ask and you will not find life here so bad."

Dylan sat back in his seat to watch the lad eat. There was more to this boy than met the eye. At times, he acted almost feminine. He had heard of a person being a man with a woman's mind, but he did not think this was the case. The lad had courage and strength, but his hands were small and slender, his face delicate, and he moved with a gentle grace. The bare skin of those knees below the kilt was smooth and well rounded.

If indeed a female, why would she dress as a man and fight in a battle? He could not understand a woman doing something so absurd and dangerous. Also, there was the strength of character and honor he had never seen in a woman. Mayhap she had followed her lover to the battle. Many women did, but that still did not explain the disguise. She could be a thief stealing from the dead. With winter just past, many were without and they took any means to feed their family but it was all speculation.

He raised the mug of whiskey to his lips, taking a sip before setting it down. His gaze caught on his hounds. How strange this! They seemed to find the youth acceptable. They were loyal to him and only tolerated others by the showing of their teeth, until now.

His male hound Bain sat close by his chair, yet watched every bite of food the youth took. The bitch Kyna seemed less reserved. She stood at the captive's chair, whining and putting her front paw on the other's lap. Kyna received a pat on her furry head for her efforts.

As he watched the hostage with his pets, a growing need to know without a doubt if this person was man or woman ate at his gut. If he had to, he would have her stripped naked to appease his curiosity and end the game. However, for now he would let her keep the disguise and see what she wanted. Having come to a decision, he relaxed slightly, leaning back in his chair.

"What is your full name? I have yet to hear it," Dylan asked.

Quickly, so she would not have to answer, Rhiannon took a drink from the mug, and fire filled her lungs. She coughed and tried to bring air to her starving brain.

"Be you all right, lad?" Dylan asked, laughing and slapping her on the back, nearly knocking her from the seat.

"I will be if...you stop hitting me."

Dylan immediately removed his hand. "'Tis sorry I am. I am too heavy handed at times."

"Do you naught have water to quench my thirst instead of fire to burn my dry throat?"

"Here," he said, handing over another mug. "'Tis not water but ale. 'Twill have to do."

She took the cup and drank greedily until it was empty. Placing the mug down, she sighed and leaned back in the chair.

"Now, let us see about getting you a place to bed down," Dylan said. The scrape of wood on stone sounded as he pushed back his chair and stood.

Rhiannon was all too happy to follow. She needed time away from him to think clearly. With her stomach full and her thirst quenched, sleep would be welcome.

She followed Dylan and the hounds upstairs. He opened the first door to his left and stepped in. The warmth of the room surrounded her. A fire blazed in the hearth to her right. Furs covered the floor and sweet rushes filled the air with a pleasant scent. She would find comfort here.

"You will sleep in my room. I will see a mat placed by the fire for you until the cubby can be readied."

"This is your room?" she asked in surprise. She could not stay here. She would be far too close to him. How could she keep her secret?

"Dylan?" A soft feminine voice came from his bed.

Rhiannon watched wide-eyed as a naked leg emerged from beneath the covers. Was she to witness the copulation of the Laird and a whore? She narrowed her eyes and fisted her hands in her kilt. *She would not!*

"Come. Out with you, wench. I did not summon you," Dylan commanded.

The woman threw back the covers to expose long blonde hair and naked curves of ivory skin. One hand lay just below her breast. The other twisted a strand of blonde hair. Her knee was bent and fell to the side so she lay open to his gaze. "Do you like what you see?"

Both hounds growled and pushed forward. Bain circled the bed, baring his teeth. Whoever she was, the hounds voiced their contempt, and Rhiannon wished to join them. If this man were to be hers, she would not share even the brush of his hand with another.

Rhiannon's tightening gaze moved to Dylan. His brows lifted and his lips had parted in surprise. "Enid?" Then in a blink of time, his eyes narrowed and a hard twist curled his lips. "Holy Smite! What do you here in my bed?"

Enid sat up on her elbows. The heated glow from her eyes sparkled from beneath long lashes. "I would think that is obvious. I wished to welcome home the victor." She applied action to her words and held her hand out to him. "Come, let me ease your body."

"What has changed that you now wish to grace my bed?"

Rhiannon was about to back out the door when Dylan picked up the discarded quilt and threw it over Enid's nakedness. Enid did not answer.

"This brings you naught." He sighed. "The day is long and I am weary."

Ignoring the cover, Enid slipped from the bed and pressed her breasts against Dylan's chest. His gaze ran over her, but no fire filled his blue eyes.

"Take me," Enid breathed across his lips. Her hand ran up his chest and into his hair, pulling his head down to her mouth.

Taking her arms in each hand, he pushed her back. "You are my brother's wife. So cover your nakedness and see yourself to your own bed."

"I am no longer a wife, but a widow and have been long without a man. I care for your house and your servants. Am I not good enough to care for your body as well?"

"Have you no shame, woman? There is another present."

Rhiannon thought Dylan had forgotten her. For the first time Enid glanced in her direction and seemed surprised, someone else was in the room. Then a sneer replaced her pout.

"He wears the McKay colors and smells foul. Send him away," Enid demanded, waving her hand in dismissal.

"The lad serves me 'til ransoms are paid." Dylan grabbed Enid's arm, bringing her gaze back to his. "Know this, none that is mine will you have, so take yourself off and let me not see you 'til morn when your senses are not addled."

Enid's teeth clenched, and a spark of anger filled her gaze. Quickly, she pasted on a smile. Rhiannon knew Enid was as false as she was beautiful.

"You are bewitched. You have been unmanned since coming back from the forbidden forest with that wreath." Enid pointed to the dried circle of buttercups and violets that hung over the fireplace mantel.

"Mayhap you can not perform as a man any longer?" The barb was thrown, caught, and thrown back.

"I function well. I am only choosy with whom I care to share it. Now go, woman! And leave my private life to me."

"I will go to appease you, my Laird, but I am here if you have need of me." Enid stormed out, bumping into Rhiannon on the way.

Dylan McGregor was under a spell. Rhiannon could not get over this bit of information. How was she ever going to get him to mate with her if he was enchanted? Moreover, if that did not happen, how would she fulfill the destiny Dela had set for her? She would not have much time to win him away from another. Robbie would see that someone came for her.

Dylan straightened a quilt on the floor in front of the fire. "This will have to do 'till the morrow. Sleep well, small one."

"Thank you." She stretched out on her side. The heat of the fire warmed her back. The cream-colored hound lay at her feet and the brown one lay on a fur by his master's bed.

Dylan unwrapped the plaid from around his shoulders and tossed it on the mattress. He took the bottom edge of his shirt, pulling the whole thing over his head.

Rhiannon gasped at the strength and contours of his muscled back and shoulders. She had seen men's bodies before, but only with the distracted purpose of a healer.

With this man, however, she was extremely conscious of his virile appeal. When he reached for his kilt, her heart filled with anticipation. A tingling started in her stomach. Heat shot through her body as the fabric fell away, revealing the firm curve of naked hips.

Then she spotted the mark. A dragon's head the size of her fist darkened the skin of his upper thigh. He *was* the *one* prophecy had foretold. Here was her proof. Dizziness filled her head and she moaned.

He must have heard the sound because he turned to look at her over his shoulder. "Are your muscles as tender and stiff as mine, lad?" He rubbed and rotated his shoulders with his back still to her. She was seized with a desire to move toward him, the need to touch growing strong. She grabbed the quilt she lay on to hold her in place.

"Shall I order water drawn for you to bathe? 'Tis helpful to soak in hot water." A mischievous smile crossed his face, making her frown.

Rhiannon almost said aye, but caught herself again. "Nay, 'tis sure to be better in the morn."

She had no doubt that when he was clothed, she would be all right again. His stance emphasized the force of his thighs and the slimness of his hips. His attitude of self-command and relaxation as he stood naked before her made her insides clamor with sensual awakening.

The feeling was like running through the forbidden forest. Her heartbeat raced, her breath came fast, and her soul exploded with excitement.

"What is your name, lad?" Dylan asked, turning around to face her. "I would have an answer this time."

The part of him that made him different from her lay soft among a nest of dark curls. Though it was the only thing soft about him, she found the image of his male rod burned into her mind and felt the rush of blood to her face.

Rhiannon quickly lowered her head so he would not see the conflicting emotions of desire, modesty, and wonder revealed upon her face.

"'Tis Rhi," she said.

"Well, Rhi, I have decided you shall work in the stables

when I have no need of you. What say you to this?"

She heard the crinkle of the straw mattress as he settled into bed. Then came the rustle of linens as he arranged the bedding.

"I love animals," she confided, barely able to speak.

Rhiannon raised her gaze to see him lying on his back. The covers fell to his waist. His ribs and stomach muscles rippled with every breath. A long old wound scarred his broad chest, yet it did not take away from his attraction. He was a Highlander, a warrior who carried scars as badges of strength.

Now that she knew he was the one, she felt the sands of time slipping past, as she must see the mating through before evil stood upon their door. But how to accomplish the task. Not only did her innocence stand in the way, but she was disguised as a lad and her smell was daunting.

He had both arms behind his head. His long black hair fanned over them to the pillow. "Perhaps you have a gift with animals," he said.

She cleared her throat. "Why do you say that?"

His answer came slurred as sleep wrapped itself around him. "'Twas the hounds. You are the first they have taken a liking to."

What a tangle her life had become! Just how was she to reveal her deceit without hurting his pride? Somehow, she had to find a way. Too many counted on her. As her mind still searched for answers, she followed Dylan into a troubled sleep.

Lightning flashed and dark storm clouds rolled rapidly across the night sky. The dark robe of the hooded Sorcerer flipped and snapped around his form as he stood in the raging wind, looking at the McGregor stronghold. He had followed her from the battlefield.

The glass globe at the top of his wooden staff glowed with orange fire. She would soon be in his grasp, and all the power of the gods would be his. He would rule the great beasts of the skies, and no mortal would dare oppose him.

He sneered at the twisting clouds and raised his arms to the sky. Fingers of jagged lightning groped through the darkness like tentacles. The wind's fury swallowed his laugh of pleasure.

Chapter Four

"You are as beautiful as ever! But I prefer your true image to this illusion you show everyone."

Dela looked up from the mortar and pestle as a tall man stepped through her door. The moonlight cast his face in shadow until he moved farther in, and firelight filled his face.

"Gian." Dela placed her hand over her chest. He could still make her heart beat fast. His silky blond hair hung long and fanned over his shoulders in waves. Green mint leaves hung braided into the silver streak at his temple.

She remembered so well running her fingers through that thick hair. How long had it been since she had seen herself in his forest green eyes? He had only to appear to turn her world upside down. Her nostrils flared taking in his special scent of wind, trees, and earth.

"I am interested in this illusion. Why do you wear this face and form?" Gian asked, closing the door.

"People only see what they wish. 'Tis easier to move about unnoticed as an old woman." She waved her hand, and her long white hair became fiery red. Her tawny eyes changed to warm brown surrounded by thick brown lashes. The wrinkled skin became smooth, and the bow to her back straightened. A mature beauty erased all signs of the hag as she transformed into Meg, the Giver of Life.

"Ah, there's my love. You have been too long from the

land of *Tylwyth teg*."

"'Tis a long time since hearing you call me that." She set the mortar and pestle on the table. "And you know where I have been. I have a duty to Rhiannon."

"Aye, how is our maid?" Gian inquired, moving closer.

She stood and moved toward the hearth. "I fear for her, Gian. She is innocent of the betrayals and the dark forces surrounding her life. She has yet to develop the powers needed to combat them."

"Have you told her of her parents?"

Meg turned to stir a bubbling pot over the fire. Guilt kept her mouth closed.

"You have not?" he guessed. "Woman! What are you about? With the darkness among us, she needs this knowledge. The powers will come with this gift."

Gian watched Meg pull a bench out from the table, then stand on it to reach for some drying herbs hanging from the cracked and weathered rafters. A trim ankle emerged from beneath her kirtle. His gaze followed up her pleasing form, from her narrow waist to rounded breasts straining against the fabric of her chemise.

His lower half stirred to life. He had been too long without her. He wanted her now.

"'Twas not the time," she answered.

He blinked, thinking she had read his mind, and then remembered his question. She had always been able to addle his thoughts with her beautiful curves.

He adjusted a certain annoying body part. "You think only of yourself in this matter, Meg. You fear to lose her. Well, think on this, woman. You shall lose her if the darkness prevails, and her death will haunt you more than her tears."

He was right, but she would not boost his arrogance by

agreeing. She changed the subject. "She will marry. The goddess has shown this to me. She will marry a *human*."

"I will see him dead first!" Gian shook his fist as he stomped over to stand below her. "By all the forces within me."

Meg smiled. "What is wrong with taking a human? You did."

"That was different," he grumbled, not so easily dissuaded.

He pulled her off the bench and into his arms. Her body slid along his, as he slowly lowered her to the floor. "You are Meg, the Giver of Life. The gods chose you to weld the gift of healing. And I wanted you."

Such arrogance! She dismissed his remarks with a wave of her hand. "And who is to say the man chosen for Rhiannon is not without his gifts?"

"I will seek this man out and judge him for myself. If he is found unworthy, I will kill him."

"And doom us all with your jealousies." Anger born from fear sharpened her voice. "The two must mate. For only by their union will darkness be defeated."

"Not all things are so easily fixed sweet love. The outcome will still depend on how great the power is in both of them. You must be sure this human *is* the right mate."

"I will see to Rhiannon. Do not stumble into this mystery and attempt to sway things your way."

"Meg, you may be a Druid priestess, but I am king of all *Sidhe* and have a knowing beyond you."

"Humph!"

When she was about to refute him, he put a finger across her lips. His face grew haggard with worry. "You know she can not fully understand her fate unless she is instructed. And without the right man, naught but pain and death awaits her."

"I have every intention of telling her all, but not 'til she is ready to hear it."

Gian threw up his hands and stepped away. A spasm of irritation crossed his face. "How could I love such a stubborn woman? Know this, Meg, if anything happens to Rhiannon it will go hard with you."

"Are you threatening me, Gian?"

He sighed. "Nay sweet, Meg. I but speak of a mother's loss of her child."

"She is daughter to a king and the light is her guardian."

"Listen well. Put away your emotions, and see that Rhiannon is prepared, because the evil one *has found* her."

Meg gasped, slapping the back of her hand over her mouth. A cold fist closed over her heart. "Nay! Take me to her."

He shook his head. "'Tis a day's ride away. You would do better with the Druid sleep. Speak to her in dreams."

"Will you go to her?" Meg pleaded.

"Aye, I told you, I will judge the man you deem her match."

Meg placed her hand on his arm. "Do not stay away. Come back to me—soon."

He took her in his arms once again. "Soon, lass, for I have missed the flavor of you on my lips." He brought his mouth to hers in a deep kiss; one made of magic and enchantment, then left as quietly as he had come. Meg's hair grew gray and wrinkles marred her face as the hag once again took her place. If Gian thought she would stay here, he was mistaken. She had her own plans to see to.

Dylan awoke, but lay still. What had disturbed him? He

glanced toward the window to see lightning flash across the night sky. He rolled to his side searching out his hounds, but they both lay at peace, unbothered by the storm.

Next, his gaze found the lass, lying before the hearth. Her chest rose and fell with an even cadence. She had kicked the quilt off, and he could see an involuntary shiver move along her body. The fire had burned down; he needed to add a few logs to warm the room and cover the lass again.

Throwing the covers back, he slipped from the bed and padded over to the hearth where he stooped down between Rhi and the fire. He took logs from a basket nearby and added enough wood to the dying flames to see them through the night. The dry saplings caught with a roar, filling the room with dancing light.

He turned toward the lass to watch the firelight play like caressing fingers over her slender form. She lay on her back with her face turned away. With a need to see more of her, he reached up and pulled the cap from her head only to discover a wealth of fiery hair that was braided and stuffed down her shirt.

The soot on her face could not cover the long dark lashes that lay pillowed on smooth cheeks. He wanted to run his finger along the edge of her dainty ear, but resisted the urge. How could so much courage be contained in this one woman? She had stood up against the blade twice, yet did not complain, or beg anything from him.

As his focus fell to her slowly rising chest, he noticed the nearly flat and misshapen swelling where her breasts should have been. He narrowed his brow. *Mayhap she is deformed in someway.*

The oddity compelled him to touch her. Softly so not to awaken her, he ran his fingers over her chest. To his amusement, he found she had bound herself so no womanly curve could be detected. A smile curled his lips. Here was solid proof of what he had suspected earlier: a woman in disguise.

She intrigued him. The longer he was with her, the more questions formed, and the answers were not forthcoming. Through the stench of stale clothes came a sweetness all her own. The scent reminded him of lavender, violets, and the forest.

The heat from the fire scorched his skin, urging him to finish his examination and go back to bed. He would find no more answers tonight, so he pulled the quilt over her, making sure her arms and legs were covered. He stood to leave her, but held his ground as she started to mumble words in her sleep.

Her brow crinkled into a frown, and she twitched as if troubled by some demon in her slumber.

"Rhiannon, 'tis Dela." The image of dreams shifted, and a white-haired witch stood before her. *"We must talk, child."*

"Dela?" Rhiannon questioned confused at the intrusion. They now stood on a green hill overlooking a valley shrouded in mist.

"You are but dreaming, yet listen well."

Rhiannon quickly adjusted. "Speak. What news do you bring?"

"There are things you must hear. The darkness is upon us. He has found your door."

"Nay, I have not had the time or knowledge to see the mating done." Apprehension settled in her stomach like a stone from the tower.

"The mating is a simple thing. You have seen the breeding of animals. 'Tis the same, except there is a ritual you must do

'afore the mating. Bathe in spring water, rubbing yourself with dried lavender and rose petals. As you bathe, you must sing the song of enchantment. Afterwards present yourself to him unclothed. He will know the way of it from there."

"Dela, 'tis the McGregor the fates have chosen for me, yet under a spell he is. I heard he is bewitched and will not take another to his bed."

The old woman smiled and ran fingers down Rhiannon's cheek. "All will work out, dear one. I shall pray that the gods will look with favor on you.

"Now...there is another matter of importance," Dela sighed. Her face grew haggard with worry as she wrung her hands. "I would not tell you what I must if it were not for the gift that comes with the telling. You will need these powers when facing evil. I would speak of your parents."

"My parents?" Rhiannon asked breathlessly. Dela had never spoken of them before. No matter how she had pleaded, the woman would never give any detail.

Dela sighed. "I have known from your birth who they are, but have kept silent 'til you were ready to hear the whole of it. With the telling comes great responsibility. You have a gift of magic within. You carry the blood of our goddess, Rhiannon. Your father is the king of the faeries and your mother, Meg, the Giver of Life."

Rhiannon groaned, trying to control a quaver of panic. "Nay-nay, 'tis not so. What game do you play?" She could not be the daughter of a faery king and the greatest healer of all time. They were legends. The journey from a common, orphan girl to an unwanted princess, abandoned daughter of the inner realms was too much.

Dela reached for Rhiannon, her face etched in desperation, but Rhiannon backed away. "I fear there is more, young lass. With the knowledge, the spell is broken. The power's released."

Rhiannon fisted her hands in the hair over both ears. The whirl of emotions threatened to overwhelm her. "Nay, leave me and say no more!" Rhiannon cried. "Say no more, I beg you!"

The sound of crying woke Rhiannon from sleep. She twisted over to come face to face with a scowling and very naked Dylan.

"Are you all right, lad?" His gentle voice was a calm in her turbulent thoughts.

"'Tis naught but a bad dream," she whispered on a hiccup, but knew her words were a lie. A shiver ran down the length of her, and she turned her back to him. Her nerves frayed, emotions in a jumble, she hadn't the strength to deal with Dylan on any level. She wrapped both arms around her knees and pulled into a fetal position.

A humming filled her mind, and she squeezed her eyes shut; yet, a flood of unseen forces filled her body. The strength of the faerie's gift made her muscles twitch and jerk. Rhiannon fought against the power, the energy of nature. Pain burst within her chest and tortured her mind, making her cry out. She clutched at her temples fearing her head would burst open.

Dylan's warm hands pulled her into his strong arms. The gentle caress of his soft breath took away her chill. "Shh, little one. 'Twill be all right. Take some deep breaths and relax. My arms will hold you safe. There is naught here to hurt you."

The slow rubbing of Dylan's fingers up and down her bare arms soon eased the quaking of her insides. His rich deep voice soothed her chaotic mind. As she relaxed, the pain faded until a deep sleep took all thoughts and confusion away.

* * *

The pounding on his bedroom door awoke Dylan to the hardness of the floor, a warm body, and the smell of a barnyard. As he got up, he made a note to see the lass bathed soon.

Caring nothing about his nakedness, he opened the door to one of his guards. "Laird, there were homes burned on the northern hill before daybreak and people are dead. Your brother and I await your instruction."

"I will be right down."

A sinking feeling in his gut told him the past had come back to haunt him. His father's words seared through his brain, a brand he must forever endure.

"'Tis sorry I am you are a son of mine, for there is evil in you. Born under the waxing moon, you were, and you carry evil's mark upon your flesh. Destruction and death follow you." Dylan rubbed the back of his neck. No matter how unworthy, he *was now* Laird. But at times, he felt the darkness of his soul, a twisting mass in a black pit, a beast clamoring to be set free. He feared the powers that grew inside him.

What if he should lose his hold on them? Would he become a monster unfit for hell? He gave a short bark of laughter. His clan already thought him that. However, with this evil befalling his hillside the deed would fall upon his head.

Five minutes found Dylan riding out of the castle with his brother and many guards. Their swift ride caused the early morning mist to swirl up from the ground and dance round the horses and riders. The thud of hooves meeting the earth echoed on the crisp air. Steam blew from his steed's nose as it labored.

Dylan's thoughts remained not on the mysterious mutilation and fire but with the lass he had left sleeping in his room. He did not need the complication of this woman and her difficulties. What he wanted most was to find the enchanting forest faery he had come across one month ago. He knew if she stood beside him, he could destroy the fear his clan felt for him. He could wipe out the curse he was under. She was pure, innocent magic. She was of the light, while he carried the darkness. Surely, her cloak of righteousness would cover his robe of corruption.

He rubbed the back of his neck trying to ease its stiffness, while images of Rhi invaded his thoughts. Her innocence drew him towards her, wanting to protect and comfort her. He admired the bravery and honor Rhi showed yet the unwelcome feelings she brought out in him would not change his mind. He would have only the Lady of the Forest.

When sight of the charred earth and remains of the hut came into view through the trees, Dylan pulled the horse to a stop and raised an open hand to halt his men.

The stench of burnt flesh overrode the smells of seared trees and scorched earth. He detected another odor, one he could not put a name to.

An eerie quiet hung over the scene. No bird or animal sounds filled the air. Even the breeze seemed to hover silently, as if to suck the breath from his lungs.

"Owain, have the men scout the surrounding area for live stock and clues to who did this crime."

Seven villagers stood nearby, but none came to greet him. Fear and anger marked each face. Dylan swung his leg over the horse's back, making his kilt swing about his bare thighs. The ground crunched under foot, sending up small puffs of ashes, as he strode over to the peasants.

Looking over the gathered crowd, he voiced his anger. "So easily have you thrown away all I have done for you and the victories visited upon you. You now return to the ravings of my father, an old man, gone these last eight winters, placing this evil on my head."

His jaw tightened, and his lips curled in disgust. The villagers shifted, faces tightly pinched, but only Drew lifted his head to meet Dylan's gaze. "'Tis sorry I am, Laird, but these deaths have the look and smell of evil. Fear has us worried for our families. We remember well the deaths of Ethan and Dearg but one month ago."

"Aye, 'tis always wise to be cautious, Drew, but knowing your enemies from your friends gives you the advantage."

"Aye, Laird."

Dylan was the Laird of all he surveyed; yet, words and deeds from the past still pierced him. He lowered his brows in contemplation. In truth, that same past made him the man he was today. He had worked hard for all he had and was not about to let it be taken.

"Tell me what you know of this. What time was the burn found?" Dylan waved his hand over the charred hut.

"'Twas not me who found it. 'Twas the old one over there."

Dylan let his gaze follow where Drew pointed to an old woman with long white hair, a frail bent-over form, gripping a wooden staff. He knew everyone in his clan, but this woman was a stranger. Without taking his eyes from her, Dylan placed his hand on the other man's shoulder.

"Cover the beehives with black crepe so they will continue to produce, and make sure all animals are taken away. The souls of the dead must find their path to the gods."

"The animals seem to have disappeared, but I will see to the hives."

Dylan grunted in response. "Also see that Coira's and

Angus's families are told of their deaths so they might prepare them for burial."

"A messenger will be sent."

Dylan left Drew and the others to step up beside the old woman. "Sweet mother—" He gave the address of respect. "I hear 'twas you who found this burning."

As she turned to face him, he was surprised to see tears shining forth from her pain-filled, tawny eyes. "Aye, see you not what evil has done." She pointed to the charred remains of two humans clasped together in death. A platter of salt with the crossed twigs of ash had been placed on their twisted bodies. Rush torches burned in a circle around them to avert the possibility of evil spirits interfering with the dead. Black smoke twisted from the tops of each torch.

Dylan stared at the still couple. His nostrils flared, the breath coming raw in his throat. He had performed their marriage and eaten at their wedding feast but three months past.

They still clung to each other, even in death. A young, true love had been ripped apart by this foul deed. He would reap justice and see like for like. Those who did this would burn for their crimes.

On closer inspection, he realized they lay outside the hut. Broken pottery and mugs lay at their heads. Dylan frowned. "Why not run? They have no bindings to hold them."

"Tell me what you see, young Laird."

"They lie outside. Anyone coming could have been heard."

"Aye. Look closer." The old one pointed a bony finger toward the intertwined couple.

Dylan did not understand what compelled him to do as she asked, but he stooped down to examine further and was surprised. "The pottery and mugs are not broken. They are melted."

He glanced up at the woman. Her sad eyes sparkled with encouragement, so he asked, "What kind of fire would melt stone yet leave part of the wood hut and the bones of humans?"

Humph! "I would say a very hot one. A short blast of heat lasting only a few seconds."

Dylan frowned. "What you suggest is impossible."

"Are you so sure?" She shook her head, as if disappointed with his opinion.

Anger rolled over him at this affront, yet he somehow knew he was wrong. He had heard of such a fire, but it was only legend.

"Tell me where or how the fire started," the woman said.

He stood and planted his fisted hands on his hips, scanning the area, walking this way and that, looking for something to indicate how the blaze began.

"I see naught." His eyes narrowed with suspicion. The old woman knew more than she was telling.

"Think, McGregor. Use the powers the gods gave you. Many lives may depend on it, yours included."

He stared a long time into the old one's golden gaze but found no censure there, only encouragement. The sun slipped from behind a cloud, illuminating the area. After the storm last night, the sun's warmth melted the chill in his veins.

Surveying the charred ground again, he noticed a strange thing. The burn was long and thin in shape, as if a large hand swiped the earth, leaving a path of fire some thirty paces before ending.

Dylan turned back toward the old woman but found her gone. He quickly glanced north and south then back to the east, but there was no sign of her. A wave of apprehension washed through him, and a sense of unreality scattered his thoughts.

His gaze fell again to the lovers. They would hold one another for all eternity. A fleeting notion crossed his mind. When his death came, there was no place he would rather be than in the arms of the woman he loved.

"Eternal rest be unto you," he whispered to the silent pair.

A throat cleared. "Dylan, forgive me."

"Aye, brother." He answered, without removing his gaze from the couple.

"There is something you should see."

Owain's tone caused unease to crawl down his spine as he followed his brother south along the burn until the grass turned green.

There, just before the trees, were four long slices in the dirt that came together in a shallow hole of torn up earth. The slices were parallel to each other, as if some giant had clawed up the ground.

"I would guess 'tis eight paces wide and runs about fifteen paces in length," Owain stated.

Dylan frowned. The smell he could not put a name to hung heavier here. "Have you no idea what made these marks?"

When Owain's gaze came around to meet his, they held until Owain's eyelids flickered, and he glanced away.

Dylan hung his head. He was as unwilling to speak his thoughts, as Owain seemed to be. The old tales of dragons brought images of fire and death to mind, but if the answer laid that way, how could he protect his clan? And in truth, if this was a dragon's attack then the blame would be put on his shoulders, calling it the curse.

He sighed. He could not even put the blame on their

enemy the McKay, for no human could build a fire that hot.

Owain's voice broke the silence that had grown between them. "I fear to guess."

"Aye."

An eerie prickling along Dylan's neck made him glance toward the west just in time to see the form of a black-cloaked figure disappear behind a cluster of trees.

"Owain, there among the trees." He pointed to the disappearing figure. "Summon the men. I want that guard."

Chapter Five

Waking to a rough shaking of her shoulder, Rhiannon realized she was still in the McGregor's bedroom. A young girl with an intense gaze bent over her. Rhiannon immediately sat up to meet this new challenge. A draft from the cold grate made her try to pull the kilt down to cover her legs, but she found it too short. The fog of sleep lifted, and she remembered the part she played.

Spying her wool cap lying at her knees, she grabbed it and pulled the fabric down over her head to conceal her hair. She glanced around, seeking Dylan, but the room was empty except for her and the lass. Hoping the girl had not discovered her deception, Rhiannon asked, "What is your name?"

"I am Nessa. Are you a McKay?"

The question was thrown back with such enthusiasm; Rhiannon laughed, releasing some tension. "I am not so sure any more," she answered, thinking of the dream just past. "But I grew up with the McKays and called them cousins. How old are you? Eleven? Twelve?"

"I am fourteen and of an age to marry." The girl's chin came up with arrogant pride, and she straightened her spine, planting fists on her hips.

Rhiannon tilted her head to one side, bringing her brows down and a finger to her chin, as if she was thinking hard on the matter. "Aye, this I can see. Have you a man picked out?"

Rhiannon asked, straightening to stand.

Nessa's frown quickly turned to a smile. "Oh, aye. If Dylan would approve," she said, twisting back and forth at the waist. Her hip length black hair was tied to hang like an ebony rope down her back. She wore a white linen blouse and a plaid skirt, one she had grown out of from the length of it.

"While we wait for this approval, would you be kind enough to lend me your help? I have the healing gift and find I am in need of dried lavender and rose petals. Where might I search for them?"

"There may be some in the cookery where we keep the herbs. But beware; I will watch you closely so you have no chance to poison us."

"I have no wish to harm. As I said, I am a healer..." Her voice trailed off as her gaze caught on the wreath in the light of day. There was something familiar about it. It was not the flowers. Anyone could make a flower wreath. However, the weave and the ribbon were hers, a design she had worked hard to perfect. She had created this wreath, but where had Dylan found it?

Enid's words of the previous night drifted back to haunt her. She had said Dylan was bewitched the day he came home carrying that wreath. The idea was staggering. Could he have seen her in the forest? A heat surfaced around her heart. She had often gone to swim in naught but the skin she was born with. Had he been there to see her naked in her secluded pool?

"I will show you the way, but then you are to go to the stables." Startled, Rhiannon turned to see Nessa raise her shoulders in a shrug. "I was sent to tell you thus."

"Where is the McGregor?" Rhiannon asked.

"He rode out. There was a fire in the north," Nessa said just as she disappeared through the door. Rhiannon, though fleet of foot, had a difficult time keeping up with the girl, as she ran down the dark stone hallway taking one turn then another. Rhiannon thought Nessa might be part faery, so swiftly did she move.

At the kitchen, Rhiannon soon found the herbs she sought and took a bar of tallow soap scented with rosemary and violets. She would glory in removing the filth from her body before using the sweet flowers.

As she followed behind the young girl, Rhiannon wondered how Nessa could be related to Dylan. She carried the McGregor coloring. Rhiannon knew Dylan had no wife, but mayhap he had sired a child.

It was a common practice for men to have bastards, though the idea of Dylan sharing the blessed event with another woman did not set well with her. Somehow, over the past two days, she had begun to think of him as hers. It could be the reoccurring dream of the warrior, so like him, that filled her sleeping hours, or the dragon's mark along his hip. In any case, she would soon see if he was hers in truth.

She followed Nessa out of the castle and into the cool morning air. The courtyard was walled in and gated. To her left were four stables and a stone blacksmith building. Glancing opposite, she found a roped off practice field for honing sword, pike, and archer skills. Straw targets, a rope ladder, and slicing posts ringed the sides of the area while the center was open for swordplay. Beyond that, a garden followed the wall until it disappeared from her view around the castle corner. The area stood quiet with only a few people in the garden, two young boys learning the bow, and a guard or two at the gate. Unusual for this time of morning. Dylan must have taken the men with him.

"Quickly now," Nessa urged, waving her toward the

closest stable. "'Tis here you are to work. Dylan's own steeds are boarded here. I must go. Enid will wonder what has kept me for so long."

"Wait!"

Nessa disappeared back into the main hall, leaving Rhiannon to stand alone, unsure of what to do. Turning to step through the stable door, the smells of dried hay, wet earth, and horse filled the air. The dark interior stood waiting.

Her gaze darted around, barely able to pick objects out of the gloom until a horse whinnied and shuffled. It could not be so hard. She had seen the stable-boys clean and feed horses many times. Surely, she could do this.

First, she would have to find a way to light the interior. She ran her hand along the planked wall until she found a barred window. Finding the latch unlocked, she pushed and it swung open. She noticed a stick lying on the sill and used it to prop the wood shutters open. Sunlight filled the stables, showing her six stalls, two of which stood empty. She found three other windows and opened them.

Picking up a pitchfork that was propped against the wall near the door, she raked filthy hay out of the empty stalls and spread fresh, dry grass.

With the steady scrapping of her rake, her mind wandered again to Dylan McGregor and this task of mating. Was she strong enough to see it through? She shivered with apprehension. How hard could offering her body be?

He was a handsome man, but what drew her was his kindness. He had offered her, an enemy, all the food, and drink she wanted and had given her a warm and safe place to sleep. She was not mistreated in any way. She remembered the warmth of his arms as he held her through the night. No one had ever done that for her. To think of him now left warmth around her heart, and she found herself looking for his return with a bubbling excitement.

The hours passed to afternoon. Her back and shoulders ached, but she was learning many things about herself. She had not wanted to face the reality of who her parents were, but she now realized all the signs had pointed in that direction. Her love of the forest came from her father. Her gift with healing came from her mother. She was part of them whether she wanted to be or not. There was also the gift she had with animals. Mayhap the animals had always known her as a kindred spirit. With the knowledge came understanding. She felt no different, only stronger with a buzz of energy within.

A horse leaned over to nudge her shoulder, and Rhiannon reached up to rub its velvety nose. A fly buzzed around her head and she swatted at it, nearly knocking over a pail of water. Bending over to grab for the pail, she caught her reflection on its mirrored surface.

She had often noticed the brilliant green of her eyes and wondered if they came from her mother or father. Dela had said they were a gift from the forest. Nature had built a fire within and changed her eyes to a magical green.

At times people had been struck senseless by her gaze; like poor Teg, some three months past. She smiled as she pictured the scene. He was a man in his early fifties, yet still healthy and of some wealth. A stranger among them, Teg had mistaken her for a serving wench and ordered her to tend his manly needs.

She turned toward him and pinned him with an angry stare. His mouth dropped open. He backed up, tripping over the watering trough, falling in with a splash and a yell. The water had been iced over, as winter had not yet given way to spring, so the chill saw to his manly needs. The poor man had avoided her until the day of his disappearance some two days later.

"What have you to smile about, McKay?" A sharp snarling voice broke through her musings.

Rhiannon glanced up to see Enid standing just inside the door with one hand propped on her hip. She looked annoyed. "Naught of importance," Rhiannon offered, standing up.

"Are you so used to playing in manure that the feel of it brings fond memories?"

This was all she needed, a jilted woman in a sour mood. She sighed. "What is it you want, Enid?"

"You will not address me by my given name. I am addressed as mistress here by all servants."

"As you wish."

A smile touched Enid's lips, and she shortened the distance between them. "I wondered, are you a strong lad?" She reached out squeezing Rhiannon's arm. Rhiannon stepped away, not sure what game the woman played. "Have you known the passion of a woman, young McKay? I am told I am very good. 'Twould please me to teach you the ways of it once you have seen a bath."

By the light! This woman was daft. Would she take anything to her bed?

"I am here to do the Laird's bidding. If you are in need of manly comforts look elsewhere."

A murderous glint passed over Enid's eyes, but her expression was one of calculating assessment. "Who are you to tell me, the lady of the house, what I can and can not do? If I wish to have you there is none to stop me."

Rhiannon had to step carefully. She did not know how far Enid's power went. Dylan was not here to help, even if he would. Moreover, if Enid found out she had tried to seduce a woman. Rhiannon shivered, leaving the thought unfinished.

"I was but saying that I have no interest in what you speak of. 'Twas not my intention to harm your feelings."

Stalking over to stand in front of Rhiannon, Enid darted a glance at the door before a malicious gleam lit her eyes.

"Beware, McKay! Those who cross me find the end of a whip. No one here will lift a finger to help you."

Rhiannon's breath caught in her throat, and she flattened her palm over her chest, seeking the reassurance of her talisman lying hidden under her shirt. If Enid was not evil, she was its apprentice.

The thundering roar of many horses' hooves pounding the earth broke the tension building between them. Hearing loud snorts and yells of greeting, Rhiannon prayed Dylan had returned.

"I am under the Laird's protection."

"He is not always here."

A shadow fell across the door, followed by a man and his horse, but it was not Dylan. Instead, it was the large man Rhiannon had crossed swords with on the battlefield.

"Lad, I would speak—Enid, what do you here?"

"I was but giving instruction," she answered, her expression once again under control. "You must watch these McKays all the time or nothing would get done. Now that you are here, I will leave the lad to you." Enid walked to the entrance and darted out the door, leaving Rhiannon alone with the giant Highlander.

"You wish something?" Rhiannon inquired, still shaken by Enid's malicious threat.

"Aye, I am called Owain, brother to the McGregor."

Rhiannon's eyes widened with surprise, then she remembered Dylan calling him brother during the battle.

He cleared his throat. "I but ask after your health, lad." He moved his weight from one foot to the other.

She swallowed the urge to smile, realizing he was uncomfortable and in his own way, trying to apologize for his actions the day before.

"Be at ease, Owain. I am well."

He nodded. His gaze fell to the ground, then back up to meet hers once more. She got the impression he wished to say more. "'Tis not right a lad your size should fight in a man's battle, but you held your own."

Taking his mount, he turned and left. Though the moment had been awkward, it was better they were friends and not foes.

Moving to the door, yet keeping to the shadows, she obtained a clear view of the courtyard. Horses and men crowded the area as well as a few women to greet them. The clang of steel on steel from the practice field rang above the noise of snorting horses and conversations.

However, all that faded when she spotted Dylan striding her way, leading his horse. The late sun winked in and out behind evening clouds, bathing him in dark and light. The wind tossed his long black hair about his shoulders, like raven's wings. His brows were furrowed, and his gaze earthbound.

He worries, she thought. Had someone been hurt in the fire? He raised his gaze to meet hers. His frown deepened, and a spasm of irritation crossed his face. His lips pursed, making his chin more pronounced. She stiffened her spine, waiting. Had she displeased him in someway?

Even angry, he was handsome and strong, yet dangerous like a predator. The closer he came, the faster her heart beat.

"Here, lad." He handed her the horse's lead. His large hand barely brushed over her smaller one, before he turned away.

Not wanting him to leave, she reached out for him without thought. "What burden weighs upon you, Laird?"

Her touch was gentle and warm, like a leaf on the water, yet he felt unable to move away. He reached up and rubbed the back of his neck. Why should she show him concern? She was the enemy, yet she cared to ask what burdens he carried. He glanced down to where she touched him, her hand soft on his battle-scarred flesh.

Some demon twisted his gut. "You brave the curse with your touch, lad. Have you not heard evil will befall you?"

"There is naught evil about you. Here I stand unharmed and well-treated in the enemy's camp. I have no fear of you, Laird."

He met her gaze, and again the green eyes called to something deep within him. Something he did not wish to answer or could not. With a certainty, he had seen those eyes before.

"Mayhap I make life too easy. Should I strip you naked and tie you to a pole? Growing up is tough for a smooth soft-faced lad. Some might take you for a lass." With a gasp, her hand had come up to her chest in a protective gesture. She was letting the woman inside show. Then the wind shifted and he wrinkled his nose. "Yet others might take you for a sow from the filth and smell. You will bathe this night."

"I will bathe when I am ready."

"You will bathe when told, or I will see it done now in yonder horse trough."

At her wide-eyed expression, he shook his head. He had no time to play these games. Nor did he want to share his ill temper with her. He was still annoyed that the man in the woods had gotten away, as well as finding no leads to explain how the burning started. With his warm feeling gone he indicated the reins and said, "See that my mount is fed and watered." Turning, he walked over to the practice field where his brother stood, a weapon in hand. With a quick jerk, Dylan pulled his tunic over his head and tossed it on a wooden bench.

"Are you ready to get beat this eve? Owain asked, a smile creasing his face.

"There is more of a chance that the sun will not rise in the morn, brother."

Owain laughed. "Bring it on."

Rhiannon gave feed and water to the horse then moved back to the doorway when she heard the clang of swords. Dylan's muscles strained and bunched with every sword thrust. Sweat glistened on his skin in the late sun. The kilt swung around iron thighs and bulging calves. His back arched as he dodged the swipe of his brother's sword.

Dylan twisted and brought his sword to meet Owain's, the clang vibrating with force. The powerful muscles in Dylan's arms and broad chest rippled. His movements were swift and full of deadly grace.

She could not look away, nor did she wish too. She felt a quickening deep within, an exciting anticipation of the night to come. Only a touch of unease rippled through her thoughts before the image of running her hands over his muscles, and scars, blowing it away.

Dylan ducked, then quickly twisted, knocking the sword out of his brother's hands. The sword slid a few paces and came to rest near a cart of grain.

He put the tip of his sword to Owain's neck. A mischievous smile replaced the frown he had been carrying. "Concede. The victory is mine."

At his brother's curse, Dylan threw his head back and laughed. A few of the other men on the field joined him.

Dylan swung his sword down and clapped Owain on the shoulder. "It could just as easily have been me conceding."

"I do not remember the day when 'twas I who won with you," Owain said, smiling. "But you are getting older, and I will see victory soon."

"I am but four and thirty. Would you see me in my grave?"

"Nay, Dylan. I but enjoy taking you down a peg from your lofty height."

Dylan spotted the lass watching from the stable shadows, and a fire lit his veins. Her bright emerald eyes burned with seductive innocence. She had become sexually aroused while watching him, and the knowledge stroked his own desire.

Her steady gaze bore into him in silent expectation. From a distance, he let his gaze travel over her face, then over her concealed breasts. When he raised his gaze to meet hers, her mouth parted. His body responded with stirrings he should not have for anyone but his Lady of the Forest. The frown creased his brow again.

"Do you want to give me another chance at victory?" Getting no answer, Owain looked in the same direction as Dylan, but he saw nothing in the shadow's gloom. "Dylan?"

Dylan turned to face him. "Not today, Owain. You will have another day to win your victory."

"Wait. 'Tis something else I wish to speak of. 'Tis not right the way others fear you and think evil follows you. At times, I want to lay the flat of my sword along side their thick skulls. It may knock the dust from between their ears."

"Give them no thought, Owain. I hope to soon have the right woman at my side, then mayhap they will turn their thoughts to pleasant things."

"You will take a wife?"

"Aye, if I can find her. She seems to have vanished, or is unwilling to spend time in my company." Owain saw the dark closed-off look fall over his brother's face and wanted to kick himself for putting it there. He had tried and failed to comfort.

"Now," Dylan said, "I need a mug of ale and a bath." Dylan sounded as if the world rested on his shoulders. Weariness set in lines around his eyes.

Owain watched Dylan storm off to disappear inside the keep. He shook his head with helpless torment. When he glanced toward the stable, again, it was to see the lad silently watching the door to the keep.

A raw and primitive grief overwhelmed Rhiannon when Dylan turned away. His eyes had told her he had seen through her disguise to the woman beneath. He had warmed to her. She had felt the intense physical awareness, an invisible web of attraction building between them, but then he had broken away. Why?

The first person Dylan saw as he stalked into the main hall was a kitchen maid. "You there, I'm in need of a hot bath. See that water is sent to my room." Without waiting to see if she heard, he grabbed a pitcher of mead from the table and ascended the stairs to his room.

Dylan poured a mug of the brew and sat down in a chair near the fire. Only minutes passed before he watched a parade of servants carrying steaming buckets of water to the large wooden tub set before the hearth, but his mind centered on the McKay lass.

This lass had nothing visually appealing, yet he had been physically aroused by just a glance from her. The last time he had been so moved was when he came upon his forest faery.

Suddenly a thought hit him like an arrow in the gut—her eyes, those brilliant green eyes. He had seen that same color in the eyes of the forest faery. Mayhap he felt this attraction for the lass because she reminded him of his Lady of the Forest. Somehow, the idea justified his lust.

"There you go, Laird."

"Aye, thank you, lass. Now tell the McKay lad I have need of him."

Left alone, he tipped the mug to his lips, downing the mead and letting the cup dangle from his fingers. He was in need of a hot soak to ease his sore muscles and troubled mind. He stood to set the mug back on the stand, glancing out the window as he did.

"You called, Laird?" Rhiannon asked, stepping into the room.

He turned toward her. "Aye, lad. I am in need of a bath and wish assistance."

Rhiannon sucked in a silent breath. Surely, he could not want her to bathe him, but his steady stare told her he did.

"I can not." She backed up, pressing against the door.

Dylan stood away from the window and strode toward her like a hunter after prey. Her whole being urged her to flee, but the light in his eyes held her immobile. He stopped inches from her.

"Aye, you can."

His towering height was intimidating, yet the warmth of his sweet breath filled her soul with such need. She wanted him to touch her, warm her. As he raised both arms on either side of her, the anticipation was almost more than she could stand. She swayed toward him slightly and held her breath, waiting for the heat of his hands.

The door clicked shut behind her, and she heard the rasp of the bolt. The realization that he had only meant to close the door made sharp fingers of regret run through her heart.

When he had yet to remove his arms, she met his gaze again. His eyes narrowed and burned with fire. One side of his mouth turned up in a lopsided grin. He had seen her response to him and was not unaffected by it.

He held her imprisoned between his arms a moment more. His eyes lowered to her lips, and she could not help but moisten them. As his gaze slid to her concealed breasts, her breathing quickened. Every place his gaze touched, she was as affected as if his fingers had traveled there.

He broke away, dropping his arms and turning back to the tub of steaming water. The chill of the room replaced his warmth. She stood as if made of stone, not knowing what to do. He was destined to be hers, yet how could she make him understand that?

Rhiannon watched him remove his clothes and step into the water. The set of his wide shoulders and a strong back tapering to lean hips and muscular thighs filled her gaze before he sat in the tub with his back facing her. Steam rolled up to crown his dark head, causing her to feel the heat from across the room.

"Rhi," his deep voice poured over her. "I am not a man who enjoys boys sexually. Is there aught you wish to tell me?"

The silence hung thickly as he waited. She cleared her throat. This was a perfect time to tell him everything, but the words would not come.

"I needed protection."

Without glancing her way, he held up a bathing cloth. "Come, if you will speak no more, wash my back."

She crossed the distance that separated them and reached for the wet cloth. He leaned forward giving her his back. Kneeling down beside the tub, she asked, "How did you know I was a woman?"

"Little things that first day gave me cause to wonder, then that night you had kicked the covers off and the room grew chilled. When I added logs to the fire, I noticed your long hair and how your chest was uneven. Your breasts wrapped tight to conceal them."

She used the cloth to caress his back and up along his shoulders. "Why didn't you speak of it?"

He sighed. "I had hoped, in time, you would share it and why you needed the disguise."

"I wished to tell you, many times, but had not the way to keep your pride intact. Forgive me."

"There is aught to forgive. I find you refreshingly clever as well as brave. I find a lot to recommend you."

His words brought a thrill to her heart as she worked the cloth over his skin. A comfortable silences fell between them as her gentle fingers, moved aside his long black hair so it wouldn't get wet, letting its silky coolness slide along her hand.

His back was smooth and hard. As he moved, the muscles bunched under her hand. He was wondrously made. It was no wonder the goddess favored him.

Rhiannon smoothed the soap over his back, and then moved over his shoulders and arms. Many a scar marred his perfection, but it suited him. He was a warrior of his own right. When she moved to wash his chest, he leaned back against the tub. She could feel his gaze on her, watching every move her hands made.

The spicy, fragrant soap mingled with his male scent and filled her senses. A private world of scent, touch, and sight wrapped itself around her. With a will of their own, her hands moved to wash his chest. She no longer had the cloth. She used only her bare hand on naked flesh. Moving lower, she ran fingers along his tight belly. The heat from his skin moved through her to land between her legs and stir a growing need.

She moved lower still and he hissed grabbing her wrist. She raised her heavy-lidded gaze to his. His eyes burned from an inner fire. One, she realized, she had lit.

Her chaotic breathing and the trembling of her lower limbs told her that she too was affected. She wanted to learn all that he could teach.

Suddenly, as if a cold wind blew across her mind, she remembered the cleansing ritual. Dela had given detailed instructions. Rhiannon could let nothing happen here.

She jerked her hand from Dylan's grasp and backed away. His eyes narrowed and sharpened on her. "Woman?"

"'Tis not the time," she answered, backing toward the door. When he made to rise, she turned, threw back the bolt and flew out the door. A deep menacing growl followed her.

The hounds bounded in just as Dylan finished putting on his kilt. They both circled the room, no doubt searching for what had angered him, but the culprit was gone.

Dylan paced, stopping before the wreath over the mantel, his loins painfully full. He had not wanted a woman in a long time. Mayhap his desire was affecting his mind, or mayhap she had cast a spell over him.

If he needed a woman so badly, Enid was there for the taking. She was considered beautiful by most, but he favored red hair and green eyes.

This disguised lass may be shapeless, but her spirit drew him by her honor, unseen in many, and by the fire of her consuming passion. By right of war, she was his, and he wanted her.

There was no getting around that truth. He walked to the window. The moon hung low on the horizon, almost full. Its golden face, larger than usual, lit everything with a warm glow.

A flicker of movement from the woods caught his attention. It was unusual to see anyone near the forest after dark. Narrowing his eyes, he watched the lass who had invaded his thoughts disappear among the trees.

"By the cross! She is on the run."

Dylan growled. She was his, and he was not about to let her escape. Taking up his sword, he ordered the hounds to stay, then left the room. His brisk stride took him through the castle, passing Owain as he headed for the gate.

"Brother," Owain shouted. "What has brought on this ill mood?"

Dylan's facial muscles tightened into a deep frown. "I am off to hunt."

"Care for company?"

"Nay, 'tis prey I must seek alone." Owain's knowing laughter followed him. He passed through the gate, nodding to the watch on duty. The woods were but a few paces from the gate, and he entered without a backward look.

Dylan had no problem in following the lass. Her body called to his, heating his need to touch her, to make love to her.

As he approached her position, Dylan spotted a small fire through the trees. Next, a flash of white linen caught his eye. Rhi stood with her back to him. She had removed her deer-hide boots, leaving her feet and calves bare. Her cap lay with her boots. Her soft compelling voice, as she sang, pulled at his soul and wrapped around his insides.

He stayed in the shadows, leaning his shoulder against a large tree. With arms crossed over his chest, he watched as she pulled her shirt over her head and dropped it to the ground. The anticipation grew nearly unbearable, as she slowly unwound the cloth from her breasts.

He wanted to see what she had so carefully kept hidden.

When she added the strips of white linen to the pile of discarded clothes, his loins tightened.

Dylan saw the red pressure marks along her back where the material had been wrapped. He wanted to rub the blemishes from her creamy skin and taste the curve of her neck. She threw a wealth of fiery red hair over her shoulder and removed the kilt from around her hips.

His heart skipped a beat. Wonder filled him. Could it be? 'Twas certain no, two women could look so alike. Had his Lady of the Forest been within his grasp? His all this time?

He should be furious at this deception, but the discovery that she was human and his rightful possession was more than he had dreamed. He wanted her to turn toward him so he could see her face and body, but instead, she stepped into the pool, carrying a bar of soap.

Dylan smiled. She had not been trying to escape, only to bathe. She waded in no deeper than her waist. Golden moonbeams danced on the small ripples made on the water by her movements.

On the far side, rocks formed the pool's shore, but here grass and a few shrubs lined the edge. Trees stood as a curtain, protecting the small pool and the woman who bathed there.

She cupped her hands and splashed water on her face. Taking the soap, she scrubbed her face and arms before disappearing under water.

Dylan stepped from the shadows into the firelight. He would not lose her again. When she resurfaced, he stopped. She arched her neck, flipping her wet hair over her head. A spray of droplets filled the air. She had turned slightly, revealing more of her body to his hungry view. Her eyes were closed, and a smile of pleasure touched her lips. Raising her arms to her hair, she soaped it and then leaned her head back to rinse.

The arch of her body thrust her breasts forward. Drops of water hung like golden diamonds from each rosy nipple. Dylan moved to the water's edge. He needed to fill his hands with her and savor the water off her breasts. He had waited a lifetime. He would wait no longer.

"Rhi?"

Chapter Six

Hearing Dylan's husky voice so close, she gasped and jerked her gaze toward him.

"Rhiannon," she confessed, unsure of herself.

"Come here."

He stood, holding his hand out. His sultry command warmed her, but it was the flames in his eyes that beckoned, bringing her from the water. The song of enchantment she had been singing stuck in her throat. She was as nervous as a bird on its first flight.

Her steps were slow and unsteady until she took his warm hand. She leaned over, picking up the small pouch of dried lavender and rose petals, before she stood to face him.

He took the pouch from her. "What is this?" His long strides brought them to a grassy spot near the water's edge.

"'Tis dried flowers. They must be rubbed upon my skin. 'Tis a ritual I must finish 'afore we are blessed."

"We?"

She nodded her gaze never leaving his face, waiting for him to lead.

His gaze ran over her body, and a smile touched his lips. "Would you lie with me then?" The intense longing in his gaze made her heart ache. His smile so loving her breath caught in her throat.

"Aye." A word so small yet it held a wealth of meaning.

"I will not force you. If you say nay, I will stop."

She smiled at his kindness. Even though this was expected of her, she found she wanted it. To be loved, to touch, and to hold this strong god standing before her filled her every wish.

He unwrapped his kilt and spread it over the grass. Looking over his male form in the flicker of fire and moonlight, her insides heated, melted, and brought forward a liquid flame to settle between her thighs.

His hair shone jet-black and blew wild and free in the night's breeze. His blue eyes sought to persuade and cajole. Her gaze slid down his chest, watching the sinew bunch and tighten under bronzed skin, but it was the firmness of his manhood that made her draw in a breath. It looked wrapped in soft velvet, and she wanted to touch it, but feared to make the first move.

Dylan's large hand took her chin and tilted it up gently. He brought her face close to his. Like a whisper, his lips touched hers before he nibbled at the edge of her mouth. He was coaxing her to respond, to follow his lead, and she was more than eager.

"Open for me," he urged, running his thumb over her bottom lip. Delicious sensation filled her as she parted her lips to meet his.

He ran a hand up into her hair to rub her neck. He was warm and hard, and she needed to be close. She raised her hands, placing them on his shoulders for support.

With her touch, his grip tightened, and he became more demanding more forceful with his kiss. A moan rumbled through his chest to play havoc with her heart. His other hand slid down her back to curve around her hips, pulling her up against him. She felt the hard evidence of his need pressed to her belly and gloried in it. Her breasts pressed into his chest, the feel of flesh on flesh, bringing a gasp of wonder. She never knew it would feel so good.

His tongue slipped between her parted lips, stoking her mouth, tasting her. Following his lead, Rhiannon gently touched her tongue to his then became bolder, exploring the sweetness of his mouth.

Mingling with the rustle of the trees and the crackling of the fire, she could hear the seductive music of their lips meeting in a hungry rhythm.

Running her hands into his hair, she urged his head closer. His hot breath caressed her cheek. She inhaled, pulling his scent deep into her lungs. Then she exhaled only to have him inhale, as if taking her very life into himself. Rhiannon moaned and grew faint, her legs shaky. He must have sensed her need because he picked her up and placed her on his plaid.

Through the haze of passion, she remembered the ritual. But Dylan surprised her. He took the pouch and brought forth a small amount of the dried petals to warm them in his palm.

Rhiannon tilted her head toward him as he took her hand. He began rubbing the flowers up her bare arm, around her shoulder and down again. The heat of her body mixed with the dried flowers to bring forth the sweet scent of lavender and roses.

She trembled at his warm touch, but found she could not keep from touching him as well. Running her hand along his thigh, then up along his belly to rest her palm over his heart before moving lower again. Glancing toward him, she saw he was watching her boldly. Slowly and seductively, his gaze slid downward, over her breasts to her womanhood. As his eyes lingered, a wet heat pulsed there, igniting a fire in her belly.

His naked thigh brushed against hers. He slid his hand

beneath her elbow and along her other arm, barely touching the sides of her breasts.

"Lie back for me, and I will worship your body."

She reached out to run her fingers across the ridges of his chest and along his scar in a caress as soft as a whisper. "Might I too, worship thy form?" she asked softly.

His smile held a mischievous delight, as he coaxed her to lie back on the plaid that was cushioned by grass and violets. He braced himself above her. His hair fell over his shoulders to curtain them. A sparkle lit his gaze.

"First, 'tis my turn."

With gentle movements, he stroked her shoulders and neck, causing her breasts to tighten, wanting his touch. His large hands slowly smoothed around them, cupping each breast and slid up to roll her hardened nipple between his thumb and forefinger.

She sucked in a long breath, arching her back. A pleasure she had never known raised her senses and heightened need. She covered his hands with her own, holding them to her; afraid he would stop.

"You respond as if you were born to be loved and I was the one to set the sleeping passion within you free," he said wonder lacing his words.

She closed her eyes, trying to hold back a moan, as he slid the palm of his hand over her nipples before moving lower. "Do you approve?"

"Aye, sweet one. I could not be more pleased."

She caressed his hair-roughened cheek, running a finger along his jaw and giving a small shy smile.

He returned the smile as he ran his hands down her ribs, moving his thumbs along her stomach. He cupped both her hips, and passed his fingers down each leg. He coaxed

Rhiannon to bend her legs at the knee until her feet rested flat on the plaid beneath them.

With his eyes holding hers, he put his hands on her knees and pushed them part. She resisted but a moment before allowing him to reveal her most private haven.

She closed her eyes and dug her hands into the plaid. Fear of the unknown raised its ugly head, and she became tense, unsure of what he would do or say.

"Look at me," Dylan demanded. "Know that 'tis I who love you and none other."

She opened her eyes to behold his and saw vulnerability mixed with his need. Could he have fears as well? Somehow knowing this made her own disappear. She smiled and ran her hand along his cheek. "I see only you, Dylan."

"Then let me pleasure you, My Lady of the Forest." Dylan reached between her parted thighs and slid a finger along her parted wet seam. She groaned and moved her hips, seeking his touch.

A soft smile curled his lips at her innocent response. He had no doubt he was her first. This knowledge sent a storm of heat and pleasure through his veins. She was his. No other would have this gift. Wanting to give her more pleasure, he inserted a finger within the folds, stroking her, bringing more cries to her lips. She was wet and tight, yet he twisted and inserted another finger.

He watched her experience each new sensation. The moistness increased and a quivering shook her straining limbs. She pressed herself into his hand causing his fingers to go deeper. With his thumbs, he parted her folds, then ran a wet finger up and over the hard nub of pleasure.

She jerked and whimpered, calling out his name, as spasms of intense pleasure forged through her body and she leapt off the edge into paradise. No greater pleasure could she have given him at this moment. The answering jolt in his body was savage, primitive. His body hardened painfully and the need to be inside her consumed him. He would wait no longer to find the heaven he sought. Dylan leaned over and took her nipple into his mouth, sucking hard, while his finger moved inside her moist heat once more before he would replace them to thrust himself deep within her.

"I will have you, Rhiannon. Now."

She whimpered, tossing her head back and answered a breathless, "Aye." He was the master, and she his instrument. She was being swept away by an earth shattering current.

Suddenly, the warmth of his body was gone, and she lay confused and in need. Her blood rushing in her veins. She watched in dismay as he rolled away. He grabbed his claymore and stood with his back to her, scanning the woods, every muscle strained in readiness.

There rose a deep empty ache inside her. She needed him to finish what they had begun. There was more to this act, she knew, and he had raised a hunger that stood unsatisfied. "Dylan? I am in need of you."

Dylan glanced at her and recognized the sexual need burning in her eyes. He, too, felt the wound of unfulfillment, but satisfaction would have to come at another time.

"'Tis glad I am to hear, lass, but many are coming. Cover yourself. Make ready to flee."

She quickly sat up and grabbed the plaid, wrapping it around her body. She looked past the firelight into the trees. The Moonstone lay cool and quiet upon her chest, giving no indication of evil.

But it was too late to flee.

Men dropped from trees and stepped from behind twisted

trunks. All carried weapons but none had them displayed for battle. They had been well hidden in their green tunics. A blonde man wearing leaves braided in the silver streaks of his hair moved closer to them.

Dylan reached one arm round Rhiannon to pull her close behind him. "Stay at my back so I know where you are at all times."

Rhiannon placed a hand on his bare shoulder, while trying to hold the plaid together about her nakedness. Her heart in her throat, she peeked around Dylan's naked form to study the invaders.

There, she came face to face with bright green eyes so like her own. She blinked and blinked again. Glancing from one man to another, she saw that they all had green eyes. Curious, she stepped around Dylan to have a better view, but he quickly pushed her back.

"Stay behind me," he ordered through clenched teeth, yet his gaze never left the leader. "State your business, stranger."

Dylan's muscles tensed and bunched under her hand. He was wound tight, ready to defend. Strange, even outnumbered she had no fear for herself, only for Dylan. A sense of urgency prickled over her skin. Something vital was about to happen and she must protect Dylan at any cost.

"I come to see if you are worthy," the leader stated, rubbing his chin.

Dylan frowned. "You speak in riddles. What clan are you from? From your dress, I would say Lowlanders. This land belongs to the McGregors."

Dylan noticed the leader shifted his eyes to glance around him. "I also come to see Rhiannon."

She gasped. "You know my name?" Again, she peeked out from around Dylan's back. Her eyes widened with surprise.

"How is it you know me?"

The blonde leader's gaze slid down her barely concealed body. Dylan grabbed her around the waist this time to control her actions. He had only just found her. He would not lose her again.

"Feast your eyes elsewhere. The maid is mine. Take your riddles and leave my lands."

"Would you die for her?"

Rhiannon gasped, slipping closer within the circle of his arms. Dylan squeezed her, giving reassurance.

"Are you challenging me?"

"'Tis just a question."

"Aye, no one will have her while I live."

The blonde man raised his brow. "We will see." He pulled a blade from its sheath. The steel had a bluish green tint to it and glowed in the firelight. *The Singing Sword.*

"Nay!" Rhiannon placed her hand over Dylan's heart, but kept her gaze on the leader. "I see no evil in you. Why do you do these things? We harm no one."

Dylan could not look at Rhiannon. He needed all his wits to face this foe. "I would ask one thing. No matter the outcome, my lady shall leave here unharmed."

"Your Lady?" An instant change came over the blonde man. He grew tense and growled, pointing his sword at them. "You have taken her maidenhead?"

Dylan narrowed his eyes and snarled. "'Tis none of your affair."

The leader yelled, "Aye, 'tis. You may well have doomed us all." He waved to his men. "Take her!"

Three men advanced on them. Dylan pushed Rhiannon behind him, and spread his feet for better balance. He would take down the man that reached them first. But before anyone could reach them Rhiannon closed her eyes, dropping the plaid to clasp the Moonstone between her hands. She stood naked. Her ivory skin glowed in the moonlight.

A wind stirred up around them and a hush fell over the forest as if all nature waited. The wind grew more powerful, whipping their hair about their shoulders and faces, as well as a few dried leaves. Dylan glanced from the leader to Rhiannon, then back to the leader.

The forest men who had been advancing halted, watching. Their hair and clothes lay still. No wind touched them.

Dylan's gaze fell again to Rhiannon. He could hardly fathom what he was seeing. If his eyes did not deceive him, this phenomenon came from Rhiannon.

He frowned, wanting to step away, but men encircled them and he must protect her at all cost. For whatever reason, she had included him in this play of nature, and he would see it through. As a light surrounded her, she threw her head back, her mouth parting on a gasp. The pillar of light encompassing her ran into the heavens, clothing her in a robe of brilliant white.

A buzz of energy tingled through him, yet he stood in darkness. The sword in his hand glowed like lightning. The power of the light was blinding.

When he glanced back at the men, they were all kneeling with heads bowed and swords laid upon the ground, the hilt of each sword offered up to him in honor. Only the leader stood, his eyes lit with emotion, his sword ready to strike, yet he waited.

"Dylan."

He turned to meet Rhiannon's glowing gaze. Tears pooled around liquid emeralds. He could not look away, nor did he want to. The heat in her gaze seemed to build to an incredible fire, a blaze that coerced and seduced.

She spoke loud and clear, making a vow before all the heavens. "Dylan McGregor. 'Tis you I choose above all others. May the light grant you strength and wisdom to defend and defeat thy enemies. Take my gift and in so doing become my champion." She raised her hand and placed her palm over his heart.

Intense heat nearly brought him to his knees. He staggered a moment, fighting the need to move away. Struggling through the heat's power, he could not draw air and feared his chest would burst. With a mighty roar, he raised both arms to the heavens; his sword brandished above his head.

Queasiness gripped his stomach. Closing his eyes, he gritted his teeth against the assault.

The beat of his heart sung loudly in his head. The rhythm grew slower until he thought it would stop bringing his death. His gaze moved with a fierce hunger to the woman before him. They both stood naked in the ring of light. The sluggish blood traveling through his veins brought a weakness to his limbs.

A second beating heart joined his, and the two hearts took up rhythm, converging to make one strong heartbeat. Power and strength seeped into his body like steel and fever. The beast within moved, and he inhaled bringing it under control once more.

With Rhiannon's next exhale, the wind and light left. The woods seemed unnaturally dark with only the moon and fire to light the area. Dylan felt the heat of her hand leave his chest and caught the whisper of his name before her body went limp.

"Rhiannon!" He caught her to his chest before her knees touched the ground. Laying her gently on the grass, a great fear boiled up within him. He covered her with his plaid and prayed to all that would hear. With gentle fingers, he brushed a curl off her forehead and felt for a heartbeat. He sighed in relief. She lived.

"You have survived The Choosing. Well done." The leader lowered his sword. "If you had not, I would have taken your head."

Dylan stood to meet the threat and wondered at the respect he could see reflected in the man's eyes.

"I am Gian." He bowed. "Now you must defeat me. Rhiannon will go to the man who draws first blood."

"Rhiannon is mine!" Dylan tightened his hand around the sword. No one would take her from him. With everything that happened, he should be confused, and weakened, but it was just the opposite. His mind was clear, and the strength of hundreds of Highlanders coursed through his veins. He would not be defeated.

From the look in Gian's eyes, Dylan knew he would not be easily dissuaded from his folly, but folly it was. The heat of the fire burned at his back, its crackle and sizzle sounded loudly in a forest gone still.

Dylan watched the other man walk steadily closer. He forced himself to loosen up. The first move came quickly. Gian lunged, forcing Dylan to step back or be run through. The slash of the older man's sword passed once more, barely missing his throat.

This was no game he played. The challenger stepped forward and struck again. This time Dylan met the attack. The scrape and slide of metal rang loud in the silence. Green sparks flew from the opposite sword.

Dylan took Gian's measure just as his own was weighed. He guessed this fight a fair match. His one worry, the sword. It had magic, he was sure of it. The advantage would not be his.

They circled each other. Dylan looked for his opening. It was his turn to attack, and the swords rang out. The strain to his forearm was intense. His muscles bunched with exertion, but held strong. The swords clanged once more with no giving in either opponent.

A bead of sweat rolled down his cheek, making him realize the effort he was using. He knew he had to finish this fight. He would use a more aggressive attack, and find a way to slip past Gian's guard. It would be a calculated risk against the older man's highly honed skills. Dylan understood the risk. One slip might see his life ended, and Rhiannon in the challenger's hands. The thought of another man touching her brought on a heat of anger and demon strength.

Dylan gave the battle cry and charged Gian striking him with his sword, keeping him off balance with repeated blows. All the other man could do was defend himself against the repeated blows. Dylan did not hesitate when an opening came. He cut a feint high, then went low, slicing the man on the thigh.

When Gian fell to the ground, Dylan pointed his sword at the man's throat. The beast within wanted to push the blade through, ending any threat this man might be to Rhiannon, but his honor held the blow. With a deep inhale and exhale, he stepped back, waited to see if Gian would be honorable and leave them in peace or if the fight would continue. He would kill the man if swords were raised again. The competitor lifted his gaze. A frown marred his face before it changed to a smile.

"Well done."

"She is mine!" Dylan stated proudly. Expecting the man to do something devious, he kept his sword aimed and ready, waiting for an answer. The man stood up and dusted the leaves from his breeches.

"Aye, you have been found worthy. Come, we must talk."

Gian turned his back and walked away.

Dylan looked over to Rhiannon still caught in exhausted slumber with her fiery hair fanned out over the grass. Purple violets encircled her head firelight played over her soft features and her body was wrapped in his plaid.

Rhiannon was his. The power of those words caused something warm to squeeze in his chest and the strength of his possessiveness surprised him.

"She will sleep awhile. The Choosing weakens the spirit of the one giving the ritual," Gian attested. "Come sit with me."

Dylan frowned at Gian and stayed standing. He was yet unwilling to leave Rhiannon's side, but he did lower his sword. Gian motioned one of his men to come forward. "Bring our young Laird a tunic to wear home." The man left to do as bidden. "The days of our ancestors the Picts and fighting naked are gone."

Dylan swept his hand down his body. "I was not preparing for battle, but for love. Now tell me of this choosing?"

"The Choosing happens to all the people of the forest when the time is right." The guard came back and handed a green tunic to Dylan, bowed and left. A gesture of respect? Dylan frowned, reaching up to rub the back of his neck.

"I have not witnessed the like."

"As I said it only comes to the people of...ah...my clan."

Dylan raised his brow. He had caught the slip. "She's not a McKay?"

"Nay," Gian held up a hand, "and do not ask more. Soon you will learn all. For now, know I am a friend."

Pulling the woolen tunic over his head and down around his body, Dylan gave thought to the words. He did not know what to make of this man. He spoke in light and shade, giving much and bestowing little. Glancing down, he noticed Gian's wound.

"It bleeds little, but I would see it tended to," Dylan suggested.

"I have you to thank for that. Your sword did not drink deep. I am duly grateful." Gian pulled a small vial from his belt. He took out the stopper and poured a few drops of amber liquid on the wound before resealing the vial and putting it back in his belt.

"I must warn you of trouble," Gian said.

"Why would you do that?" Now Dylan was suspicious.

The older man laughed, showing off a dimple. He sat back against the tree trunk, looking up at Dylan. "You still hold a grudge. Is it because I interrupted your love-play, or that I wanted to take Rhiannon?"

Anger resurfaced at the man's words, causing Dylan's hand to clench around his sword. If this fool tried to take her again, he would receive more than a scratch on his leg.

"After all that was done, do you think I would now take your counsel?" Dylan looked annoyed. Letting go of his sword, he crossed his arms over his chest.

Gian held up his sword and ran a thumb down the blade. A bead of blood swelled. The steel's bluish-green light moved like waves of lightning over its surface. "I give this warning for Rhiannon's sake. 'Tis her safety I seek."

"Then speak, I will listen."

"The McKays will attack your keep on the morrow."

"How is this known to you?" Dylan asked, his brow furrowed. Confused, he asked, "Be you one of their lot?"

Gian shook his head then stood to face him. "I know a great many things. But know this, young Laird, I speak truth."

"Then I thank you for the warning," Dylan offered.

"Beware, McGregor, there is one among the McKays your sword must not touch."

"Speak his name."

"Robert McKay. He is young and Rhiannon and him carry a bond."

Dylan's sharp gaze struck Gian's face. "They are bonded?"

"The same."

He had thought her innocent of men. Could he be wrong? Had she loved another man, or worse could she have been raped? Had she been fleeing from a cruel lover? Mayhap that was why she had come to him in disguise. She had said it was for protection. Then he remembered the man on the far hill after the battle, and the way he had bid farewell to Rhiannon. There had been a deep affection between them. He did not like the way of his thoughts and forcefully pushed them away.

"Here, a gift," Gian offered.

Dylan tried to shake the sinking feeling in his stomach by focusing on the object offered to him. Stretched between Gian's hands lay the magical sword.

Dylan frowned. "You are giving me your sword?"

"Aye. 'Tis called The Singing Sword. You are the first to defeat me. And the last."

"I have heard it said The Singing Sword was made and blessed by faery."

"So 'tis." Gain smiled, the dimple winking into view again. "It was anointed with a powerful herbal condenser to attract and hold energy and any charge given to it. Tinctures of gold and emerald have been applied to the surface and blessed with moonlight. There is no other sword of its kind." The man's voice held a note of reverence. "Now, she will sing for you. Take her."

Dylan reached out, taking the jeweled hilt in a firm grip. He lifted the blade into the air. "She is much lighter than my own." He stepped back and swung the blade with a forward slash. Then did a back slash. When he swung repeatedly, the sword started to keen with a shrill whine and the bluish-green glow nearly blinded him.

He stopped and met Gian's gaze. "'Tis a fine blade."

"She sings well for you. Take care of her. She may well save your life. Do you know her worth?"

"Oh aye. 'Tis told she will cut through anything."

"Aye, even stone, but she will not cut the flesh of her owner. I realized she had chosen you when she sliced into my thumb." Gian placed his hand on Dylan's shoulder. "I must take my leave. We will meet again. Guard the woman well, Dylan McGregor."

He watched Gian and his men disappear as quickly as they had come. He was alone with Rhiannon again.

The pungent scent of pine mingled with that of heather and wood smoke in the stillness of the night. The fire had burned low, but the moon overhead brightened the sky.

Dylan stooped beside Rhiannon, placing his elbow on his knees. The easy rise and fall of her chest, covered only by his plaid, tempted him to resume the intimacies. But he had never taken advantage of a woman and would not start now.

Running a finger down her pale cheek and over her full bottom lip, he thought about how responsive she had been with him. Blood rushed to his loins and his chest tightened. He had searched for her for many months.

To feel this deep need for someone left him vulnerable, and the fear of that gnawed his insides. He was caught between needing her to fill his emptiness, but afraid of taking it and being left open to more pain and rejection like what he received from his own clan. He desired her, but who was she really? What life had she led before him? What would he do if he found out she had a husband? To realize she may not be his tore at his gut. Nothing would part them, he vowed.

She had chosen him to be her champion for whatever reason, and it pleased him to think she believed in him like no one else did.

He sighed, knowing he needed to get them home. Daybreak was only a few hours away. All had to be ready when the McKays attacked.

Chapter Seven

Dylan pulled his plaid back to reveal Rhiannon's naked toes and slender ankles. He lifted one dainty foot and slipped it into her boot, then did the same with the other before tying the laces.

Putting out the fire was the last thing he did before gathering his weapons and picking up Rhiannon then heading for the castle. He liked the feel of her pressed close. She was warm and soft in all the right places. Her head rested on his shoulder, while the brush of her sweet smelling hair and her warm breath along his neck sent spirals of pleasure coursing through his body.

He pulled her tight against him, worried about what would happen now. He had no wish for the world to intrude upon them yet, but he had no choice.

He ducked under leaf-covered branches and stepped over a moss-eaten log before the Keep came into view. Its stone walls shone silver in the moonlight.

Walking through the arched gate, he noticed the torches had burned low, and the courtyard stood deserted. He breathed a sigh of relief. He had no wish to treat his men to the sight of Rhiannon's nakedness under his plaid, or explain how she got that way. Before he reached the main hall, both hounds came rushing out to bark and wag their tails with excited greetings.

"You missed me have you? Keep it down. I do not need

everyone coming to see what you are howling about."

Stepping through the doorway into the hall, he spotted Owain sitting at the high table and groaned. He would have to explain, or never hear the end of it.

His temper flared at this inconvenience, making his voice rough with annoyance. "Do you wait up for me, little brother?"

Owain's gaze slid over the woman then he answered with a shrug. "I was in need of a drink. I see you have brought home a woman. Was she the prey you sought?" A smile spread across Owain's lips before they disappeared in his mug.

"Aye." Dylan frowned. "Since you are up, follow me. There is much we must decide 'afore daybreak."

He took the stairs two at a time with ease and kicked the door to his room open. "Add logs to the fire, brother. I wish to chase the chill from the room."

Dylan gently laid Rhiannon on his bed. A deep sigh escaped from her rose-colored lips, but did not open her eyes. A warm feeling curled in his stomach. He liked seeing her in his bed with nothing but his plaid to cover her. He had not known how possessive he was until this night.

"Who is the lass? Is she ill?" Owain asked. Having stirred the fire, he moved to the bed.

Dylan smiled. "Nay, she is not ill, only sleeping soundly. Do you not recognize her?"

Owain blinked, his brow furrowing. "Nay, but she is bonnie. Is she spoken for?"

"Aye, she is!" Dylan answered, his voice sharp. Shaking his head, he forced the unreasonable anger away. Owain had only asked the same question he himself would have asked upon seeing her.

"Look closer, brother. 'Tis the lad you fought but two days past."

"By the fat! I would not raise my arm to a woman. What was she thinking to dress as a man and raise a sword? Is she daft? I could have killed her." He put his hands over his face and groaned. "'Twas bad enough thinking she was a lad. I am no better than those McKay swine."

Laughter broke from Dylan. For the moment, he was enjoying his brother's discomfort. "Do not moan so, there was no harm done, but the jest was on us all, I fear."

"Did she have you fooled as well?"

"Aye, at first. Now as you can see, she is in need of clothes. She will not be dressing like a man again. For if I am forced to view her naked knees below that kilt a moment more, I shall lock her away in this room with me and not come out until I am old and gray."

"I envy you that task," Owain said.

Dylan lifted his brow studying the other man's expression. His brother was taken with Rhiannon, but knew the line was drawn, so he took no offence.

"Go take some clothes from Enid. Both women are about the same in size. Enid has many gowns and can do without a few. Later, I will restore what is taken."

When Owain went to do as asked, Dylan sat alone with Rhiannon. Looking over her face and form brought unwelcome thoughts. Fear brought questions he did not want answered. With the light of day, would she regret lying with him? Would she try to run away? Mayhap he should tie her to the bed during the attack this morning to make sure she would be here on his return.

He reached for her, running his finger along the shell of her ear. He must bind her to him, so she would not leave. But how? He had no understanding of the heart or mind of a woman. His mother barely spoke to him while he was growing up, and his younger sister feared him. No doubt from his father's ranting of death, hell, and the mark of the beast.

Hearing Owain's heavy steps in the hallway, Dylan pulled in his dark thoughts. The door opened, and Owain walked in with loaded arms. With a heave, the woman's apparel landed on the bed. "I brought three dresses plus the things she would need to wear under them."

"I did not know you were so well versed in women's clothing," Dylan teased.

One side of his brother's mouth turned up. "'Tis unchivalrous to speak of such learning. The women would surely frown."

Still smiling, Dylan changed the subject to something more serious. "There is another matter we must discuss. What defense shall we use when the McKays attack at dawn?"

Owain lifted his head. "How do you know they will attack? Have you spotted them?"

"'Tis not important how I know, but that I do. I want everything ready. Awake the house, and have all prepare for the attack. Silence is to be maintained. Set the guard around the outer wall. Tell them to keep hidden so the approaching clan will see naught amiss."

"Aye, and I will open the armory," Owain added. "All will have the weapons needed. If the wall is breached, I want the women to be able to protect themselves. Also, the archers need have two extra quivers of arrows. They will not have the time to seek more if they run low."

"Good thinking. See to it."

Alone, Dylan gave in to his need to touch Rhiannon again by stroking her cheek. In sleep, she unconsciously turned into him, seeking his caress. He ran a finger along her bottom lip, knowing a desire to taste them.

He leaned forward, bringing his lips over hers gently, kissing and drinking from her sweetness before leaving her to rest. "Later, bold one. I will return to finish what we began."

The mist hung heavy over the fields and forest. The gray light of dawn filtered through dark shadows of trees. A lone bird proclaimed the morning in song. Dylan crouched on the ledge of the outer wall, waiting to catch a movement of the approaching clan. Twelve other guards plus Owain were positioned along the wall, watching as well. The McKays would not get through without being seen. The man closest to Dylan shifted his position then sat still once more.

Light drizzle dampened Dylan's hair and ran down his face to fall from his chin. He pulled his plaid closer, and scanned the area again.

He rubbed his brow and thought of Rhiannon; the way she had been last night as he held her. Her passion and responsive nature was so beautiful, so special. He swallowed, and tightness closed his throat when he thought of the possibility of losing her. Would he meet a man who had some claim to her this day?

To his left, he spotted a guard, making his way toward him along the wall. "Laird, Owain sent me. There are men spotted in the forest near the east wall."

Dylan clapped his hand on the man's shoulder. "Good. Lead the way." He followed the man back to his place then went to stoop down next to his brother.

"There at the edge of the tree line," Owain offered, pointing toward the forest.

Dylan nodded, peeking over the wall and into the forest. A band of shadowy figures gathered among the trees. A few swords reflected the morning light unknowingly giving them away. "How many?" Dylan asked.

"I would guess around two dozen."

"The number is small. They seek to enter through devious means."

The McKays seemed to make a decision and moved west. Dylan and Owain followed their progress along the wall, staying low, yet keeping them in sight.

"They're headed for the front gate," Dylan said.

"Aye."

"Are they hoping for an invitation," Dylan asked.

Owain snorted.

Two enemies stepped from the trees, one carrying a coil of rope. When they disappeared below the wall, Dylan saw another man leave the forest to join his friends below.

Dylan and Owain had only to wait a moment before an iron hook with a rope tied at the end flew over the top of the wall. It clanged on the stone and then scraped along the granite until it hooked on the wall's edge. The rope went tight. Their guests had arrived.

"Wake up, wake up I say." Rhiannon awoke to pain slicing through her cheek from a stinging slap. "Get out! This is the McGregor's bed."

Rhiannon raised her hand to her injured cheek, while her sleepy gaze met Enid's angry snarl. Pulling herself up in the bed, she grabbed the plaid to her naked breasts. The last thing she remembered was that the men in the forest had them surrounded, then there was light and Dylan.

She was not given the time to think more. Enid reached up, fisting her hand into Rhiannon's tangled curls and pulled.

"Oooh!" Rhiannon dropped the covers to free her locks from the harpy.

"Get out of his bed, you harlot. I will have you thrown in the dungeon. You are a thief and a whore. How dare you take my clothes!"

"I did not." Another stinging slap made Rhiannon defend herself. She kicked out and connected with Enid's stomach. Her hair came loose as the woman fell back to land on the floor.

Enid screamed in rage, "Guards!"

A large Highlander stepped inside making Rhiannon realize Enid had this planned. She quickly scanned the room for a weapon, jumping from the bed and grabbing Dylan's dagger from the bedside table.

"Why?" Rhiannon asked Enid, keeping her gaze glued to the warrior.

"Whoever you are, I want you out of my way."

"He was never yours."

Enid screamed in impotent fury. "Take her to the dungeon. I shall enjoy seeing the flesh torn from her back."

"I will not go without a fight." Rhiannon spread her feet for balance and bent slightly at the waist, holding the dagger in her right hand. The warrior was built stocky with a square face and chin. His bulbous nose covered most of a scarred face and his arms were thick from swinging a battleaxe. But it was his small beady eyes that held her attention. They ran over her naked form, sending a shiver of nausea through her body at his lust.

"Do I smell fear, wench?" His eyes burned with a thirst to do her harm.

"Do not do this horrible thing. Seek out the Laird."

"Sorry, I follow Enid's orders and gladly. She has done me a favor this time."

He grabbed at her. Rhiannon stepped back swinging the

blade in a downward arch. She thought she had missed until she saw the blood covering the blade.

He had not made a sound, yet his nostrils flared and a wicked curl marked his smile. He slammed her against the wall, using his heavier weight to knock the dagger from her hand.

His large hand circled her throat, holding her pinned to the wall. The smile grew large under his nose as he moved a hand to her breasts and squeezed.

"Nay! Nay!" Rhiannon hit at his hand and kicked at his legs, with no effect.

Enid jeered, "'Twill be no less than twenty lashings for this theft."

"I have stolen naught," Rhiannon yelled

Enid turned to the warrior. "Take her below. I wish to see her bled then you can do what you want with her. I care not."

Rhiannon's heartbeat raced in panic and her muscles tightened. The guard threw her over his shoulder and left the room.

The piercing scream tore through Dylan's soul. The sound of pain was so deep it twisted his gut and he bent over. He shifted and grabbed Owain's arm. A frown marred his brow. "Did you hear that?"

"Hear what?"

"That scream."

"Nay." Owain frowned.

The pain had been Rhiannon's, he was sure. "See that our guests are coshed on the head and brought to the main hall for questioning. None are to be harmed. There is a matter I must see to."

He moved away just as the first invader slipped over the

wall to be rendered senseless. As he reached the main hall, another scream ripped through his mind. The air was knocked from his lungs. A panic like nothing he had ever felt before crawled along his spine. He ran up the stairs to his room and found it in shambles. He left his room, nearly tripping over a servant. He grabbed her arm. "Where is she?"

The young maid's eyes grew large with fear and darted back and forth. "Who, Laird?"

"The woman I had in my room."

"I was told she is a thief. Enid took her to the dungeon."

Dylan jumped the stairs two at a time as he ran through the kitchen to a trap door buried in the floor. He pulled the door open, just as another scream tore at his heart.

He grabbed a torch from a basket and lit it from the kitchen hearth. They would pay! He would find pleasure in seeing to their judgment, a torturous death all.

He descended steep stairs that led deep into the earth. Damp rock lined both sides of the passageway. Water trickled down from the rock wall to follow along a small groove beside the stairs. The water collected, making part of the floor soggy black pools of crawling things. The odor of mold and mildew smelled strong in the cold dampness, and rats scurried out of his way. The scraps of broken spider webs across his path told of others passing this way.

He could not remember the last time the dungeon had been used for anything but storage. Jumping the last few steps, he spotted a flickering light ahead. He heard someone talking and the jingle of chains. The hard packed earth cushioned the sound of his footsteps as he followed the voices.

Walking through the door, he spotted Rhiannon hanging from chains in the wall. He turned to see the flogger throw the whip back to snap it forward again with curled precision.

Dylan rushed the Highlander and rammed full body into him. The man grunted as he fell to the floor. Dylan landed on him; his fist connected hard with the man's jaw and then swung back to hit him again.

While the man lay stunned, Dylan snarled through clenched teeth and pulled the bone-handled dagger from his boot, bringing it up under the man's throat.

Something splintered inside him, and the barrier between good and evil was no more. Instead, the need to kill roared in his ears. The beast within hungered for their death. It would be so easy to let the blade slide along the man's throat. Then again, torture was appealing. Mayhap he would pluck the man's eyes from his head.

"Give me the keys," Dylan gritted between clenched teeth. He wanted the man to protest; to give him a reason to take revenge. When the man did not move fast enough, Dylan sliced into the flogger's chest, drawing blood and taking delight in returning some of the pain this swine had given Rhiannon. With fluid ease, he brought the blade back to the man's throat.

The warrior's eyes widened and he gasped, giving up the keys.

"I should carve out your heart." Dylan's voice was low with malice, but his breathing was slow and even. He knew he had to cage the beast within.

"I was but following orders, Laird. Enid orders the punishment for the house."

"You will seek my counsel for all things or find your head rotting on a pike at my gate."

Standing, Dylan turned his glare on Enid, who cowered in the shadows. When she moved to speak, he narrowed his eyes and tightened his jaw. He bunched a fist in front of his face. "Speak at the risk of your life. Your punishment is assured."

She closed her mouth just as fast as she had opened it. Dylan moved up behind his Lady

Rhiannon pressed her forehead to the cold stone. The chains holding her to the wall jingled as she strained against them. The weight of her body pulled on her arms, making it hard to catch her breath. Her back burned, as if hot irons seared at her flesh, and her legs shook giving out.

She felt disjointed, as if she floated above herself. Enid's cursing had stopped, and Rhiannon could no longer feel the sting of the whip. Why had they stopped? Or were they tormenting her by prolonging the torture? Her mind hung clouded with pain.

A warm hand ran over her shoulder and up her arm to her wrist. Instinctively, she knew that gentle touch.

"Dylan?"

"Aye, sweet lass. I thought you safe in my own house."

When he released the cuffs, she found the strength gone from her legs and collapsed in his arms. He lifted her naked body to his chest, and she curled against his warmth, pressing her cheek into the curve of his neck.

"She is a thief, Dylan," Enid yelled. "And I had every right to seek punishment. I have a right to speak on my behalf."

"You have only the rights I give you." Dylan snarled, carrying Rhiannon out the door and up to his room.

She could not seem to stop shaking and clung tightly to Dylan's neck. She had no wish to let go. The security of his arms made her feel safe, as nothing else ever had.

When he made to lay her on the bed, she tightened her grip. She waited for him to object and force a separation, but instead he lay down with her, his arms pulling her close and covering them with a quilt.

Dylan ran a finger over her brow then along her cheek to her chin, bringing her gaze up to his. His eyes glittered with warmth and concern. He was a warrior used to battle, yet here with her he was so tender.

"Little Moonbeam, is there some herb or salve I might use to ease your pain? I would see to your wounds."

Her gaze dropped to his mouth, remembering the kiss they shared last night. Warmth poured like liquid amber into her lower belly. She wished he would share another kiss. Just the taste of him would surely ease her pain, but he seemed not to know that.

"There is a healer in the village. Rhiannon?"

She took a deep breath then let it out slowly. "In my bag, there is a jar of elder-bark and sorrel salve."

Dylan moved from the bed and over to the woolsack near the hearth. Inside there was a small earthen jar. "Is this the one?" He held up the container.

When she nodded, he said. "Lay on your stomach, and let me see how bad it 'tis."

She bit her lower lip. "You must wash the wound first," she said. Doing as he asked, she rolled over, swallowing a lump of shyness. After all that had happened between them, to have this emotion surprised her. Mayhap it was the bed, or that Dylan was clothed and she lay naked. She felt her body tensing with anticipation as she waited to see where he would touch her first.

Dylan splashed water on a linen cloth and sat down beside her. He noticed her eyes were tightly closed as though she feared more pain.

Pulling the quilt off, he heard a low moan. "I can not promise this will not hurt, but I will go as gently as I can with these big hands of mine."

When he laid the damp cloth over her injured back, she jerked. "Forgive me."

"Nay, Laird. 'Tis just cold."

Warmth invaded his chest and move down to settle between his legs. The erotic images she created with her innocent words caused a swift male reaction that startled him with its intensity.

Smoothing the cloth over her back and down the small indentation of her spine to the roundness of her bottom did not help his condition. Yet, he could not help admiring her luscious curves. Her skin was soft and creamy and had been unmarked until now.

The red marks of the whip's lash stood out against the paleness of her skin, and anger replaced any warm thoughts.

"I stole naught, Dylan. Please believe me."

His gaze moved to hers. She had turned her head to watch him, and he had given his anger away with his frown. "I never doubted that, sweet one. There are three marks, but only one has broken the skin. I fear 'twill be bruised and sore for a while." Dylan rubbed the back of his neck. Some champion he turned out to be. "I have some dresses here for you to wear when you feel up to it."

"Dresses?"

"Aye, here at the foot of the bed."

"But they are..."

"Laird." The captain of his guard interrupted at the bedroom door. Dylan quickly pulled the quilt back over Rhiannon.

"Aye, speak."

"We hold three McKays below."

"Find Owain and have him meet me there."

The captain nodded and left.

"I will be back shortly. Rest easy, 'twill not take long," he said, as he walked out the door.

Rhiannon struggled to sit up. The McKays were here? Mayhap she could help patch this rift between their clans. They must fight as one, or all were doomed.

When she moved to stand a wave of dizziness whirled through her. She sucked in a breath as images flashed through her mind. Fires, blood, screams of fear, and a large flying creature blocking the sun with its body. The earth fell into darkness. Her fists flew to her temples. An unvoiced scream hovered on her lips. She gasped putting her hand to her brow. Pain filled her mind, yet she whispered one name. "Dylan."

Dylan went down to the main hall. Torches flickered along the wall and soft morning light fell through the open door. A group of warriors waited near the hearth. The fire illuminated the features of three unconscious McKays on the stone floor. Bain and Kyna padded over to smell the prone men.

Having had to deal with treachery in his own keep, Dylan's mood was foul. "Wake them," he ordered, waving his hand. Anger lowered his brow, and a need to vent coil in his chest.

Owain took the bucket of water from the table and emptied its contents over the McKays. They woke sputtering and spitting. While they wiped at their eyes and shook the liquid from their heads, Dylan took their measure.

Two men were dark-haired and brawny. Not as tall as he was, but thick in muscles. The youngest of the three held his attention. The lad had dark colored hair and hazel eyes, but his features looked familiar and Dylan wondered if he held Rhiannon's son. He shook his head. This lad was too old to have come from Rhiannon's loins. Then he remembered the man who had called out to her from across the battlefield. There was a great affection between them and the knowledge felt like a dagger plunged into his gut and twisted.

"As you know from the lumps on your heads, some of us frown when you climb our walls," Dylan sneered. "I hope you were not hit too hard."

All three McKays staggered to their feet, their backs straight, and heads high. The youngest of the three stepped forward. "You have no right to hold us here. We came by invitation. You did wish to ransom our kin."

"Aye that I did." Dylan frowned, sharpening his gaze on the youth. He planted his fists on the table and leaned toward them. The maids setting the table stepped away.

Dylan's voice lowered with menace. "But 'twas not what you had in mind. I do not take kindly to being attacked 'afore I break my fast. Do you ken?"

One of the older and wiser McKays grabbed the boy's shoulder. "Hold your tongue, lad, or 'twill find us facing the dragon's ax-man."

The lad jerked his arm free. "Nay. I care not if this Laird be dragon or murderer." He slapped his palms down on the table, making Bain pull his lips back in a show of sharp canines and give a low growl. But the lad did not glance at the dog.

"Where is Rhiannon? What have you done to her?"

"Robbie?" The soft feminine voice broke through the tension. All eyes turned to the source. Rhiannon stood at the top of the stone stairs. Long locks of curly, red hair hung over one shoulder, while the rest fell in waves down her back.

She wore a topaz blue kirtle with a cream under-skirt. Dylan had never seen anything more beautiful, but she only had eyes for the lad.

The expression of naked longing on her face infuriated

him. And that feeling annoyed him all the more. She turned to look at him, and he watched her eyes widen in alarm and her cheeks grew ashen.

His brow furrowed. What did she have to fear? Her gaze shifted again to the lad. She cautiously moved down the steps; her injured back obviously paining her. He found it amazing she could dress and walk upright.

There was a shuffling of feet, and then before he could be stopped, the lad ran toward Rhiannon and grabbed her in a hug. She groaned, closing her eyes in a grimace, yet gently wrapped her arms around the boy. Dylan stepped forward to push the lad away. "Have a care..."

"Unhand her, you bastard!" The lad jumped at him, hitting Dylan with a shower of blows. The hounds sent up a terrible ruckus of barking and growling before Dylan ordered them quiet. With a well-placed kick, Dylan knocked the youth to the floor and fell over him to hold him down. The struggle continued until a sword tip appeared from one of his men and rested on the boy's throat.

"Nay," Rhiannon yelled.

Dylan looked up. "Fergus, 'tis not needed... But, my thanks." Fergus nodded and withdrew his sword. Rhiannon moved up next to Dylan. Her warm hand ran over his shoulder and her shirt brushed his thigh.

She said not a word, and that meant more than everything to him. Rhiannon trusted him enough to handle this situation and not bring harm to the boy. But more than that, she sided with him. His heart swelled with satisfaction.

"McKay, I am but protecting Rhiannon from farther pain. Her back is bruised. If you but calm, I will let you up."

Even though the fire of anger still burned in the lad's eyes, he nodded agreement. Dylan stepped away. The youth stood up, brushing rushes from his hair and back.

"Laird," Rhiannon broke in. "I would have you meet my brother, Robert Mc—"

"Your brother!" Had he heard her right?

Her brows wrinkled. "Aye."

There was no other man to stand in his way. She was an innocent yet, untouched, and the joy that filled his soul made him burst out laughing. He wanted to pick her up and swing her around, telling her how her innocence pleased him. The torment he had felt these many hours melted away.

"You find this amusing?" Rhiannon asked, a smile touching her lips.

Seeing the sparkle of bewilderment in her beautiful emerald eyes, Dylan knew he had to explain his actions. Part truth would have to do. He had no wish to speak of intimate matters now.

"I had no idea you had a brother, and I am pleased I did not lop off his head as he climbed over my wall."

Her smile grew. "And I as well, Laird."

"Come," Dylan said, taking her arm. "Let us break our fast, while Robert and his two companions are fed. Afterward, you two will have some time alone."

Dylan nodded to one of his guard. "Take our guest over to the lower table."

The guard stepped forward, taking Robert's arm. He led the boy to a corner where his clansmen already sat eating.

Robbie jerked his arm from the guard's hold and plopped down on a fur-covered bench. The smells of wood smoke, sweet breads and roasted boar enticed him, but most of all, a hot anger filled every pore of his being. Robbie watched the easy manner with which Rhiannon dealt with the Dragon Laird and felt betrayed. He had come for her, fearing the worst, yet she walked freely about and wore fine clothing. What was going on? How could Rhiannon be kind to the man who had killed and maimed so many of their clansmen? This was unlike her. Mayhap she was under a spell. No matter what it was, it would be up to him to see her home safely. Soon—was his goal.

The two men he had followed seemed to eat as if they would never eat again. Which might be truth, but he did not feel like eating. His stomach cramped in knots. He watched the McGregor seat Rhiannon next to him before taking the head position.

What was wrong with her? There was a change. What, he could not place. It was not like her to sit and smile at the enemy. The Dragon Laird had done something to her.

"I am here to see to your head wound."

Robbie turned to meet a pair of pretty blue eyes. Long black hair hung in a braided rope over the shoulder of the bonnie young lass. Her head was tipped to one side, studying him. He swallowed and his heart struck a double beat. Then he reminded himself she was of the clan McGregor. "Leave me alone."

"Oh, but I can not 'til I see if you are well."

Robbie turned, giving her his undivided attention and sighed. "I said I am fine."

"Nay, you did not. You said, leave me alone." She raised her chin and looked down her nose at him. "There is a difference." She stepped closer and started poking around his head.

"Stop that! You might—ouch!"

"See, you are not fine." She smiled triumphantly.

"Not with your tender care." He sneered.

She slapped a cool cloth over the lump at his temple.

"Mayhap I should give you dried iris root. 'Tis a purge that might cure your grumpiness and make you sweet-tempered."

"You are a brat."

"And you a boar."

He smiled, the first time since the battle and Rhiannon's capture. "What is your name, brat?"

"Nessa. And yours?"

"Robert. I have a wound from the battle but four days back. Would you look at it too?"

"Oh, aye."

He pulled up his kilt to show her his thigh. She gasped, grabbing at his plaid and quickly covering him.

"What do you, sir?"

His smile deepened. "I was but showing you my wound. You did want to view it."

"You are wicked. You know well and good that a maid should not view what lies beneath the kilt."

When she reached for the cloth at his head, he took her hand. "So I do." He stared into her blue eyes and found fire running through his veins. When she spoke, his gaze dropped to her gentle pink lips.

"I would ask a boon," Nessa asked shyly.

"I am a prisoner here, but will do what I can for you."

"My brother has seemed lighter of spirit since your sister came to us. Please watch with an open heart and say aught that will bring pain to them."

He dropped her hand and put the frown back in place. "You are the McGregor's sister?"

"Aye."

"Leave me."

"I was right the first time. You are a boar and care only for yourself." She smeared lavender oil over his cut; none too gently.

"Ouch!"

He expected some sassy remark, but instead, she turned and stomped off.

"Brat," he stated again, tearing off a hunk of hard bread. Robbie slipped the crust onto the platter of venison to soak up the juices then popped it into his mouth. His gaze moved again to the high table to see his sister watching him. She smiled. He did not.

Rhiannon had watched the by-play and had seen Robbie smile at Nessa. Turning to Dylan, she asked, "How is Nessa related to you?"

"She is my sister."

That surprised her. "Your sister?"

"Aye."

"Do you have any children?" It was not uncommon for Lairds to have sired bastards.

He smiled and leaned closer. "Nay. Would you like some?"

She felt heat rise to her cheeks. "I think you need your wine watered. You should not ask a maid such."

"'Tis but a simple question."

"Aye, to the ear, but your eyes speak of what lies behind those words."

"I was thinking of a starry night and the pleasures of the flesh: my fingers traveling and seeking. I would have you there again."

"Silence. Someone will hear." She quickly glanced around as she raised the cup to drink.

"I will speak no more on it here, if you but grace my lips with yours."

She smiled back at him. He was a rogue. She leaned

closer, and a sparkle of triumph lit his warm blue eyes. When she was close enough to kiss him, she brought forth a piece of cheese and pushed it into his mouth.

Rhiannon laughed at his childish pout. Taking another piece of cheese, she kissed it then brought it to his lips. His smile returned, as did the heat in his eyes.

He opened his mouth to receive her gift, and when she placed the offering between his lips, he took her hand and kissed each finger. The moist heat made a shiver of pleasure run up her arm and into her breasts. Next, he kissed her palm.

"I...I wanted to ask," Rhiannon started but found her thoughts centering on what Dylan was doing with his lips.

"What?"

"Ahh,"

He chuckled. "You wanted to ask me something."

She gently pulled her hand from his. He made it difficult to think. "Aye. How is it Robbie is here?"

"I think I mentioned this 'afore. He climbed over my wall along with his companions."

"Oh, aye."

"There is even now a group of men in the forest waiting. They are being watched. I think Robbie and the others were to unlock the gate, so they could storm the castle."

"What will you do with them?"

Again, he saw fear reflected in her eyes and realized why he had seen it the first time. She feared for her brother's safety.

"Be at ease, sweet one. He was caught 'afore any harm was done. The punishment will fit the crime."

"Thank you." She closed her eyes and bowed her head.

"How are you feeling?"

"A little stiff and sore...but well. I have been wondering how we escaped the men in the forest."

"They let us go and I carried you home." Dylan grabbed a boiled egg and bit it in half, his gaze averted. He liked the idea of her making this her home.

"You are not telling me all there is." She raised an eyebrow.

He waved one hand through the air, then sliced off a hunk of meat. "'Tis all that is important. Here, eat, 'tis a choice piece of boar." He raised the juicy meat to her lips. She opened her mouth just enough to take his offering.

Rhiannon's moist lips sliding over his fingers brought heat to his insides, and mental images of her lips on another part of his body, causing him to groan.

The episode in the forest had only increased his desire to claim her. None other had ever moved him so. Her emerald eyes looked right into his soul.

He brought her fingers back to his lips to savor her sweetness. Her eyes widened, and she inhaled deeply.

"'Tis sweet you are, like honey and heather wine. What have I done right to have you here by my side? I can not think of a thing, yet here you are, and I am blessed," Dylan marveled.

She ran her hand down his beard-roughened cheek. "'Tis who you are inside that makes you special. In just a few days, I have seen the man you are. You have my trust, for you are fair and just in all things. 'Tis I, who am blessed to sit beside so great a Laird."

He smiled at the warmth in her eyes and the praise heaped upon his head. Dylan's chest swelled but the experience felt uncomfortable. He feathered his fingers through his hair. He had been cursed since birth and carried the beast. She did not know about the darkness that grew inside him. If she did, the warmth in those eyes would turn to fear and she would run away, leaving him once more alone. Now that he had experienced her closeness, sharing, and loving, he could not go back to being ostracized again.

He had to find a way to bind her to him. Then when she found out about the evil, she could not leave.

Suddenly, Dylan realized the hall was too quiet. All conversation had halted. He glanced around to see one elder after another enter the main hall. Soon all eleven stood inside the doorway.

Owain moved closer to Dylan's left. "What's afoot?"

"I do not know." Dylan answered. "But 'tis not good I fear."

Chapter Eight

"Is something amiss, Laird?" Rhiannon inquired.

Dylan frowned. "The elders only gather when there is a matter of importance to decide. But I am always forewarned of the meeting and what charges are to be set forth to discuss."

"And you have no knowledge of this meeting?"

"None." Dylan leaned back against his chair and tightened his jaw.

Owain frowned. "There is mischief about. I like not the feel of it."

"Nor I, brother. We will soon see what brews."

Dylan did not have long to wait. Enid walked in and over to the elders. They nodded and approached the high table. Dylan lowering his brow spoke first. "'Tis poor manners to interrupt the Laird's meal. This must indeed be a life and death matter. For surely you would not meet over a woman's grumbling."

One of the elders cleared his throat. Another shifted his feet. "My Laird," McDonald spoke bowing his head. "Someone has brought us word of treason. A most serious charge."

"I agree." Dylan stated, grinding his back teeth. "Who is this traitor?" The silence was deafening as all waited for the answer.

"The charge was brought against you."

Loud gasps floated around the room. Rhiannon stood up. Her fiery curls bouncing about her shoulders. "Nay!"

Dylan grabbed her hand to stay her.

Owain rose from this seat, his hand on the hilt of his sword. "Bring the man forward who would dare level such a charge against my brother. I will challenge him."

"Nay, Owain. Hold your sword." Dylan had thought he made things clear to Enid. But it would seem she wanted to bring Rhiannon's pain and shame before everyone and stab at him as well. Now it would seem, Enid would play her hand of revenge, but Dylan would see her ride the pole instead of his lady.

"But they have slurred your good name," Owain said a frown marring his brow.

"'Twould not be the first time. Sit down both of you." Rhiannon sat and tucked her hair behind her ear. "I am Laird here. Until someone puts a knife in my back, I am the law. Now have my accuser step forth to face me."

The elders opened a path to Enid. Without blinking, she walked toward the table her expression calm and flawless as always. She had mastered that art well. One never knew what went on in that head of hers. Dylan clutched the arms of his chair to hold back his anger.

"Enid, speak truth. Why bring the elders and lay the word traitor at my door?"

"You choose the enemy over your own clan," she said.

"Be careful, Enid, of what you say." Owain tensed.

"Easy, Owain. Let her speak."

He turned toward Dylan. "She spouts lies."

"Aye, but I wish all here to see this as well." Dylan's gaze met Enid's again. "Explain how you come by this charge."

"I found out that the McKay slut is a thief. I found her

with things stolen from me and had her whipped." She pointed a thin finger at Dylan. "You cut her down 'afore the punishment was seen through and threatened *me*. *Me*, the wife of your brother slain these two years and the lady of this house." Again, murmurs swept through the room.

At the mention of Thomas, his oldest brother, Dylan felt a stab of grief so intense it was like the slide of a knife between his ribs. Thomas, with a few others, had gone to spy on the McKays; only to take an arrow through the chest and die shortly after returning home.

The scraping of a wooden bench on stone, and a yell from the far corner of the room made Rhiannon and Dylan glance in that direction. Robbie was being restrained by a guard, his eyes sparkling with anger. "You bloody bitch! Rhiannon doesn't steal."

Ignore the outburst, Enid's voice rose again. "I am sure all of you remember the night of the battle when the McKay prisoners where brought 'afore us." She walked around the room, seeming to have everyone's attention. Her hands where perched on her hips, and her chin was lifted. The glint of power sparkled in her gaze. "There was a lad with a big mouth. He was no lad, but a woman in disguise. She insulted us, refusing to bend the knee. Now we find this woman sits at the right hand of our Laird, a place of honor. And she has stolen my belongings, for which the McGregor will refuse t punish." Enid swung back to face Dylan.

"Laird, did you know this?" One of the elders asked.

"Know what? That she is a McKay or that she was in disguise, or that Enid accuses her of thievery?" Dylan asked with raised eyebrows.

"When Rhiannon arrived all knew she was a McKay. And what crime is there in dressing like a lad for protection? So, we come down to Enid, accusing Rhiannon of being a thief. That leaves only one problem. Is the accusation true?"

Dylan felt Rhiannon tense under his hand, but he continued.

"If 'tis proved Rhiannon is not a thief, you punished her unfairly and while under my care. And there is the accusation of treason you have laid at my door. That will go hard on you, Enid."

"I caught her with the things she took from me."

"Let it also be known the wrath of a scorned woman can take many faces. Enid was found in my bed the night we saw victory over the McKays, and I rejected her." Dylan knew what Enid was about and had no sympathy for her. She had chosen her path.

Enid sucked in a long breath. "Nay, Nay! 'Tis not true."

"You chose to make this an open trial. You have brought this on your head. The clan must have all facts, so they know where your heart lies and why these charges were brought forth. Now, I ask, what were the things Rhiannon took?"

"Gowns. Three in number." Enid glanced toward the accused. Her face twisted in anger as she pointed at Rhiannon, her hand shaking with her emotions. "The brazen harlot even now dons my blue topaz." Dylan took notice that two other maids nodded in agreement.

Owain grabbed Enid's arm as she surged forward toward Rhiannon.

"You whipped an innocent, Enid. For 'twas I who gave Rhiannon the dresses," Owain announced.

"You!" Enid stopped to glare at Owain through narrowed eyes. "Why do you cover for her? Has she spread her legs for you as well?"

Before Dylan could reach Enid, his brother backhanded

her. Enid raised a hand to a reddened cheek and glared. "You had no right, Owain."

"Aye, he did." Dylan spoke softly despite the anger boiling through his veins.

Enid's seething gaze rested on Dylan. "What say you?" she hissed.

"Lady Rhiannon was without female apparel, and you being somewhat the same size, I bid Owain fetch some dresses from you with the understanding that I would see them replaced."

"Nay!"

"Aye!" Dylan continued, "'afore you could be told of my decision, we had intruders at our walls. I cared not that you grew angered, but you crossed a line when you took Rhiannon from my room, and my protection, and had her whipped." The thunder of his voice echoed off the stone walls. A deathly quiet fell over the room. A few observers crossed themselves as if the cursed Laird would kill them all in his anger. "You have no right, but what I give you."

"I had no way of knowing any of this." Enid offered in her defense. She jerked her arm free of Owain's grasp and stepped back. "She is a McKay, I had every right to punish her."

"Enid, in all this time have you not learned that I am law here? You do ought without my say." Dylan ran his fingers through his hair. Some of his anger cooled. "Because you took the law into your hands and punished an innocent, I must pass judgment. 'Tis only fair you have the same punishment as you inflicted on Rhiannon. An eye for an eye."

"Nay. She is an enemy." Enid swept the room with wide eyes, looking for someone to support her. Finding no one, she backed toward the doorway.

"I, as Laird, decide who is friend or foe. *All* judgments come from me. I need two guards. You and you." Dylan pointed out men he knew would see the task done. "She is to be stripped naked and chained to the dungeon wall. Three whip marks only."

"Nay!" Enid screamed as the warriors advanced. She dashed for the door, bumping into one of the elders. A guard cut across her path and grabbed her arms. The other man came up behind her with a dagger to slice through her blouse. "Unhand me! I am the lady of this house. Touch me naught! 'Tis the devil who has ordered this evil." She scratched one man, leaving bloody grooves down his arm. But she was no match for them. Stripped of her clothes, she struggled as the warriors dragged her from the hall. The echo of her screams rang through the room. "A curse on your head, Dylan McGregor."

"Someone bring me Tavish," Dylan ordered. "'Twas his hand that held the whip. Let us be done with this. I wish to have the rest of the day in peace."

Quickly, a man moved to do as bid.

Dylan sighed. Weariness seeped though his bones. Sleep called to him. He lifted the chalice of wine and took a long swallow. His gaze moved to the elders, staring at them one by one, waiting for them to speak. They had always watched in hope he would make a mistake. He was the cursed one after all, and they would see evil appear in all he did.

Each elder bowed reluctantly. "Your judgment is fair."

"Aye, but what of your charge of treason? What say you of that?" Dylan asked.

The head elder's gaze moved to Rhiannon.

Dylan slapped his palm down on the table. "Look to me and speak!"

"We hope your heart has not betrayed our clan. As to the charges, we see ought to make them stick."

Rhiannon placed a gentle hand on his arm. He set down the drink to meet her gaze.

"'Tis sorry, I am, to have brought this trial on you," she said.

"'Twas not you, sweet one, but the greed of others and vindictiveness." The man who had gone after Tavish rushed up to Dylan. "He is gone, Laird. His uncle said he packed up and left, telling no one where he had gone."

"Then he has chosen banishment. No longer is he of the clan McGregor. Take what possessions he left and give them to those who need them. If he shows his face again, 'twill be his death. No McGregor will choose dishonor." Dylan's gaze did not waver from the elders as he spoke. "Owain, see to it. Take what men you need."

Owain nodded as he stood and wrapped his plaid over his shoulder. He pointed to two men who followed him out.

"I go to my chamber, Rhiannon. I think your brother would enjoy your company, but then again, so would I." The sweet curve of her smile made him nearly groan from the power of it. "Take what time you need." Dylan offered begrudgingly, pushing away from the table. The scrape of wood on the stone floor brought the hounds to their feet. "But, do not leave the castle," he ordered before leaving the hall.

On the way to his room, Dylan stopped at the foot of the stairs and waved Fergus over.

"Aye, My Laird?"

"Lady Rhiannon is free to go anywhere within the castle walls, but she is not to leave."

Though he had told her to stay in the castle, he would make double sure that no danger befell her. Rhiannon was prized above his own life. He was a cautious man who left nothing to chance. That was why he still lived to draw breath in a castle full of snakes.

"Aye, My Laird." Fergus bowed then moved to stand at the main entrance.

Satisfied all was well, Dylan climbed the stairs to his room.

Rhiannon glanced toward Robbie. His scowl was still in place. There was much he did not know, and it was his right to hear it. He must know she had not betrayed him. She was following her life's path. The one Dela had foreseen.

She stood and walked over to stand in front of his table. "Will you talk with me, Robbie? There is much I would share."

Rhiannon paced the confines of Dylan's room. The bright warmth from the hearth brought beads of moisture along her hairline. She nervously pulled at a ribbon on the front of her dress as she thought of her brief time with Robbie. The talk had not gone as well as she had hoped. He refused to believe anything she had said, yelling she was under a spell before he was taken to the other prisoners and assigned a task.

Shortly after that, she discovered a guard watching her. To test her suspicions, she moved toward the outer door, and just as she would have stepped out the guard blocked her way. She could not believe Dylan trusted her so little. She came straight away to voice her complaint but found his room empty. Questioning a passing maid, she found Dylan had been called out to see to a matter.

Disappointment touched her soul as she realized her hope of sharing his bed this night might be for naught. They must join their bodies soon so they would have one spirit as well as one heart. Now, she stood alone unsure of herself, and what to do. She knew the prophecy. With every hour that passed, evil came closer to tearing them apart.

She had had a taste of passion in Dylan's arms and the idea of making love excited her, yet fear welled up also. To be so open and vulnerable to a man, to Dylan, brought uncertainty.

Mayhap she should tell him all that was at stake. If she wanted him to trust her, she needed to trust him. He would help her, wouldn't he? She sighed. She knew she needed Dela's counsel. Would the wise one still speak to her?

Leaning her forehead on the window, she viewed the courtyard below. With an evening storm approaching, gusts of wind played on the unwary. A stable boy fought a spooked horse for control, pulling on its lead rope and yelling.

A soft radiance came from inside the stables. Then her gaze moved to an orange glow coming from the blacksmith's shop. No doubt the fires for the iron still burned. Two warriors holding waving and hissing torches walked from the castle to the gatehouse. Their kilts lifted and snapped about their thighs.

Another beam of light drew her gaze to one of the courtyard fires. She knew they would burn through the night so warriors could keep warm.

Then she noticed a cloaked figure in the shadow beyond the light. He had a small frame and stood shorter than most clan warriors. The firelight flared and Rhiannon saw he held a dagger. At that moment, a gust of wind ripped the hood off the stranger. He turned reaching to replace the hood, and Rhiannon got a good look at a face.

"Enid."

What was she doing? Everyone in the hall had been told she was abed. The pain had been great, and she would not be up until the morning. Something was amiss.

Rhiannon chose to follow Enid. She pulled her cloak from the iron hook behind the door and stepped out into the passage.

Because the evening was overcast from the approaching storm, the sconces had been lit. A draft blew up from the main hall passing over the gray stone, making the flames dance.

She glanced in both directions, but did not spot the Highland guard. Dylan had asked her not to leave, but surely, he would understand why she had to. Enid had proven untrustworthy, and Rhiannon did not want Dylan to be caught unawares again. She would be back before anyone noticed her absence.

As she passed through the empty hall, the rushes crushed underfoot, sending up the scent of dried rosemary. The clang of iron on stone and mumbled voices came from the kitchen but no one entered the passageway.

She grabbed hold of the heavy wooden door and pulled it open just enough to slip outside. A gust of wind grabbed at her cloak and skirts, whipping them one way then another. Dark clouds passed with speed overhead. It would storm soon.

Rhiannon looked toward the courtyard fire for Enid and found her gone. She quickly scanned the area and saw the woman disappear behind the stables.

Picking up her skirts, she gave chase. She came up to the corner of the building and peeked around the edge. She watched Enid glance around before touching a stone at shoulder height in the wall that surrounded the castle. There was a clanking of metal and a grinding of stone as the wall opened enough for Enid to slip in.

Rhiannon moved over to the opening and peered into the darkness beyond. Thundered rumbled in the distance. A shiver of apprehension passed over her. She hated dark places.

But this was too important to let fear stand in her way. She took a big breath and slid inside. It was cold and dark. The smell of rotting earth filled her nose, but she soon made it through the short passage.

She followed Enid into the woods, and crept up behind a thick tree trunk. Enid stood along the back road just past the village. Whom was she waiting for?

Lightning flashed, thunder cracked with a rolling boom, shaking the ground. Gusts of wind violently bent the trees and caused the leaves to slap and rattle in a tortured dance, but the dark clouds had yet to let go of the rain they held in their bloated bellies.

Enid glanced in her direction, and Rhiannon stepped back behind the tree, holding the hood of her cloak tightly over her head. If the wind got hold of her hair, it would shine like a red flag, and she would be caught spying. She laid her cheek against the rough bark and filled her lungs with the crisp scent of pine.

She caught the faint sound of an approaching horse before the wind whipped it away. The horse and rider exited the shadows of the wood and onto the open road. As the rider neared, he seemed familiar.

Teg. The man who had fallen into the icy horse trough last spring. She held her surprise by covering her mouth with a hand. He stopped before Enid and dismounted. Rhiannon leaned forward, striving to hear what was said.

The roaring wind carried only part of their conversation to her.

"Here is your coin…Laird McGregor…kill him."

A pouch was handed to Teg. No, doubt the blood money to betray Dylan.

"Tell no one."

Teg took the pouch, and slipped it onto the belt at his waist. "'Twill be done. My master wishes it also."

Rhiannon turned to lean the back of her head against the tree and made fists at her sides. How could Enid do this? Dylan had cared for her, giving her a place of honor in his home. He was her brother by marriage.

The sky had turned black and ugly and the angry clouds chose now to flood the earth. She heard the rain hit the leaves before drops landed on her face.

She looked once more toward Teg and Enid. They were in a heated embrace apparently unmindful of the rain. Having seen and heard enough, Rhiannon pushed away from the tree and made her way back to the castle. How was she to tell Dylan of this betrayal?

Enid loved the feel of Teg's hands on her breasts. "I have one other job for you. There is a woman with red hair who resides as the Laird's slut. I want her dead as well."

"You are a bloodthirsty wrench."

"Do not complain. You love my seedy passion, or you would not keep coming back for more." He moaned, as he put his hand between her wet thighs, the rain making their naked bodies slippery.

"The woman's name is Rhiannon. Make sure she suffers long before she dies. I want to hear her screams."

Teg suddenly stilled his hand.

"Why have you stopped? Continue, my body hungers."

"Is she a McKay with green eyes?"

Enid did not like the way he asked about the bitch. "Why do you care? Do you know her?"

"Nay, I do not know her. I just saw her once, but my

master seeks her blood. He is a powerful Sorcerer."

"Good. I must meet your master." Her mind busied with plans on how to seduce the Sorcerer and use him for her own needs. This was a wonderful night. She sighed, opening her legs wide. "Play with me, Teg. I am very hungry tonight."

Her laughter blended with the rain.

Dylan sat at the head table, then motioned for a maid. She quickly stood before him and bobbed a curtsy.

"I thirst. Bring me a tankard of scotch whiskey."

"Aye, my Laird."

He sat his elbows on the table and rubbed his eyes with his thumb and fingers. He did not want to think about what he had found earlier in the village. It was much like the disaster yesterday.

More than fifteen sheep had disappeared from a herd without sound or tracks. All that had been left were a few heads, shoulders, and front feet. It was as if the rear half of each beast had been severed cleanly with one strike and was nowhere to be found.

There had been no blood-smeared trail or discarded bones: nothing. The villagers were becoming irate, and who could blame them. They depended on their livestock for food and clothing.

The rumors and murmurs against the evil of the Laird were once again being spoken openly. He had no way to help them. He could not track something that left no tracks.

What evidence he had gleaned from this attack pointed to something he himself did not want to believe in, yet he could feel it twisting in his blood.

He pulled the Singing Sword from its sheath and held it up to the candlelight. The blue green glow pulsed with energy.

He turned the blade and the candle flame flickered.

Dylan moved the blade back and forth over the small candle. The fire bent and flickered each time. Then he made another discovery. Below the sword's handle, in a ring of silver, was a clear crystal sphere. The light from the candles passed through it to make rainbows. The sword had a special beauty all its own, one that was rivaled only by Rhiannon.

It would not be long until the whispers reminded her that she had chosen a Laird under a dark curse; a curse that would be with him forever. Would he lose her? A chill invaded his heart.

The maid interrupted his thoughts by setting a tankard before him along with bread and cheese. She bobbed again before retreating. Dylan returned the sword to its sheath with a hiss of sound then grabbed the cup and took a long swallow of the fiery brew. The whisky warmed his cold heart and quenched his thirst.

He wearily rubbed his brow then brought the cup to his lips again, but held it in mid air as he watched his man Fergus rush in to kneel on the floor at his feet.

"Forgive me, Laird," he said with a bowed head.

Fear the like Dylan had never known pierced his head and wrapped its talons around his innards. He set the whisky down. He found it hard to get words through his stiff lips. "Where is she?"

"She is not in the castle, my Laird. I have failed you."

Dylan hit the table with both fists, making the tankard jump and spill. His roar filled the room and echoed through the halls, causing the hounds to leap up and move away.

"How long?" he gritted out.

"But an hour or two, Laird."

Dylan stood, his fists still planted on the table. "Bring me something that she wore from my room. The hounds will find her scent."

"Aye, Laird." Fergus left quickly to follow orders.

Alone in the quiet, Dylan heard the drip, drip of whisky as it ran through the boards of the table to hit the stone floor, the rumble of thunder, the crackle of the fire and the racing of his heart. The beast within wrapping itself around his chest was something evil and ugly.

He could not lose her. She had brought joy into his life, something he had never known from his father, mother, or the people he fought so hard to protect. Rhiannon and he were connected in a way he had yet to understand. She was his lifeline. He could not go back to being alone.

The squeaking of the iron hinges brought his head up. He frowned as the main door opened. A cloaked figure stepped through, the wind, and rain whipping the material around the small figure until the door closed.

Turning around Rhiannon stopped and gasped. "Dylan!"

He left the table and marched toward her with purposeful strides. She had never seen that glowering mask of rage on his face before and fear curdled in her stomach. Here was the Dragon Laird she had heard tales about.

"I—I brought you news." Panic rioted within her, making her want to flee. Surely, he could kill her with one blow. "Dylan, please," she begged, holding up her hands to ward him off.

He did not slow. She backed up against the door. "Listen to me, please."

When he raised his hand toward her, she covered her head in defense. "Do not hurt me."

Her words and actions shocked Dylan. They penetrated his anger and fear. He had only meant to take her arm. It was the curse. Somehow, she had heard about it. His greatest fear had come to pass.

"Rhiannon."

She glanced through arms still covering her head. He watched her expression until he saw when she realized she was not in immediate danger.

"I have never struck a woman in anger. I will not start now!" A thin chill hung on the edge of every word. He took her arm in a firm grip and pulled her across the main hall and up the stairs to his room. Dylan came face to face with Fergus in the doorway, a torn chemise in his hand.

"You found her," Fergus stated.

"Aye."

Dylan walked past the Highlander and slammed the door in his face. The rough bump of the bar sliding across the wood door told Rhiannon that Dylan had locked them in.

His angry blue eyes ran over her from head to foot. Why hadn't he slapped her? Her cousins had always done so when they were displeased. She found another quality to like in him.

"Take off your clothes."

His sharp order caught her off guard. Rhiannon placed a hand over her throat. "What?"

"By the rod! Take off your clothes 'afore you become sick."

His expression was cold as he turned away.

She hurried into the dressing closet. She could hear him pacing as she quickly pulled off her wet kirtle and chemise. Picking up an old shift, she hurriedly threw it over her head and let the hem fall to the floor. Finished, Rhiannon stepped out and Dylan came to a standstill.

Looking at the vision before him, he found his body hardening and lust tempering his anger.

Chapter Nine

Did the woman know what she was doing to him, standing there in that flimsy thing? Her hair hung damp over her shoulder, causing the white material across her breast to stick to a hard nipple. The gown was large, so one strap hung down her arm. Her bare feet and ankles peeked from under the hem. The swells of her breasts and gentle curve of her hips showed through the thin fabric. He wanted to touch her, except he would not.

"You betrayed me," he whispered, turning from her.

"Nay, I did not." She stepped closer but stopped when he spun around angry.

"You left when I told you nay!"

"My word was not given. If it were, I would not have broken it. I had no plan to leave, but spying Enid in the courtyard, I had to follow."

"I care not what Enid does. When I give an order you will follow it."

"Dylan, hear me, please. Your life is at stake."

With anger still burning in his veins, he said. "I will have your word, Rhiannon. Now!"

Having the gift of reading people, Rhiannon realized there was more behind Dylan's anger than the desire for her to stay with him. There was an overriding fear. She stretched out her hand to implore him.

"Please understand there is a task I must finish." It was evident by the narrowing of his eyes he would not listen to anything she had to say until she gave her word.

"I can only say that I will stay 'til I am called away. The prophecy is to be fulfilled."

That she should torment him now made his anger increase. He had to put a stop to this power she had over him. He took a step closer, his gaze never leaving hers.

Pushing her back against the wall, he brought his face only inches from hers. "I care not for prophecies, curses, or assassins plots. You will stay at my side 'til I tire of you."

His fingers plunged into her hair then to the back of her neck. He helped her lips meet his and kissed her with desperation.

Dylan pulled the warm scent of her in to fill his mind and quiet his fear. She clung to him, while he plundered her mouth like the warrior he was. He took everything for himself, yet she too was receiving and begging more. Her moan brought him to his senses. He averted his face when she moved to taste him again.

He would not take her in anger.

He stepped away, yet seeing the heavy passion in her narrowed eyes and pouting lips still moist from his, he wanted her again. However, his strength of will stood strong. He turned away and left the room, locking the door behind him.

Rhiannon turned to glance out the window, her arms wrapped around her waist. She needed time to think. If Dylan was afraid she would leave him, mayhap he had come to care for her. Her heart swelled with a hope that was quickly dashed when she remembered the locked door. How could they work this out if he held her a prisoner?

"You are very brave."

Rhiannon turned from the window. She had been so deep in thought she had not heard Nessa open the door and stepped inside.

"Why do you say that?" Rhiannon asked, wondering if Dylan had reconsidered and she was to be freed.

"Because as angry as Dylan was, he could have turned his curse on you."

Rhiannon frowned. "What nonsense."

"You do not fear death?" Nessa's eyes rounded. "Everyone knows that Dylan was born under a dark moon and he carries the mark of the dragon. Evil rides with him."

Dela had told her long ago that darkness held him.

"Our father used to warn us to stay clear of Dylan or bad luck would befall us. All fear him."

Rhiannon was shocked. "And everyone here and in the village followed this advice?" she asked. Now she understood why he seemed so alone in a room full of people.

"Aye. Even though I love my brother, I must have a care for myself. As must you."

"Nessa, everyone fears death, but 'twill not come from Dylan. Has he ever hit you or mistreated you?"

"Well, nay."

"And has he seen to your welfare and that of your brother?"

"Aye."

"Then why would he curse you, or anyone he has cared for...?" She paused, as she realized why Nessa might be concern. "You heard him yelling?"

"Aye, everyone below heard him."

She wanted to groan upon hearing that. "Well, he was very angry, yet here I stand unharmed."

A frown marred Nessa's face, as she seemed to

contemplate those words.

"I am new here," Rhiannon continued. "And I have not spent the time with Dylan as you have, but I do ken he would not hurt those he loved."

"You give me much to think on." Nessa dropped her gaze to the cup she held. "Here. 'Tis a mug of warm milk. Dylan thought you might enjoy it."

"So I am to stay here?"

"Aye. Sorry, Rhiannon. Things will be better in the morning."

Rhiannon took the mug, never saying how much she hated the stuff. "I thank you for the kindness. Sleep well."

"And you too, Lady."

Rhiannon realized she was more than tired. It was an emotional tired as well as physical. She set the mug down and crawled up to recline on Dylan's bed.

How long had he sat here, four, five hours? The torches had been put out and all were abed. He sat with his elbows on the table in the main hall, his face in his hands. With his anger gone, there was only the fear to eat at his soul.

He wanted Rhiannon with every fiber of his being. He needed her. He hungered for the smiles she bestowed, every word of praise, every touch or look of tenderness, but all this scared him as well. He had been an outcast all his life, cursed to walk alone.

Oh, he had Owain and Nessa, and they cared for him in their own way. But at times, he had seen fear in their eyes. He had never wanted to see that same fear in Rhiannon.

The iron hinges on the front door moaned as someone entered, but Dylan cared not who. He turned away, gazing instead into the flames at the hearth.

The Dragon Laird

A warm hand on his shoulder brought him around to face its owner. He recognized the old woman from the village fire. She smelled sweetly of rain. Her white hair hung over one shoulder and her yellow eyes held wisdom far beyond his.

"Your soul is heavy, but the light will soon come to see it lifted," she offered.

"Again you speak in riddles. Why have you come, old woman?"

"So the Dragon snarls and snaps at all when in pain." Her smile grew. "You will address me as Dela for the time being."

"Leave me, Dela. I am unfit company."

"First there is something I would show you." Dela brought forth a golden chain from a cloth purse. Link by link it was revealed until a multi-faceted crystal caught the firelight. As it spun, rainbow sparks glittered on the walls and across his face, creating a profusion of colors.

He could feel the crystal's pulsating brightness behind his eyes. Waves of heat passed through his body until he could not move, but that did not keep him from trying.

Dylan's attempts to fight the hypnotic sleep pleased her. "Do not fight the dragon's eye, Dylan. Let go and sleep. There is ought to fear."

"Damn you, witch," Dylan whispered as his head fell to his chest.

Dela helped the sleeping man lay his head down on the table for a more comfortable rest before going upstairs to Rhiannon.

Rhiannon lay in the middle of Dylan's bed. Even as tired as she was, sleep would not come. She struggled with idea after idea on how to make things right but nothing seemed perfect.

Now that she had the whole story, she suspected Dylan thought it was the curse she feared and that he had the power to hurt her. If only she had Dela to talk to.

Just then, a bump on the door made her sit up. Then came a sound of something sliding along its wooden surface.

Rhiannon stood up, waiting. A fog seeped from under the door to wrap around the bolt and iron hinges. Had evil found her? There was no escape from this room. She stood alone.

She grabbed the Moonstone at her breasts, but it lay cool and quiet. Sparks shot out around the door edges, blinding her for a moment before it swung open.

An old woman stood in the hall. Her back bowed with time, she gripped her staff with one hand while waving at the smoke with the other, coughing. "Always too much smoke."

"Dela," Rhiannon greeted with a laugh. She stepped over a guard who slept stretched out among the rushes and wrapped her arms around the woman's frail shoulders.

"'Tis so good to see you," Rhiannon offered.

"So you are not still angry with me?"

"Nay, I have seen the wisdom in the knowing. Will you tell me more of my family?"

"Aye. Along the way. Collect your cloak. We must be off while the weather is right."

Rhiannon glanced down the hall, knowing Dylan would be hurt again if he found her gone. "I can not leave. There is much you do not know."

"Humph! 'Tis what you think. The Laird will not know you have left. He will sleep 'til I wake him." Dela patted Rhiannon's hand. "All will be righted this night. If Gian had left his nose out of this, the deed would have been seen to days 'afore."

"Gian?"

"Aye, your father. He was the one who interrupted your love play in the forest. He must always have his way. That is what comes of being king of *Tylwyth teg*. Come, we must go."

"Wait." Rhiannon gently pull back on Dela's arm. "Would my father," she swallowed over the title, "have killed Dylan had I not chosen him?"

"Oh, aye, and doomed us all. Come, come." Dela lead the way as Rhiannon digested all she heard.

When they passed by a snoring Dylan, Rhiannon asked Dela what she had done.

"I but showed him the dragon's eye. He is a strong warrior, Rhiannon. He fought the sleep. Worry not, sweet lass. No harm will befall him."

The night air blew cool, carrying the scent of rain, which had fallen hours past. The moon winked out from between each passing cloud.

No one marked their leaving, and Rhiannon knew it was Dela's doing. The trees bowed slightly in the breeze, carrying the hint of cedar, oak, and sweet rowan.

"Dela, where do we go?"

"Tonight you help me build an area of protection for you and your Laird."

Dela moved more fleet of foot than Rhiannon had ever known her to be. She had a time keeping up.

"I have no knowledge of casting. There was no time to learn," Rhiannon reminded.

"I will spell-cast, you are to direct it. Your protection has always come from the water. Have you ever noticed 'tis bathing you go when your soul is heavy? The water spirit is your ally."

Looking back over her life, Rhiannon saw the old woman was right. Suddenly, Dela stopped so unexpectedly in front of

Rhiannon that she ran into her.

"Forgive me, Dela."

"Do you love him?"

The abrupt question made Rhiannon suck in a quick breath and clear her throat. She thought a moment, her heart racing.

"I know little of what love is, but I would die to save him, just as I would do for Robbie. I would tenderly care for his feelings and wants, as I do for you, but still, there is more.

"When I am around him 'tis like finding a piece of myself. There is a oneness, a connection that fills my very soul. He but smiles, and I want to melt like butter on warmed bread. If I am gone from him too long my chest hurts and breathing is hard. Is this love, Dela?"

"Aye, lass, and I am glad to hear it." In the moonlight, Dela's eyes sparkled with moisture. "And he has feeling for you as well."

"Really?"

"Aye." Dela chuckled. "Now there are more things you must know 'afore we reach the forked river. 'Tis time we talk of your mother."

"Can you not tell me first of Dylan's feeling?"

"This you will know in due time. We will speak of your mother as we walk."

"I remember you saying she was Meg the Giver of Life."

"She is."

"Did my parents not want Robbie and me?"

"Oh, they wanted you and praised the gods for you."

"But why would—?"

"Nay, let me finish, then you may ask your questions. Your mother had the gift of healing even as a young girl, and with it came a soft heart. She befriended a strange boy from the village because no one else wanted to bother with him.

"Twas not until she saw Beiste break the legs of a duck and laugh at the poor thing's pained attempts to walk that she saw the evil festering within him. By then, 'twas too late. Beiste thought Meg was meant to be his.

"When she married your father Gian, and went to live in *Tylwyth teg,* Beiste could not get to her. Therefore, he swore to all things unholy that if Meg had a child he would use its blood to tip the scales between good and evil and rule the world.

"When you were born they kept your identity hidden and fostered you with your distant relations, the McKays."

The roar of the water told them they had reached the beginning of the forked river. Dela stopped and turned toward Rhiannon. "Can you understand and forgive your parents for this life you have had to live?" Dela paused before continuing. "I hope you can."

Rhiannon's mouth fell open when Dela's form started to shift and melt away, leaving a beautiful middle aged woman with long red hair the same shade as her own, and soft brown eyes. She spoke with a voice as soft as a morning dove.

"I have never deserted you, my own, but this was the only way we could protect you and still share your life."

"Who are you?" Rhiannon asked, but instinctively knew.

"Meg, your mother."

Tears clouded Rhiannon's vision. Her mother had been with her all these years, loving her, teaching her, and sharing her woes. Meg, too, had tears in her eyes, no doubt waiting for her daughter's reaction.

Rhiannon fell to her knees and clasped tightly to her mother's legs. "Mother," she cried, fearing this was a dream that would soon end. "Pray you, do not leave me. How long I wished your arms around me, holding me."

The song of joyous weeping filled the gentle breeze as Meg knelt to enfold Rhiannon in her arms for the first time with no secrets between them.

"How I have longed to hear you call me thus." Meg wiped tears from Rhiannon's cheek. "I thought often on this moment and feared your rejection."

"Oh, nay. I have loved you as Dela, now how much more I love you as my protective mother. Speak no more of rejection."

"Aye, come my own, there will be time later to talk in full. The moon will soon set, and we must be back 'afore then. Remove your clothes and enter the water. Face the river's fork."

Rhiannon followed Meg's instructions just as she always had Dela's.

"This river circles your laird's castle and lands. Close your eyes and listen to my voice. You must do everything I tell you."

Rhiannon nodded, took a deep breath, and exhaled slowly. The cool air of the forest calmed her.

"Picture in your mind the river circling the castle. The water seeps into the earth, caring for all within its circle. Sit Dylan at the center of it all. Do you have all this pictured?"

"Aye."

"Good. Do not lose that image. As I chant, the spell will pass through you to fill all you hold within your thoughts.

"Mother Earth and gods above, we raise our voices in need. We seek the powers of the north, the west, the south, and the east. May all living things hear our plea. May this river, bringer of life, ally and friend to the chosen one, give protection to all she holds dear."

Meg repeated the chant until it became nothing but a hum

surrounding Rhiannon with warmth. In the midst of that warmth, Rhiannon centered on Dylan, and nothing else. She called to him, and he raised his head to meet her gaze.

The fire of passion in his eyes burst upon her like a wave. She gasped and gloried in the sweet emotion. The bond between them was a golden thread unseen by any save them. The thread could never be cut. Not even time or death could break them apart.

"Rhiannon." Something cool passed over her face. "Rhiannon, wake love. We must be away to the castle."

She slowly opened her eyes to see the moon disappear behind a cloud. Meg bent over her as she lay on the forest floor having once again taken the form of Dela.

"Did I dream everything?"

"Nay, my own. I must wear this disguise a while longer. Come, we must cross the river and enter the circle."

The nervousness in her mother's voice made Rhiannon sit up and look around. The burning at her breasts caused alarm. "My Moonstone." She grabbed it, the heat intense. "He is near. How could the Sorcerer find us?"

"He knows every time magic is invoked. Hurry now, he can not harm us once we enter the circle."

Standing, Rhiannon picked up her cloak and shift and took her mother's hand. Together they stepped into the rushing water. Being fully dressed, Meg had to struggle to keep upright. The currant tugged at her clothes.

They were half way across the river when a lightning bolt struck a tree on the bank where they had entered. With a thundering crack, a large branch severed from the trunk and came crashing down, just missing them.

One of the small branches scraped along Rhiannon's left arm. The force of the limb entering the water knocked Meg off balance. Rhiannon saw her go under and a scream erupted from her very soul. She reached into the water's depths, searching desperately for anything to grab.

She reached further, swinging both arms side to side. Something slid through her fingers. She grabbed again, catching it this time and giving a mighty yank.

Her mother broke the surface, coughing and frantically wiping wet hair from her eyes and nose.

"Rhiannon."

"Aye. I have you. We are almost there."

"My dress got caught and I could not free myself."

"My ally the water spirit and the gods above have blessed us this night by saving your life."

As they struggled up the opposite bank to safety, two hooded men rode into view on the far side. The taller of the two pointed a finger at Rhiannon, his voice a roar in their heads.

"I will have you, daughter of Meg. Your blood is mine."

Rhiannon covered herself tightly with the cloak, feeling unclean where his gaze had touched.

"Come, let us leave this place," Meg whispered. Both of them shivered, not from the night's cool breeze, but from the stench of evil.

"No power on earth will keep me from you, Rhiannon," the man vowed. "I will cut the life from you and feast upon your flesh."

Grabbing her mother's arm, she turned and ran with her, but the evil one's words echoed in her mind and a shudder of dread crawled through her belly.

Dylan awoke with a start. His breathing became fast as he surveyed the hall. There was no one present except the old woman, whose clothes were dripping wet. From the window, he could see darkness still covered the earth.

His gaze came to rest again on the woman he believed to be Dela, and he narrowed his gaze. "You cast a spell on me."

"'Twas nothing but sleep." She leaned toward him, her eyes glowing. "I have much you must learn and little time."

"And what makes you think I would listen."

"Dylan McGregor, if you wish to keep Rhiannon healthy and at your side, heed my words with care."

"You have my attention. Speak. But know this, witch. If you ever use your spells on me again, you shall reap my wrath."

"So be it." Meg worried more about Gian's wrath, when he learned she had told Dylan everything. It was time the Dragon Laird had the knowledge. She spared no detail of the prophecy, the identity of Rhiannon's parents and what lay ahead. Dylan sat quietly, rubbing his chin with thumb and forefinger.

"Rhiannon is yours, Dylan, take her 'afore she is ripped from you. Light and darkness are two sides of the same coin. They make a whole that is unbreakable. Go. Love her, my Laird."

The ancients foretold she was his. He could not begin to express how that knowledge thrilled him. Dylan left the old woman to her own devise and took the stairs two at a time. He opened the door to his room and spotted Rhiannon sitting in front of the fire drying her hair. Startled, she glanced up. He knew she was nervous from the way she grabbed the chair arm with both hands, as if to hold on should his temper burst forth. But the flame of anger had blown out and another, stronger fire lit in its place.

He closed the door, leaving the hounds out in the hall.

One of them scratched at the entrance, no doubt Kyna. She would miss her warm bed by the fire this night.

"You went out?" Dylan leaned back on the wooden door, taking in the view of her as the firelight passed through the chemise to reveal the curves of her body. Hot blood pulsed in his loins.

"Aye."

"But you returned here...to me?"

"'Tis where I want to be."

His heart beat faster. "You have been told I am cursed." At her nod, he continued. "Yet, you want to stay?"

"Aye, if you want me."

"Because the prophecy said you must?"

"Nay…aye…I mean, I must stay. However, I am glad 'tis you the gods chose for me. I am pleased with their choice of mate."

He closed his eyes and nearly moaned. Her innocent words hitting their mark, he met her gaze again. He could feel a tangible heat emanating from every cell of his being.

"Come here." The command rolled off his lips with a deep intensity. He wanted her to come to him. He needed her to come to him. She stood slowly. Her hair, still tangled from the night's breeze, fell in disarray to her waist.

The sway of her hips and the bounce of her breasts enchanted him as she moved closer. When she stopped, she stood close enough for him to feel her shallow, uneven breath on his neck.

Her warm, sweet female scent filled his head and caused blood to race to his loins. She held his gaze with her blazing emerald eyes, waiting. He found himself spellbound and unable to move.

"I am here, Dylan. I am yours to command."

He did moan then. Air grew impossible to draw, thoughts difficult to order, and words impossible to speak, yet his need to touch her was great.

Dylan ran his hands into the silky hair framing her face. She let her head fall back exposing the soft flesh of her throat and thrusting up her breasts so they grazed his chest.

Intense heat curled to life in his groin until he hardened with it. Her flesh so tempted him that he slid his mouth over her throat and along the collarbone to the back of her neck.

He gently pulled the hair away from her ear to kiss its tender rings and warmed it with his hot breath. She gave a shiver and moaned. Her hands came up to rest upon his back.

He smelled the musk of sensual ripeness upon her and became intoxicated with the awareness of her need.

Dylan ran one hand down her back to her hips and pressed her soft feminine folds to his hardened rod, giving in to his raging desire. Her fingers dug into his flesh, and she gave a whimper of pleasure.

He lifted one of her legs to wrap around his hips then rubbed himself along the seam of her covered womanhood.

She became weak in his arms and called out to him. With one move, he turned and had her back pressed against the door lifting her higher so he had better access to the treasure between her legs. He pulled the ties on her chemise loose before sliding it off her shoulders to bare her breasts.

With greed built of lust, need, and a heart's wish, he brought his lips to the hard peaks of her nipples. He filled his mouth with the ripe fruit, suckling and kneading her tender globes. Rhiannon ran her hands into his long black hair and held his head to her.

With eager fingers, he pulled his shirt over his head. One tug freed him of his kilt. Deft fingers made impatient, he pulled her chemise the rest of the way off. Now skin to skin, he held her close. Her soft damp curls tickled his rod, making him clinch his hips and press closer.

The magic of her mere touch tantalized him. He moved his fingers down to spread her. She was slick, warm, and no doubt sweet. The very thought compelled him to seek the truth. With lips and tongue, he worked his way from her breasts to the softness of her belly and lower still. He knelt before her, his thumbs opening the sensitive folds of her secret haven.

His kiss was deep and open mouthed, seeking the hidden nectar between her thighs. He explored every mound and crevice, finding her most sensitive nub to suckle and flick with his tongue. Her fingers tightened in his hair. Her cries made excitement surge through him.

Rhiannon opened for him, desperate for his caress. Passion rose and intensified. There was power in his touch, for all her thoughts centered on what his mouth was doing. She felt like she was in the place between earth and heaven. A place of ecstasy.

Rhiannon could hear her own cries of pleasure, as she raced through suspended time to reach the heavens and the earth moved.

She sank to her knees on the fur-covered floor. Dylan followed her, spreading her legs, his fingers moving and stretching her wider before his hard silken shaft pushed in slowly into her welcoming moist heat, filling her. He made her complete as nothing else could. They became one. The beat of their hearts sang the same song.

When he made to withdraw, she held on tight to his hips, a whimper of protest on her lips.

"Sweet love, I will not leave you." So saying, he plunged

within her again. "Here I am home." His mouth met hers hungry as he built the rhythm with each thrust.

The heat in his gaze commanding, his hair fell over his shoulders to brush over her sensitive nipples with each thrust, before his lips met hers. She would refuse him nothing.

The rhythm built. His muscles flexed and she felt again his magic. Sweat made their skin slick, his body sliding along hers with each thrust. His movements came faster and harder. They worked together to find their pleasure. Then he jerked once, twice, throwing back his head, shouting out his release and she followed with a cry of her own. His warm seed filled her womb. He kissed her tenderly before resting heavily upon her, but she had no wish for him to move. She rubbed her cheek along his dark head as it rested on her breast. The softness of his hair and the smell that was so uniquely his comforted her. Holding him tight, she fell asleep.

Dylan knew when she slept. He gently picked her up and cradled her naked body against his chest, as he walked to the bed.

The sun had breached the night's sky, but he had no wish to give up this moment. Seeing her now in his bed with the sun pouring through the window to touch upon a bare breast, he hardened again with need. He ran a finger around her nipple and watched it tighten.

A banging at his door shattered their privacy. Rhiannon sat up, grabbing for the covers just as the door flew open. Dylan's roar of rage echoed through the halls.

Chapter Ten

Owain rushed into Dylan's room, a worried frown on his face until he spotted Rhiannon's naked curves barely wrapped in Dylan's bed linens. She sat facing him the sheet draped over her breasts. His gaze turned heated at the sight of her hair tossed over one bare shoulder, while the rest of its fiery mass fell along the pale skin of her back to pool around her hips.

The sun pulsed through the window, highlighting its strands of golden fire. Her lips were moist and red from a night's passion, and her dark lashes rested on flawless cheeks.

He had come to adore her spirit and honor, the way she took any situations that life gave her and beat it. Now to see her as a seductive woman stirred his feeling even more. Here was a woman he could love, given time.

Dylan stood by the foot of the bed, watching his brother lust after Rhiannon and felt the talons of anger wrap around his innards.

He glanced back at Rhiannon. She smiled at Owain, signs of a pink blush coloring her cheeks. Then she pulled the linen up closer to her neck.

Was she being receptive to his brother? He had no understanding of a woman's mind. A picture of the two of them together in a heated embrace came unbidden to his mind, and he felt an uncontrollable jealousy consume him.

"Rhiannon—," Owain whispered, just before a roar filled

the room. Owain turned in time to see his brother's fist connect with his chin.

Pain shot through his head, making him stagger. When he righted himself, he took in his brother's twisted face. Anger marred every line.

Understanding dawned, and he felt as if he had been hit again. Dylan had taken her innocence. With a cry of anger, he returned Dylan's punch with one of his own. Then he swung again, Dylan ducked and landed a blow to his stomach.

When he bent over, Dylan's fist connected with his left eye. Lights fanned out in his head, and his legs grew wobbly, but he swung again, hitting Dylan in the chest. Dylan's hard fist smacked the side of his head.

Rhiannon gasped with each punch. This had to stop. They were going to kill each other. Clutching the sheet to her breasts with one hand, she slipped from the bed, dragging the cover with her. Her angry strides took her to the washbasin on the nightstand, and filled the basin with cold water from the pitcher.

Taking the basin, she walked over to the fighting men and threw the cold water over their heads. They parted to stare at her, wiping water from their eyes and faces.

Owain flipped his hair back and rubbed at his chin, looking uncomfortable.

"What the hell was that for?" Dylan ran a hand through his wet hair to smooth it back out of his face.

"'Tis the only way to stop a dog fight." Her jaw was clenched. "Fool man, why did you hit Owain?"

"He knows."

"Aye, you are jealous and have no reason for it. If you will remember, I chose you." She turned to Owain. "Why did you come to see Dylan?"

"He never sleeps late, and when I heard how angry he was at you last night, I came up to check on his health, as well as yours."

"You thought he had hurt me?"

"Aye,"

"Both of you are fools." When he moved to speak, she raised her hand. "Stop. Please leave, Owain. I would speak to Dylan alone."

"Aye, go, and the next time you fear for my health, I shall have your eyes plucked from your head." Dylan balled his hands into fists.

"I am going, but you should not tarry here. Others will seek you out, Dylan for castle needs." He turned back to Rhiannon. "I beg your pardon." At her nod, Owain turned and left, dripping water on the floor as he went.

Dylan slammed the door and bolted it. He crossed his arms over his chest, frowning.

"*Och!* Dylan, what are you about?"

"You are mine, by the gods."

"Aye, by the gods," she said, taking the sheet and throwing it at him. "Our union is written in the stars. I have given myself to you this night, and you cheapen my gift when you think I would fall into the arms of another."

He grabbed the sheet, running it over his face and body, drying off.

A warm hand slid over his tight shoulder, tender, soothing. "There is no reason to be angry," she whispered.

He glanced in her bright eyes, so innocent yet so expressive. Tender possessiveness filled his heart. "I will not have others viewing what is mine."

His deep voice was once again caressing, the words perhaps his way of trying to right his wrong.

She smiled, running her hand over his chest. He uncrossed his arms, letting them fall to his sides, waiting to see what she would do and enjoying her boldness.

"Now, am I yours, My Laird?" She asked, tilting her head to one side. She ran a finger over his nipple. Pleasure brought blood pounding into his loins.

He smiled. "Have you forgotten? I have not." He pulled her to him and ran a dark finger through the moist heat between her legs.

"Good," she moaned, as he pushed his finger deep within her. "'Twas never any doubt," she sighed. "That I was yours. 'Twas how you felt, that concerned me."

Dylan leaned forward kissing her neck where her heart beat. "Explain," he ordered in a hot whisper, moving his finger in and out of her, enjoying the sweet shivers of pleasure that ran through her body.

"When I gave myself to you, my heart and soul were given as well. I tell you this, so you know 'twas not for the prophecy or any other thing. I have been yours from the day you brought me here and showed me kindness."

At her words, he stopped his play and raised his head to meet her gaze. Had her life been so troubled? Mayhap they were kindred spirits.

"I have known little kindness and often a man's fist," she continued her voice low and heavy with desire. "So know, My Laird, I do not care about curses; only your kindness and how you might think of me."

Dylan took her face in large, battle-rough hands, running his thumbs along both sides of her jaw. "I have been alone in this life and have not the talent to speak words a woman should hear." He cleared his throat. "But to me you have more importance than any gold or battle victory. You have become the very air I breathe."

Moisture filled her eyes. He wiped a tear from her cheek. "See, I have injured your soft ears."

"Oh, nay." She slid her arms around his neck. "No bard could have said it sweeter. You have touched my heart most deeply." She took his face and brought his lips to hers, giving a gentle whisper of warmth from one to the other, but Dylan would have none of that.

He crushed her in the protective shell of his arms and his mouth opened on hers, feeding his need to taste her response again. His manhood was stiff and hard and as their mouths mated, he stroked her woman's softness with his silken blade.

The banging at his door had him growling again. "Must I be beset with all the castle's wants this morn?"

Rhiannon giggled and received a scowl. He was like a boy with a new toy, one he could not play with until finishing his chores.

A smile touched his lips. "Be quick, and dress. We are off to ride."

She caught his meaning and smiled mischievously. "Should I bring an extra cloak in case we tire and wish to rest in some gentle meadow?"

He burst out laughing. "Oh, aye."

Dylan dressed quickly then left Rhiannon to wash and clothe herself for the day. There was something he needed to do. Spotting Owain slumped in a chair sipping a drink; he went over to stand beside him.

Owain lifted a mug to his mouth and drank heavily before speaking. "What do you want?"

"I would not have hard feelings between us," Dylan stated.

"I was wrong," Owain offered. "She has ever been yours, and I see the caring you have for her. I will be no trouble, brother, but do not ask me not to feel for her. 'Tis too late for that."

"Aye, she is a woman to fill a man's heart. 'Tis a hard road you chose."

"Aye."

The best thing was to keep him busy. "I need your help. See that all McKays are brought to the courtyard." With that, Dylan left for the stables and ordered his mount readied.

Now, he stood waiting in the courtyard, holding his mount's reins. He had not meant to cheapen what Rhiannon had given him last night, but jealousy chases reason away.

He had suffered with that emotion over the years, so he understood what it was. His fear of losing the first selfless gift someone had given him had triggered his temper and possessive nature, hurting her unintentionally.

Now, he wanted to give her something that might show her how much she meant to him. What he contemplated doing was unheard of. People would grumble because of the lost coin, but he could deal with complaints. He had heard them all his life, but he could not do without Rhiannon.

The door to the Keep opened, bringing Dylan's gaze around.

One by one, the prisoners stumbled out to stand quietly in a close group, no doubt fearing for their lives. Only one stood straight and glared at him, Robert McKay.

Owain stepped up beside Dylan, causing him to turn and face his brother. "That is all of them, Dylan. Mind telling me what you wanted them for?"

"Soon, Brother. Do you feel as bad as you look? The left side of your face is swollen and black, and your chin has an extra lump, while your eye seems to be swollen shut." Dylan smiled.

"Well, you are not so handsome yourself. You wear the same colors on your jaw. And aye, it hurts like hell, so do not make me smile." Owain grumbled then broke into a smile. "Ouch! Be damned." Owain frowned and rubbed his cheek.

"There she is," Dylan stated, watching Rhiannon appear in the doorway. She spotted him and smiled, but it slipped to a frown when she noticed her clansmen.

Dylan motioned her over, then spoke loudly so all would hear. "McKays, today is a day of celebration. I give you your freedom to go home or stay as you will."

A mighty chorus of voices rose in cheers, but he had his gaze glued to Rhiannon. Her expression registered surprise then joy. When the ovation calmed enough to be heard, he continued.

"This honor was not from Laird McKay for no ransom was paid." Quiet fell over everyone. "It comes from your lady, Rhiannon. We hope this act will bring peace to our clans so we can be allies.

"Food and water will be provided for your trek home. Those who stay will be welcomed into our clan."

Again, cheers rang out over the morning air. Dylan watched Rhiannon accept bows and handshakes of thanks, but her gaze always returned to him. As she made her way to his side, there was such tender emotion in her eyes. It pleased him to know he had put it there.

When she reached him, she took his hand. "Why did you lay this deed at my feet? I had no knowledge of this."

"They would not have believed 'twas my doing. I did this for you, a gift to honor the one you gave me."

"Oh, Dylan." She laid her head on his shoulder. "The gods have blessed me greatly in their gift of you." When she raised her head, there were tears in her eyes. "That others can not see the man you are, is unbelievable and unbearable."

The smile he bestowed upon her held genuine warmth. He ran a finger down her cheek and over her bottom lip. "Let us be away. I would have you to myself."

She ran her hand tenderly over his bruised jaw. "By all means."

"Rhiannon." She turned to see her brother running forward. Guilt lanced through her. She had given no thought to Robbie.

"Rhiannon, what route shall we take home? They wish to follow you," Robbie volunteered, beaming with pride.

"She stays with me," Dylan stated, placing a possessive arm around her waist.

"You can not keep her prisoner," Robbie snapped, grabbing her arm.

"Please, stop," Rhiannon ordered, caught between the two glaring men. She did not want the two most important people in her life at each other's throats.

Turning to Dylan, she laid a hand over his heart. "Please give me a moment to speak to my brother."

Anger sparkled from his blue eyes half hooded in a frown. She feared he would refuse, but he gave a reluctant nod. Rhiannon took Robbie's hand and led him a short distance away.

She glanced over his face, then pushed the hair back from his forehead. How would she explain why she would not go with him this time?

"He can not keep you here, Rhiannon. I will kill him if he tries."

"Robbie, please try to understand. He is not forcing me. I want to stay. I want to be with him."

"You are not making sense. Where is your honor, your

loyalty to your clan? You are a McKay."

"Nay, I am not and neither are you. I told you who our parents were and how we came to be there."

"I care not who our parents were." Anger burned his cheeks. "They did not want us. The McKays took us in and gave us a home and a name. Now that some old hag has spouted tales you turn your back on the clan."

"Robbie, you have been my whole life for many years and will continue to be a part of me, but you know how my life was. I was naught but a servant to them. Here I am not mistreated and I have found a man I love.

"You have shown me you can care for yourself. You are a grown man and will find your own way as I wish to do."

"He has cast a spell over you. You are not the Rhiannon who followed me to the battlefield. You would not have let anything part us." He tightened his jaw and his hands balled into fists at his side. "I will not stay here and desert my clan."

Guilt sailed through her heart, but she would not leave Dylan.

"I am different, aye, but so are you. There is no spell unless 'tis love. The McGregor is kind. Have you not seen this? All are well fed, even the enemy. No one is hit, and the punishments are fair."

Robbie glared at the Laird. Rhiannon noticed Dylan's frown and realized his patience was running thin. She knew it had been hard for him to let her handle this, but he had. He was used to giving orders and seeing them carried out, not letting others have the power of decision. He was giving her another gift. A gift of trust.

Turning back to Robbie, she said, "I have a prophecy to fulfill, and Dylan was chosen to stand by my side."

"He is cursed and marked. Would you follow that same

path? See reason, Rhi. I want you with me. I will not see you hurt," Robbie stated.

She took his hand, her gaze blurring with unshed tears. "You are flesh of my flesh, and I love you, but let me be happy. I know not what the future holds for any of us, and neither do you, so take happiness were you find it."

Robbie looked away toward the gathered clans. She followed his gaze. "Others will stay also. See, many gather food and water for the trek, but others stand back against the wall. They will stay to join the McGregor. Won't you stay?"

Robbie looked at the divided McKays, then down at his boots. "There is another burden you must think on." Robbie said, meeting her gaze again. "Has he spoken of hand fasting or marriage? If not, then he has made you his whore. For that I should kill him. He shows you no respect."

"Look at his life, Robbie. Dylan has never been accepted. He does not have the knowledge of the rights and wrongs of relationships. He has a good heart, and when he thinks on it, he will do right by me. I have no doubt."

Robbie frowned. "You have put a lot of faith in him. I hope you are not disappointed and left in the cold with child." He sighed, running a hand through his hair. His shoulders slumped forward. "You are truly happy with him?"

"Aye." She smiled.

"When will I see you again?"

"The doors here will always be open to you." Tears blurred her vision. She did not want to say goodbye. She did not know when she would see her baby brother again. If the McKay continued this feud, mayhap never. Robbie would not turn his back on his clan.

"'Twill not be the same with the McKays. They will mark you a traitor and bar the doors."

"Aye, this I know, but if you can help us unite the clans, as allies, the way for our visits will be clear."

"Aye," Dylan said from behind them, putting his arm around her. "'Tis my wish as well."

Rhiannon gazed up at Dylan. He had lasted longer than she would have thought and had given her the time she needed with Robbie.

Robbie glanced at Dylan with narrowed eyes. "You will see to Rhi's every need, or find my blade between your ribs."

Dylan lifted his brow, and gave a sultry smile. "Aye lad. 'Tis my greatest pleasure."

Rhiannon felt fire in her cheeks, yet could not help laughing.

"Come, Rhiannon, I would be off," Dylan said impatiently.

She pulled Robbie into her arms and they clung together. As she laid her face along his, she whispered words of parting. "I love you, Robbie. May the gods go with you and keep you safe."

"As I love you, Rhi. Let this parting not be long."

Tears filled her eyes, to tumble out and roll down her cheeks. "Aye, not long, brother." They kissed, and then Robbie turned and with long strides disappeared among the mass of people.

She watched the crowd, hoping for one last glimpse of him, her heart breaking. The stone of separation set heavy in her stomach. There had only been the two of them for as long as she could remember. She prayed this would not be the last time her eyes beheld his tall form.

"Are you all right?" Dylan asked, concern deepening his voice, his large hand rubbing up and down her arm in a comforting rhythm.

"Aye." When she was in his arms, everything seemed right.

Dylan pulled her around and wiped at the tears running down her cheeks. "Come."

He mounted his horse first then reached for her. His muscled arm bulged as he pulled her up to sit across his thighs. The horse sidestepped, but Dylan righted him easily with one hand. With the other, he pulled Rhiannon tight against his chest.

"Do you see my brother?" Dylan asked.

Looking around, she spotted Owain watching them from the stable door. Sadness marked his bruised face, until he noticed she looked his way. He smiled, with a wince, and inclined his head.

She knew he had tender feelings toward her, but would not compete with Dylan, yet tormented emotions poured from eyes so like Dylan's. She wished she could bring ease, but that was something only time alone would heal.

"He stands by the stables, my Laird."

Dylan glanced where indicated then brought their horse over before his brother. "Owain, we will be back 'afore dark. 'Til then, you will be in charge." Owain nodded, and Dylan turned the mount, walking it through the gates and down the dirt path into the hills. They were soon concealed from prying eyes by a grove of trees. The fragrance of new growth and wet earth after the nights rain opened her soul, pushing the sorrow from her thoughts.

Rhiannon leaned her head back on his shoulder and closed her eyes. She did not know what the future held for any of them.

She knew she made the right decision in staying with Dylan. There could be no other choice.

Dylan leaned his cheek down and rubbed it along hers. The warmth of his strong arm around her made her feel secure. The soft stroking of his thumb along the underside of her breast brought a fire to her blood. The passion, still new, ran hot for both of them.

She turned her head to kiss his jaw and bury her nose in his neck. He smelled of spice from the soap he used. She closed her eyes and inhaled deeply, savoring the mixture of spice and musk that was his special scent.

Dylan turned taking her lips with nibbles then ran his tongue along her bottom lip until she opened to receive him. She reached back and ran her fingers through his hair. His strong hand covered a breast, kneading it and pulling softly at the hardened nipple.

She moaned. "Think we might find that meadow soon, my Laird?"

His deep husky chuckle broke over her. "Oh, aye, lass."

Then as if an icy wind passed through her, she sat up, stiff; all attention focused on the unnatural cold.

"What is it?" Dylan asked, casting a glance around them, examining every tree and rock carefully for signs of danger.

"'Tis a feeling only. Something is not right."

They had not passed from the circle of protection, she was sure of it. She could hear the water, to her right, as it ran over rocks in the riverbed.

With each step the horse took, Rhiannon felt a sense of oppression. Finally, the heat of her Moonstone answered her question. "The Sorcerer is near."

Dylan pulled Rhiannon up hard against his chest and removed the Singing Sword from its sheath. He directed the horse with the pressure of his knees.

The air hung thick with malevolence. Her breathing

became labored. She grabbed Dylan's arm as fear overcame her. Her gaze darted around the trees.

"There is evil here. Do you not feel it?"

The horse laid back its ears and tossed its head, then it stopped, standing still on the path.

"I feel power emanating from the ground. Our mount feels it too, but I see naught amiss."

"Nay, my Laird, the evil comes from within those trees. Look at the Moonstone. It glows."

On its own, the horse turned to move off the path and head toward the spot she had pointed too. Dylan tried to direct the horse back to the path with his knees. When that failed to work, he pulled the reins to the left, but the horse would not turn. He pulled again, trying not to damage its delicate mouth but determined to remain on the path.

"Had I not trained this horse myself, I would swear 'twas unused to commands." He pulled left again, and a quiver shook through the animal's body, yet it continued toward the stream through the trees.

"The horse is being lead by another. We must get off 'afore we are taken with it. We must not cross the stream, or we leave the protection of the circle."

A loud clap of thunder filled the air around them, yet no clouds darkened the sky. All birds hushed their singing. Then they took to the skies in a mad dash of squawks and flapping wings.

The vibration coming from the ground reached Rhiannon through the horse. "Dylan?"

"I feel it."

Their mount blew from his nose and danced as if it stood on hot coals. Then the stallion reared.

Rhiannon leaned forward and grabbed for the horse's

mane, but missed and fell back into Dylan, causing them both to slip from the saddle. Dylan grabbed her around the waist, taking the brunt of the fall.

He grunted as they met the ground. Her head connected with his chin and bright lights filled her vision.

Rhiannon turned just in time to watch their mount stumble once, before he disappeared among the swaying trees. She rolled off Dylan, but held on tightly to his chest.

The tremors were growing in strength. The ground dipped and swayed. She felt as if her innards would soon spill from her body and join with all the rocks that bounced like grease in a hot pan.

"Dylan."

A loud rumbling echoed through the forest. Apprehension gnawed at her stomach. Glancing behind, she saw a hill of rocks sink into the earth and disappear. Dirt clouds swirled through the area where the hill once stood.

The sting of falling pebbles, made her lean over to protect Dylan. "Dylan, please." She pushed the hair from his face and found his eyes closed. Fear made her clench at his arm and give a shake, but he did not move. It was up to her to find a place of safety.

She pushed away from him to stand, but the earth became unstable and she fell to her knees. It heaved and swayed affecting her balance like the time she had been on the sea in a fisher's boat.

Loud crackling made her glance up. A large limb crashed through branches to hit the ground to their left and burst into splinters.

Other branches fell splintering around them. One small piece hit Dylan and he moaned.

"Nay. Dylan, wake up!" Panic welled in her throat.

A ripping sound drew her gaze to a small tear in the earth's crust that moved like a slithering snake. Then like an arrow it ran under the base of a tree. It widened, and the snapping of roots breaking came from the darkness below.

Hissing steam shot up from the jagged rip, and a scream escaped through her lips. The ground split again off to her left, shooting steam upward with a whining force.

A tree, having lost its hold on the rocky dirt, toppled. The massive trunk raced to meet a rock face, crashing through smaller trees as it fell.

Rhiannon watched in horror as it hit a tree directly overhead. A large branch nearly the size of Dylan's chest cracked and descended toward them. There was no time to move out of its way.

Chapter Eleven

Growing up, Robert had always thought he would fight his first battle, marry, and have children, and Rhiannon would be there to share those things with him. Now, she had been charmed away by the McGregor, and some old hag's tale of woe and prophecy. He had no idea what life held for him, but he was now on his own.

Nessa stepped up next to him to help pass out bread and water skins. He glanced at her from the corner of his eye. He admired her easy smile, and the way her hips swayed as she moved.

Here was a woman to please any man, but she was a McGregor. The name put a foul taste in his mouth, but still it did not change the fact she was generous and had a fire for life. Moreover, he found he enjoyed sparking that fire.

He caught her glancing at him from those blue eyes and felt a stirring in his loins. He could feel her gaze slide over his length and knew he was headed for trouble.

The gentle curve of her breasts would fit his hand. Thick black waves of hair danced around her face and shoulders. His mind filled with her many assets, he reached for a loaf the same time she did, their hands meeting over the bread.

Nessa quickly removed her hand from his and met his warm gaze. Air was hard to find, and when she stood near him, her heartbeat grew faster.

He was a McKay, and yet he plagued her thoughts since meeting him the other day. She wanted to brush back the hair that fell over one brow and run her fingers over his broad shoulders.

A fluttering worked its way into her stomach as she admired his lips. She had never been kissed. Now, she wanted to learn how, and have Robbie teach her.

Surely, she would burn for her wicked thoughts, but they stayed. Even though it was pleasurable to think of kissing him, she knew it would never happen. They were enemies. Anyway, he probably had a girl or two, already. She gave an unladylike snort, practically throwing a loaf of bread at a warrior. She would not be added to his list, yet when he gave that devilish smile, it heated her blood, and her heart wanted to jump from her breasts.

"Well, Brat, we meet again." One side of his mouth came up, and a twinkle of mischief gleamed in his dark green eyes. The wind lifted his dark hair to tap it playfully at his shoulders.

"I see the Boar has been freed from his cage." She smiled, impishly.

"Ouch, she has claws." He frowned and stuck out his lower lip in an expression of hurt, but the affect was lost when his mouth twitched in silent laughter.

"'Tis good you noticed. How is your wound?"

"Which one?" he asked, suggestively.

"I do believe your confinement did ought for your manners." Nessa handed another person some cheese.

Robbie leaned over to pull her hair back and run his finger along the edge of her ear. She shivered in pleasure.

Then he put his lips close to her ear and whispered. "I will gladly show you my wounds any time you wish. All you need do is ask."

She gasped, turning to meet his leer. *The rat.* Did he think he could win her over with such talk? He was just too handsome for his own good.

She put her hand on his chest and in a soft whisper, "I would not flutter and faint at the sight of your rod."

He drew in a sharp breath, and she smiled, then pushed hard on his chest, making him take a step back. Then raising the volume of her voice, she continued, "Peddle your wares to someone who wants them, Boar. I have no interest in boys, only men."

So saying, she turned and stomped away. Those close enough to have heard the exchange, chuckled.

"She did it again. The Brat got the last word." His laughter rang out over the chattering crowd. "Not this time, Brat." He would show her the difference between boys and men. He set the water skin down on the stone walk and chased after her.

Robbie spotted her near the castle wall just as the tremors hit. There was immediate silence from everyone in the crowd. All turned their attention to the ground as first pebbles rolled, then the earth heaved and rent with jagged tears. Sudden hysteria broke out. People screamed, running into the castle, the stables, or the forest. Others stood frozen in their fear.

Robbie watched in horror as small pieces of mortar tumbled down the castle wall and landed only a few feet from Nessa. She stood with her back pressed against the stone turret's base.

Glancing up toward the tower, he saw movement and realized that several blocks had loosened. Any one of them falling from that height could kill the young woman.

"Nessa!" He ran toward her but tripped over a large crack in the ground that had not been there a moment ago. Loosened rocks rolled down the hill from his left. He looked again at her. The distance was too far. He was not going to make it. Pain filled his chest. "Nessa, run!"

She turned toward him, and he saw the stark terror in her wide eyes. She was frozen. The stones above let loose and started their descent.

Nessa heard her name called from a great way off. Sheer black terror swept through her. She could not seem to move anything but her head.

Hearing her name called again, she looked up to see fear on Robbie's face as he ran to her. A scream rushed in to fill her panic clouded mind and ring in her ears.

Nessa felt a sting to her shoulder as something hit her, but she kept her gaze locked on Robbie. He would help her. She formed his name on her lips, but no sound passed them.

"By all the powers that be," he screamed. "Let me make it to her!" He could not see her crushed. Then, as if his feet had wings, he dove for her, knocking her to the ground and rolling out of the way just as stone and mortar hit the ground with a resounding *thunk* and *clatter*.

He pulled her beneath him, shielding her from any stray pieces. Her soft whimpering tore at his heart. "Shh, Love, I have you." The earth shook only minutes more before all quieted.

He lifted his head to inspect their surrounding. The tower stones had made a deep hole where they had landed, and Robbie marveled that he had made it to her in time.

Glancing down at the woman in his arms, he found her eyes tightly shut, while tears escaped from the corners. She shook uncontrollably and her breathing came hard and fast just like his. Only hers was from fear and his from exertion.

He laid his forehead on hers, bringing the sweet smell of

her into his lungs. Her softness felt so right next to his hardness.

"You saved me." Wonder laced her words. Her bright blue eyes opened searching his face.

"Aye." Feeling her small breasts pressed into his chest, and the warm softness of her body, he was in no hurry to move away. She brought a hardening to his groin, and sweet emotions to his heart.

"Why?" Nessa asked between gasps. He had no liking for the McGregors, yet he had risked his life to save hers. Did he hold some tender feeling for her as she did him?

He raised his head, and that devilish smile was back. "Whom else would I get to tend my wounds?" He reached up and removed a strand of hair from her cheek.

His answer was so unexpected it broke through her shock to ease some of her fear. She giggled then covered her mouth as she broke into laughter, but the laughter soon turned to tears.

Robbie pulled her up tight, and she clung to him as her tears washed away the fear that remained. "'Tis all right, love. Are you hurt? Talk to me."

He did not know the first thing about crying women. Therefore, he held her, enjoying the feel of her in his arms.

"I am sorry," she whispered on a sniffle.

"For what lass?"

"I could not move. I was so scared."

"It happens sometimes. I feared I would not reach you in time."

"You flew, Robbie. I saw you fly." He heard the wonder in her voice.

"I was always fast of foot, but I have to admit today put that to the test." His intent scrutiny, traveled over her face, coming to a stop at her mouth then went back up to her incredible eyes.

"Thank you." She admired his strength and tenderness, but most of all, she wanted his kiss.

"Robert McKay." They both turned toward a stout Highlander who was waving him on. "Come! Let us be away from this place."

The McKays were on the move. Some had already disappeared among the trees.

"I need to go." Robbie stood with a reluctant frown and helped Nessa to stand. She was still a little shaky and was glad when he put his arm around her.

"Be you of good health?"

"Aye, not but a scratched shoulder and a bruised bottom thanks to you."

"'Tis said, once you save a life, that life is yours to protect. You are mine, Nessa McGregor." Pulling her back into his arms, he captured her lips with a hungry urgency, as if he wanted to possess her soul.

His lips were warm and sweet like heather wine.

His hand ran into her hair, while the other moved down her back to press her closer to his hardness. She wound her arms around his neck and stood on her toes to reach him.

Then he pulled away. "You are mine, Nessa. Wait for me. I will come back for you." He turned and left.

She stood alone, watching him run after his friends. Half way up the hill, he turned to look at her. The breeze lifted his dark hair while his kilt swung about his strong thighs. He raised his hand in farewell before disappearing into the trees.

Her heartbeat raced in a chaotic tempo and the tightness of unreleased tears settled in her chest. She reached up and ran a finger over her kiss-swollen lips. Her first kiss. She would wait for him and dream of this day forever. She would never forget.

* * *

Pain!

Dylan slowly opened his eyes to see panic etched in every line of Rhiannon's face. She lay over his chest, as they both were prostrate on the ground. Her breathing came rapidly. He wrapped his arms around her holding her close.

She buried her face in his shoulder, then whispered along his neck. "Dylan, I could not rouse you." Her voice quivered with anxiousness. "Then with all the shaking this tree fell right for us, and I could not move you in time. Then another tree fell against the first, pushing it to the right of us. I was so scared." The fear was making her rattle on.

He groaned while reaching up with one hand to feel a sore spot on the back of his head. When he brought his hand around his fingers were wet with blood.

"Sweet Mary, what have you done," Rhiannon scolded, quickly moving out of his arms to examine the cut.

"'Tis naught, leave it."

"It may fester. 'Tis best to clean it now."

He jerked away, "Leave it, I said. I have had worse wounds."

"Then at least rinse it in yonder stream." Rhiannon planted her fists on her hips.

One side of his mouth turned up, as well as one brow while he looked her over. The fear had left her with the need to care for him. The fire in her eyes brought heat to his groin. He wanted her now, right here among the leaves.

"What are you looking at?" she asked. "Are you going to wash the dirt and blood from your head or not? Be warned, if not, I shall find a way to dump a bucket over your stubborn head."

"By the rood, woman. You have fire. 'Tis not only from that red hair, but all the way to your soul." At her frown, he chuckled. "So be it. 'Tis a small thing you ask."

He stood, and reached for his sword only to find it gone from its sheath. Looking about, he found the blade a few feet away. He stooped to retrieve and examine the steel for any nicks, sliding his thumb along the edge testing his sharpness. Satisfied, he slipped it back into the leather sheath, and walked with steady strides to the water's edge.

Kneeling down, he plunged his head below the water's surface, shook it, and lifted it out. The water dripped reddish brown from his hair to be whipped away in the rapid flow of the stream. He plunged in again. Then he jerked his head out, and flipped his long hair back, letting the icy water run along his collar and down his back.

"You can stop frowning. The blood is washed away and my wound is clean."

Rhiannon tore a strip of linen from her chemise. "I am not frowning. 'Tis concern. Here, let me tie this about the wound."

"The horse. Did it run off?"

"Aye."

When she reached for him, he grabbed her hand. "You tremble. Why? The wound is small."

"'Tis not the wound. Look about you." She pulled her hand from his and wrapped his head with the linen bandage. When she finished, he glanced around, barely remembering what had happened before being knocked out.

Rhiannon explained. "Trees fell, tearing their roots from the ground. The earth cracked to expose hell fire, and the ground rolled like the sea. I feared 'twas the end."

"And the Sorcerer. Did he show his face while I lay unconscious?"

"Nay. He seemed to have left with the shaking."

"'Twas his magic." Dylan had a distant look on his face,

as if he was somewhere else.

"Dylan?"

His gaze slid to hers. "We need to find a place of cover." Dylan stood and adjusted the bandage. "The beasts are still restless. I think more of the same will follow."

He held out his hand, which she took. "What beasts? What are you talking about?" she asked.

"I get these feelings sometimes. Thoughts that seem to appear in my mind, but they are stronger today. Everything is clearer."

Could he be having visions? They had made love last night; could the bond be strong enough to open doors in time, giving them both glimpses of the future?

"Tell me about the beasts," Rhiannon demanded, having to hurry to keep up with his long strides.

"Later. We need to leave here." Still holding her warm hand, he started back the way they had come. "I think I saw an opening in a rock wall this way."

"Would not the stones fall on us if another shake comes?"

"Not if the wall is solid."

He soon found where a long narrow cut had formed in the face of the towering rock. When they stepped up to the opening, they found it no wider then the width of Dylan's shoulders. As they passed through, the ground began to move again.

Dylan quickly pulled her into the darkness and pressed them against the rock wall. He covered her the best he could with his own body, hoping to shield her from any falling debris.

Small boulders skipped and clattered from above, then bounced along the dirt floor. He prayed they would not be buried alive.

Chapter Twelve

All motion stopped. Silence ensued as Rhiannon struggled to calm her frayed nerves. She pressed her forehead up against the stone's cool surface and concentrated on slowing her breathing.

How could she share the insecurity gnawing deep in her belly? No one must know of her fear of failure. So many questions beat through her head. The doubts haunted her. What price would her people pay should she choose the wrong path or make an ill decision? So many depended on her, and the closer she came to the time of reckoning, the more her fears plagued her.

Could she stop the Sorcerer? Remembering the dark-cloaked demon on the river last night made her light-headed with apprehension. Would she be strong enough to face that monster and defeat him?

The dust settled, but the darkness closed in around her. She was cold and damp. The sun's warmth could not penetrate solid rock.

Feeling a tickle on her head, she reached up, scratched, and found a bug among the grit in her hair. With a squeal, she knocked the creepy thing out, and gave a deep shudder. She did not mind bugs really; except this one had a hundred legs, was a foot long, and had poisonous fangs.

Why hadn't Dylan returned? Earlier he had walked deeper

into the cave to see where it led, and he had been gone for what seemed like forever.

She could not take much more of being alone in the dark with bugs the size of a man's fist. The Sorcerer's evil magic seemed to plague the darkness. Panic started to gnaw at her spirit and with it, doubts in her ability to see through this task before her. Cold crept along her arms, causing her to wring her hands. She closed her eyes and pictured the goddess.

"Oh, Lady of Light, help me see the way. Give me the courage to see this task done, no matter the outcome."

Brilliant white warmth invaded her heart, ran down her arms, legs, and lastly filled her mind. She was not alone. Dylan would be by her side. The heavens guided her, its light within her. She would not falter.

A flickering light cast her shadow on the stone's face just before she heard Dylan behind her. "Rhiannon, come. I would show you something."

She turned to see him carrying a lit torch. His dark hair held two thin braids at each temple with the rest falling loose about his strong shoulders. His eyes sparkled with an excitement that stirred her own. She had nothing to dread. "Where did you find the torch?"

"Further in. There is a stack of them."

He held his hand out, and she ran her fingers over his battle-callused hand and into his palm, while watching the firelight dance in his warm gaze. Closing his hand firmly around hers in a secure grip, he smiled.

He led her deeper underground. The path narrowed at one point with giant cones of rock jutting up from the floor and hanging down from the ceiling.

White liquid dripped from the tip of one large stalactite into a small pool. A crack in the ceiling let the sun's rays stream down and reflect on the pool. Small flower petals from above floated and spun like sparkling stars through the beam of light to land along the earthen floor.

The air carried a cool musty scent of rain, but also the gentle hint of sweet flowers. The constant splash of the water was restful in its rhythm.

"Mother's milk," Dylan stated.

"What?"

"The white fluid pouring from the nipple of that rock is called mother's milk."

"Oh." Heat rushed to her cheeks. He led her around to the back of the pool where the stone had been chipped away, forming a wide man-made trail.

"Others have been here?" she asked.

"Aye." His excitement was tangible.

The light from the torch flickered on the smooth walls, and she thought she saw something in the shadows ahead. She peered closer.

"Wait." She stopped, pulling her hand from his. "Come here and raise the torch," she said, helping him direct the light toward the wall, only to stop short. "Look." A large winged reptile with a horned head was carved into the stone. Its jaws were open in a snarl, and it blew fire at a herd of deer escaping into the forest. *Dragons*.

Their very name brought a cold stab to her heart. Chilled, she folded her arms tightly around her waist and curled her toes within her boots. Apprehension coursed through her blood.

"You spoke of beasts earlier." She inhaled a deep calming breath. "Tell me now, what beasts?" She waited for him to speak the words she feared most. She turned to meet his blue gaze. The firelight cast an unnatural flame deep within his beautiful eyes.

"'Twas dragons. The gate has been opened and they are free." His voice echoed like a death toll.

"Do you know what you speak of?" She gasped. This was the death and destruction Dela had said would come. It was part of the prophecy.

"Aye, lass. It has taken me awhile to admit it even to myself."

"I had a vision yesterday. I saw dark wings, fire, and blood. The screams were deafening." She shivered. "Now it comes together, and I understand."

"The Sorcerer's play with magic disturbed their peace today," Dylan said. "That's why the earth trembled."

"You are in tune with these beasts? You read their thoughts?" Silence sat heavy as she waited for his response only to have another realization hit her. "'Tis true then, about the power of the dragon's mark."

It was a statement of wonder. The breath left her body, and her heart pounded against her chest. "You are the Dragon Laird!"

There was a slight curve to his lips, and firelight shone brilliantly in his cobalt eyes, a magical fire. "I think 'twas what the old woman meant when she spoke to me at the first village fire. She said to use the power the gods gave me. 'Twould save lives, mine as well." He looked back toward the darkness. "Somehow, I am connected to the beasts. They call out and I hear. Come, a little further."

Rhiannon followed Dylan around a large bolder in the floor to a carved doorway. Over the mantel, Celtic words were etched in bold ancient script.

"Can you read it, Rhiannon? I do not know the old language." He held the torch closer for her to see then pulled a root away that hung over the stone.

Time had worn the words in some places, but most remained legible. With a worshipful touch, she ran her fingers over each letter. "Son of darkness, Daughter of light, One must choose the way 'tis right."

Dylan frowned. "A riddle? Mayhap there are others?"

Rhiannon grabbed his arm, pulling him around to face her. "I have been called the daughter of light. And Dela told me; I would meet a man surrounded by darkness to stand by my side. Dylan, you were born under the cursed moon. You are the son of darkness." Excitement warmed her as the full meaning hit. This was her destiny. And his.

Dylan rubbed the back of his neck. "Rhiannon, this was written years ago, well 'afore our time. It could mean anything."

She slid her hand across his check in a gentle caress. "Nay love. 'Twas written for the chosen. With all that has happened, can you not see these words were written for us? Dela once said we are two heads of the same coin. Light and darkness. That is why we will destroy evil. I see it now myself." She looked back at the ancient writing.

"You are my strength, and I am the wisdom. Standing together, the Sorcerer can not defeat us." She pointed at the words over the door, overcome with the enormity of it all. "That is the way that is right." With this understanding came a swell of courage.

Dylan stepped closer to cup her face with both hands and gently brush his lips over hers. "Aye, you have chosen the right path. There is no one I would rather be with than you. You fill the empty space in my dark existence."

She ran her fingers through his long black hair, only to have him take her hand and bring it to his lips. "Come, we are almost there."

As they stepped through the door, three different passageways faced them. The sound of water splashing and soft flickering light illuminated the opening of the passage to her right. The other two stood dark and forbidding.

"This way." Dylan put an arm around her waist and directed her to the right. "I found this as I explored earlier."

The small cavern had torches set in all four walls. The flames cast a warm golden glow, but the room itself was heated. Steam rose in soft clouds from a pool that took up most of the floor.

Carved steps descended into the clear pool. Water poured in a steady stream from a small opening in the back wall to cascade over smooth rocks before sliding into the pool. Three natural stone pillars stood as guardians along the water's edge.

Large twisted vines decorated the back wall and pillars, while another wall had clear crystal formations running through it. The torch's light touched them, spilling a rainbow of colors about the room, but Rhiannon's gaze was caught on the wall to her right. There was a picture of a red headed, green-eyed woman bathing in a pool heated by dragon's breath.

"She looks like you," Dylan whispered in awe. "I wanted you to see her."

Rhiannon turned from the drawing to look upon Dylan's strong face. He must have sensed her gaze because he turned toward her. He ran one long dark finger along her jaw then across her lips.

"'Twas like the first time I saw you bathing in the forbidden forest. There was something magical about your communion with the water making it a sensual act. I wanted to join you... Let me worship you…now…and here."

He threw the torch over toward a corner where it puffed out and took her in his arms. His gaze never left her as he pulled the strings loose on her kirtle then slid the sleeves off her shoulders. The garment floated to the floor.

Standing, dressed only in a thin chemise, she reached to untie the strings to his shirt and pulled the bottom from his kilt. She lifted the shirt over his head and let it fall to the ground, forgotten.

His chest was darkened from the sun to a golden brown. The battle scars showed up lighter, but did not detract from his sensuality.

She marveled at the ripples of muscles over his chest and stomach as she ran her fingers slowly over each one.

"I would worship you as well, my Laird." Her fingers slipped inside the belt on his kilt. "I would see more of you, touch more." She moved her hand down to boldly touch the hard evidence of his passion through the kilt.

He groaned, grabbing her hand, pressing it around himself. "Rhiannon," he whispered, his voice deep and rough, a plea.

She kissed him, parting her lips, encouraging him with the press of her tongue against his lips.

Dylan complied by invading her mouth with his tongue and running a hand down to her bottom, pulling her up against his hard staff. The other hand tunneled into the waves of her hair, giving her neck support as he kissed her more deeply.

Through the thin fabric of her chemise one of his long fingers slid down the crease of her bottom, pressing in. Rhiannon moaned. Heat roared through her limbs to land at the sensitive folds between her legs.

"I want you, Rhiannon," he whispered, already easing the top of her chemise down to bare her breasts. Her nipples were tight and throbbing, needing his care. Then he was there; his mouth, warm and wet, sucking deeply.

His lips moved up her neck to her ear. "I want to take you in the pool."

"Please," she begged, knowing she wanted him to fill her and make her complete.

The chemise had worked its way to her feet, and he removed his kilt. He lifted her into his arms and carried her down the steps and into the water. It came chest high and warm, slipping over their naked flesh like a lover's caress. Beside the waterfall, he let her body slide down along his until she stood next to him. "Turn around. Let me wash your hair."

Smiling, she did as he asked. She had never been so well cared for. Arching back, she let the warm water rush over her head and around her shoulders.

His long fingers rubbed her scalp and combed through silky, wet tresses. His touch sent shivers of warm honey through her body. Then his hands moved from her hair down her shoulders to circle a breast. His mouth followed to suckle the hardened nipple. She moaned aloud with erotic pleasure.

He picked her up again and sat her upon the edge of the pool, her legs still in the water. "Lean back on your arms." When she hesitated, his gaze became intense. "Trust me, Love." Keeping her eyes on him, she leaned back on her elbows. The river of water now ran along her back and around her hips.

Dylan took one of her long legs and bent it at the knee, then sat it on the ledge and did the same with the other. He ran his hands up to her knees and gently pushed them apart.

He felt her tense as he slid his hands down the inside of her thighs to the place he wanted most to be.

"Dylan," she sighed.

"You have made me a hungry man, Rhiannon." With his thumbs, he opened her and lowered his mouth to feast. His tongue twirling around then pushed deep, moving in and out, pushing deeper. Finding the sensitive nub, he suckled it, drinking of her sweetness, savoring the small moans and rock of her hips. He could feel the desire building as her muscles tightened. Her head thrashed back and forth until she cried out and shivered her release.

He ran his hand down one leg to her ankle, following closely with kisses, waiting for her to catch her breath.

Rhiannon was not having any of that. She sat up, grabbed his face in both hands and kissed him fiercely. She was wet and ready, desperate to feel him inside her.

Rhiannon clutched at his shoulders, feeling his muscles bunch as he pulled her off the ledge to straddle his waist. The water cloaked them in swirling warmth. His hardness probed at her entrance.

"Fill me," she pleaded, and he all too willingly complied. With his hands on her waist, he slid her down and sank deep within her. Her body convulsed with pleasure and tightened around his.

His hand moved to her bottom, lifting her then filling her again. His thrusts, hard and quick, sent spasms of fire roaring through her.

She felt the coil of heat building once more and tried to hold on to prolong the pleasure.

"Come with me love." Dylan groaned. The sweet invitation too great, she cried out, her nails digging into his flesh. Dylan stiffened and gave a long moan as he filled her with his warm seed.

He laid his forehead against hers to catch his breath. His gaze swung up to meet hers. A smile curved his lips with the knowledge of shared passion. Tightening his grip around her, Dylan moved to the steps. Climbing out, he lay down on the warm stone with her cuddled in his arms. He kissed her shoulder and neck as he pulled her closer. Then he rolled to his back, and she curled along his side.

"Are you alright?" he asked, his eyes closed.

"Oh, aye" she sighed, resting her head on his shoulder. His smile became lazily with contentment.

A sound woke Rhiannon where she lay next to Dylan. The torches had burned low, but everything else seemed to be the same. Still, the feeling of unease raised the hair on her arms.

Then a deep roar echoed through the cave's walls, followed by a thunk that shook the ground.

Terror squeezed her throat. "Dylan," she whispered, shaking him awake while watching the darkness beyond their only exit.

He opened one eye and smiled at her. "Are you never sated, fair one?" Dylan rolled over, pulling her beneath him. "'Tis good to see you will keep up with my hunger."

He kissed her, but her fist connecting with his arm made him raise his head to look at her. He saw fear sparkling from her wide emerald eyes and frowned. "What's wrong?"

"I want to leave here." Her voice trembled with anxiousness. "Now!"

"Have you seen something?"

"Nay, 'tis only the feeling of unease about the darkness beyond." She pushed at his chest and again looked toward the door.

He followed her gaze to the passageway but saw nothing. "But we have not explored the rest of the passages. I want to go deeper. See what other treasures we can find." There was something about this place. He felt a force compelling him to seek deeper, drawing him to discover the darkness.

She took his face in her hands and brought his gaze to hers. "Please, Dylan. Take me out of here. You can explore another time."

Seeing the fear in Rhiannon's eyes compelled his heart to follow her, rather than his own need. "Aye lass, let us dress and be on our way."

Rolling off her, he stood and she did the same. A silence fell between them as they dressed. His thoughts on the dragons. Their powerful magic called to him. Then, there was the Sorcerer. He must keep alert to anything that might harm, Rhiannon. If he lost her his world would fall apart.

He walked over to the torch he had thrown against the wall earlier and relit it from a burning sconce. He turned back to find Rhiannon waiting near the door. She had her head to one side, peeking around the door into the passage beyond. He wished she would tell him what she feared, but she had a good sense of things; he would do well to follow. Dylan glanced one more time at the steaming pool, picturing her open to him, and his body responded.

He took her hand, and she turned around to face him. "I would ask that we keep this pool to ourselves," he said. "I would come back here with you again."

At her nod, he raised his torch and led the way out. He wished he could keep her all to himself but knew that was a passing dream, for responsibilities hung heavily. As Laird, he must protect his clan, be it from feuding clans or dragons.

"Master, this is Enid." Teg shoved her toward the hooded figure seated on a dark horse. A black hound rested off to one side.

Enid tried peering through the shadows of the cloak's hood to see the Sorcerer's face but had no success. A dark, heavy material draped him from head to boot. She had no way of knowing if he was old or young, ugly or handsome. She did not care as long as he was a man, a powerful man.

"She has paid us to see to the death of The McGregor," Teg said.

Enid nodded, swinging her hips seductively as she moved to stand close to the Sorcerer. Finally being in his powerful presence brought currents of lust so strong her muscles contracted in ecstasy.

She wondered how forceful he would be in bed. Her confidence bolstered by lust, her seductive walk changed to a saunter. Once she satisfied him, she would hold the world in her hands. There would be no more need for Teg. He had served his purpose.

"Aye, I would see Dylan dead, and you, great Sorcerer, the ruler over all." She ran her hand up his thigh and under his cloak to the flesh of his male organ. She watched his fiery gaze build within the dark shadows of his hood as she stroked him, his staff swelled to hardness. A shiver of pleasure, so intense it was orgasmic, moved through her body. She stifled the moan. Quick as lightning, his long fingers closed around her throat, cutting off her air. She clawed at his hand and fingers. Fear and desperation ate at her innards as she tried to loosen his grip. As the need for air increased, black spots distorted her vision.

"Do not speak, whore." A deep raspy voice floated from the dark hood. Then she was freed and thrown several feet to land in the dirt at Teg's booted heels.

Enid sat in a crouched position, rubbing at her tortured throat, pulling in deep gulps of air. How dare he reject her! A flare of temper boiled just below her heart, and her hands became talons clawing in the dirt.

Teg stooped down beside her. "I would have Enid as my price. The one you offered me for service."

"You would take her over gold?" The Sorcerer sneered. "You are a fool. Take her. There is but one prize for me." The Sorcerer's voice gentled. "Rhiannon, the daughter of goddesses. Only she is worthy to hold my rod between her legs."

"That whore," Enid snapped, anger spilling forth, "has already ridden the McGregor's stump." She pushed Teg away and sat up. To have Rhiannon take again what she wanted was too much to bear.

"Enid, hold your tongue," Teg warned, glancing nervously at the Sorcerer.

"I will not. He should know she is secondhand goods."

"Slug of the earth." The Sorcerer hissed. "Speak once more and reap thy reward." The hound pulled back its lips to bare its teeth but gave no sound.

Teg grabbed her arm, but she shook him off, too angry to take heed. "You could have me. I would do anything to please you. That bitch knows nothing of man's pleasure, and she comes with the stench of the McGregor's seed on her mouth and belly."

A malevolent snarl came from the darkened hood. "You will forfeit your prize, Teg. She heeds not my warning. She is Bain's." So saying, he pointed a finger at her, and the large black hound crouched ready to spring, its lips pulled back, giving a low growl.

Enid tasted the acid of fear in her throat. "Nay, wait!"

"Take her." With the cold command, the hound leaped. Enid screamed and held up her hands in a futile effort to ward the animal off.

Sinking his teeth into her arm, the dog tore at her flesh,

shaking his head with the effort to rip. She cried out, and he released his grip. When he came at her again, he slashed at her side just below her armpit.

She hit at the hound with her fist connecting with its nose and head. Enid's breaths came in fast pants and small whimpers, but the dog was relentless and she was tiring.

She felt the teeth on her throat and knew the battle was lost. Darkness clouded her vision, and suddenly she did not feel the pain anymore. She was aware of nothing except sinking to the ground and odd involuntary jerks of her body. Then nothing.

"Bain." The hound let loose of the woman's throat. With a large tongue, he licked his nose and walked over to stand by the Sorcerer.

From beneath the robes, the Sorcerer brought forth a hunk of dried meat. The hound caught the treat in mid air and swallowed it whole. The hooded man swung down from his horse and walked over to stand above the body.

Teg knelt down picking up Enid's limp hand, still warm. "Do not waste emotion on her. She was using you." The Sorcerer's voice was flat.

"Aye, I know this, but she had such passion."

"So says a man who has not visited his wife for many months," The Sorcerer snapped. "I will not have disobedience. Step back, I would have what life force she possessed." Teg did as asked.

The Sorcerer knelt down by Enid and ran his fingers through the blood still seeping from her neck. He wiped his bloody fingers over her still lips then kissed her, running his tongue over her mouth and sucking at its fullness. Taking the blood into his mouth, he savored it. It was not Rhiannon's, but all life had power.

Teg turned away not caring to watch the Sorcerer's strange rituals. Instead, he spotted armed men coming from the trees. "Master, we have visitors." It was the mercenaries he had paid for with the money Enid had given him.

The Sorcerer was right, he had a wife to support, and should stop thinking with the flesh between his legs. After the Sorcerer got what he wanted from Rhiannon, Teg could go home with gold in his pockets.

"They are on the move." The Sorcerer stated, standing up and staring off into the trees to the south. There was no need to ask whom he spoke of. "I may not be able to touch them with magic while in their cursed circle of protection, but they can not stop arrows or blades from the mercenaries. I will have Rhiannon this night, and the Dragon Laird will die."

Chapter Thirteen

Something was not right. Dylan feared alarming Rhiannon, but his hunter's instinct put him on alert. It could have been the silence of the birds, or a snapped twig, even a shift in the breeze.

He scanned the trees and bush but saw nothing, yet the sense of danger became too strong to ignore. "Rhiannon, we are being followed. Stay close and do what I tell you."

At her nod, Dylan pointed to their right. "Run."

Rhiannon pulled up her skirts and took off like a doe in flight, darting through the trees. He followed close behind, guarding her back. His footfalls were much heavier than hers, but his long legs helped him keep pace. The unmistakable sound of metal on metal warned Dylan these were not ordinary men giving chase. "'Tis mercenaries."

"What?" Rhiannon asked, jumping a fallen tree trunk.

"Men who kill for coin."

"By the gods, the devil could not get to us with sorcerery, so he uses men."

"Over there. That rock formation will give us some protection." Dylan pulled the Singing Sword from its sheath, gripping it in his right hand. They raced through shafts of golden sunlight that poured through the leaves. The trees thinned here, so they would make an easier target.

Th-wack! An arrow struck a tree just over Dylan's

shoulder. Rhiannon ducked and cried, "Dylan!" A wave of apprehension coursed through her.

"I know. That was too close. Do not stop until you get to those rocks. We have to make a stand there."

More arrows sang by, mercifully landing harmlessly in the leaf-covered earth. "Rhiannon, do not run straight. Weave back and forth. You make a harder target. Faster love. I hear more men off to our left."

"This is taking too long." She frowned

"It keeps an arrow from finding your back," he countered.

They reach the rocks. Then glance back to see shadows of men among the trees.

Rhiannon scrabbled for a handhold on a rock as she stepped on another, slowly working her way up. Dylan followed closely.

"Go to that shelf on your left. We can hold up behind these boulders."

"I see it," she answered.

Before she could reach the cover of the large rocks, a rain of arrows fell on them. She gasped as a sharp pain pierced her shoulder, and her vision blurred. She heard Dylan curse. Looking at her arm, she spotted an arrowhead protruding two inches out of her shoulder. Using her one good hand, she sat down behind a jutting of boulders, laying her forehead against the stone at shoulder height. Dizziness assailed her from the smell of her own blood.

"Rhiannon?"

She must have blacked out for a moment. When she opened her eyes, Dylan sat in front of her. Concern marked the edges of his mouth, and he reached out to smooth the hair from her forehead. "'Tis not bad, Dylan. Do not worry." She did not want his attention on her when it needed to be on their pursuers. "How many men?"

"I counted nine." He answered, looking around the edge of their protection. "They will reach us shortly. I think I can take them one at a time from here."

"And if you can not?" He turned to face her, and she read the answer in his eyes. *We will die.*

The spark of determination sharpened his gaze, and his answer came firm and final. "I will hold them." His gaze moved to her shoulder. She moved a little, groaning as the arrow scraped against the rock.

Without a word of warning, Dylan grasped the end of the arrow and broke the tip off. She gasped and dug her fingers into the muscles of his leg. Nausea hit her in waves and she feared she would empty her stomach.

Leaning into him, she took in great gulps of air and rested her head on his shoulder. She felt his movement toward her back and realized he meant to pull the arrow free. She clenched her teeth as he pulled the arrow's shaft from her shoulder in one smooth jerk.

The scream erupted from deep within. As the sharpness of the pain eased, she felt the warmth of fresh blood run down her back. With care, Dylan leaned her back against the boulder.

"Forgive me, love. To be quick and have it done is the best way."

She nodded and watched him through a glaze of pain. He lifted her skirt and ripped a long piece of cloth from her chemise. Folding the material, he pressed it to the seeping wound.

He took her good hand and moved it to the bandage. "Hold this tightly." Their gazes met, sharing an intense longing to survive, and an understanding of what they faced.

"We will see this through." He gave her a quick kiss of reassurance then stepped away.

Tears filled her eyes, and she gulped hard. This would not be the end. "Your power will save us, Dylan."

"The only power I have is hearing the beasts and the strength of my sword arm."

"If you can hear them, might they hear you as well?"

A clattering of rocks drew his attention below. The sorcerer's mercenaries started the climb up. Their faces seemed twisted with unnatural strain. Their eyes black empty holes.

She took his hand, pulling him close once more and placed his palm over her heart, and placed her hand over his. "Call to them. You can do this," she encouraged. Closing her eyes, she reached down within her soul searching for and willing him the power of her heart. If they were to live through this trial, she needed to give him all the help she dare, without give up her life.

Dylan narrowed his eyes as he gazed on Rhiannon pained pale features. The answer came easily. He would do anything to protect her. He took a deep breath.

Loud and clear, he raised his voice to the heavens. "Hear me, ancient ones. I call on the dragons to protect the chosen one. Hear the plea of the Dragon Laird and give us aid."

Dylan waited an eternal moment for the dragons to come. But disappointment filled his belly as the first mercenary hauled himself over the edge of the shelf. With a growl, he attacked the enemy.

The sword's bluish glow pulsed to life, and the whining song cut the air. The blade sliced through muscle and bone, taking the man's head from his shoulders.

Dylan kicked the corpse over the side. It bounced off a jutting rock and knocked off one of the men below.

Legs apart, Dylan balanced on the balls of his feet, waiting for the next man. When the rock suddenly shifted, the force almost brought him to his knees.

"What was that?" Rhiannon pulled away from the rock she'd been resting on.

Dylan could neither think nor answer as another man climbed up to face him. One more was close behind.

Rhiannon's scream from behind made him turn to her in time to see a large red eye appear in the boulder she had been sitting against. Then the rock transformed into a large scaled head with its mouth open and sharp teeth bared.

With the speed of a striking adder, it breezed by Dylan to attack the mercenary. In one chomp, the man was cut in two. Blood splattered Dylan's face and shirt. "By the gods!" Dylan cried.

The dragon raised its head to the sky and chewed twice before swallowing. Then the rest of the dragon's illusion disappeared. Smooth gray stone turned to scaled, umber skin. Its large body and tail curled around the rocks.

The top half of the formation hadn't been rock at all, but the dragon. The huge beast's body and tail now surrounded them. Even lying down, the dragon was taller then Dylan. Large vertical scales rode down the center of its neck, over its back to end at its tail.

Dylan jerked Rhiannon up beside him, the sword held out to face the beast, but they were ignored as its long neck lowered reaching down over the side to face the Sorcerer's men.

Screams of the dying filled the air as the dragon fed. Dylan hoped he gorged himself so he would not still be hungry when he remembered them.

Blood covered his shirt. He knew that was all it would

take for some animals to attack, so he ripped the fabric down the front and tossed it over the side, leaving him bare-chested.

He could feel Rhiannon's fear and thought of killing the beast while it fed. Its neck was stretched over the edge and it would be easy to use the Singing Sword to make a fatal wound, but he couldn't do it. He had called the beast up, hadn't he? It would be dishonorable. Even if it meant his life, he would face the dragon only if the beast attacked them. Mayhap if they held still they would be overlooked.

Dylan leaned close and whispered in Rhiannon's ear. "Do not move."

Rhiannon couldn't move. The dragon fear held her immobile. She had heard stories of the creature's powers but thought them to be mere legends. As the tale went, when a dragon attacked, it secreted some scent that paralyzed its victims with fear. She wondered if that was happening to her.

Again, the dragon snatched a man into his mouth, swinging the victim up to chomp and swallow. When the last man fell to the dragon, all was quiet. The large beast stood upright and rocks clattered and shifted under its weight. The foot-long curved claws scraped the stone.

With a speed unbelievable for a beast so large, it swung its diamond shaped head toward them. Dylan shoved Rhiannon behind him and swung his sword up ready to defend his lady.

The dragon blew air from its nose in a grunt, then a forked tongue came out to wave up and down. Dylan could have taken the nose and tongue from the beast but held his ground, waiting to see what move the dragon would take next. Their gazes met. The vertical black pupils in the dragon's red eyes dilated. Then it turned away.

Sauntering over to the edge of the cliff, it raised its head, fanned out large smooth skinned wings, and stepped off the ledge. With a mighty flap, it lifted its massive bulk into the air. The blast of air knocked Dylan and Rhiannon to the rock shelf, causing them to roll dangerously close to the edge.

Dylan grabbed Rhiannon, holding her close then jerked his head around, frowning as he watched the dragon. "What is it?" Rhiannon asked.

"He spoke."

"I heard naught."

"He said, he who wears my mark, I save this day."

Then Rhiannon did something she had never done before. She fainted.

Dylan knew he had to find help for Rhiannon. The only way down was to climb. Now that the dragon was gone, the top of the rock was flat. The dragon must have come here to sun himself, while a few trees stood near to shade his sensitive eyes from the brightest rays.

Walking to the opposite side of the ledge, he found the way down not so steep. That would make it easier to carry her. He wiped the blood from his blade with his kilt then sheathed the sword and went back to Rhiannon.

He stooped down, checking her wound. It still seeped and that worried him. He needed to burn the wound shut but had no way to build a fire. All their supplies were still with their mount, wherever he was.

He ran a finger along her pale cheek. Certainly, the gods would not take her from him now. She lay so still. Picking her up, he gently positioned her over his shoulder. He would hold her legs to his chest with one hand and use the other for climbing.

The way down was not as bad, but it took longer than he planned. His leg muscles threatened to give out, and his head wound throbbed under the bandage, but fear for Rhiannon drove him on. Once on the ground, he worked his way east through the forest. An hour passed before a hint of wood smoke teased his senses: a camp.

With the fire, he could stop Rhiannon's bleeding. The breeze blew from the east so he continued in that direction. When the smell of smoke became stronger, he laid Rhiannon down on a bed of green moss under an oak. He would not take her into a possibly hazardous situation. Pulling his sword free, he went to spy on the camp. There were too many foes about to walk into a strange encampment.

Before he got within a few yards, men dropped from the trees to surround him. They wore green tunics, and their eyes matched the deeper green of the forest.

He counted seven, all holding swords pointed at him. Trapped, he took a glance in Rhiannon's direction. Fear for her made him determined to fight.

He swung his sword around overhead, hearing its familiar song gave him strength. He narrowed his eyes with lethal purpose. He would kill as many as he could before he died. With one hand, he waved them closer. His muscles bunched and his heart sped up as energy shot through his body.

"You want me? Come get a piece then," Dylan yelled. "I shall take the first man's head." His gazed went from one man to the next, waiting for a move.

One short man stepped forward, and Dylan gaze swung to him.

"You are the Dragon Laird."

The bold statement made Dylan nod. "Aye."

The forest men lowered and sheathed their blades, and a smile of one fashion or another curved every lip.

"'Tis the Singing Sword that gave you away. Come, you are welcome."

Unable to give in so quickly, Dylan used caution before lowering his blade. "Who leads you?"

"Gian of *Tylwyth teg.*"

Relief washed over him. He would find help here. "My lady, Rhiannon, is wounded." Without waiting for others to follow, Dylan hurried back to where he had left Rhiannon.

She was pale, but when he bent and picked her up, her eyes blinked then opened fully. The smile she gave him as she rested her head on his shoulder lightened his heart.

"We have found a camp, and I will see to your wound." Her only answer was a sigh, before she closed her eyes again.

The camp sat in the heart of a secluded grove of rowans and oaks. Iron lanterns hung from low branches. Faeries in flight, stars, and dragons were cut out of the iron to let the candlelight illuminate the night.

One large cooking fire burned in the center of the camp. Lean-tos made of tree limbs were scattered through the trees. Men and women sat about in small groups, talking, working on arrows, or weaving mats.

To the north and west, a thicket of berry brambles provided protection, as well as sweet smelling white flowers. To the east stood densely wooded trees, their large roots twisting above the ground like a nest of serpents.

It was twilight when he entered camp and supper preparations were underway. The men who had held him at sword point melted back into the trees.

Dylan searched for Gian and found him seated by the fire. Gian spotted him at the same moment and stood, making his way over to them. "Can you give us a place for the night?" Dylan asked.

He hoped for help, but he did not expect the anger clouding Gian's face. "What have you done to her?"

"You shall not want for a story. First, put a blade to the fire. I would close her wound."

Gian waved a hand at someone sitting by the fire. The man took his dagger and ran it into the red-hot coals.

"Bring her here." Gian indicated a woven mat made of marsh reeds. "Call Meg. We have need of her." He directed a small woman stirring what smelled like stew, near the fire.

Dylan knelt beside the mat and laid Rhiannon down. She stirred and opened her eyes, seeking him out, blinked twice and faded back to unconsciousness. Her head turned toward him, as if seeking his presence.

He pushed aside fiery curls from near her mouth. Taking a dagger from his leather boot, he cut away the fabric over her wound, leaving the shoulder bare.

He hated the thought of what he must do but saw no other way. "Bring me the heated knife." Dylan ordered. The dagger was pulled from the coals and passed to him. The tip burned bight red.

"What do you?" A woman's biting voice cut across the camp to halt Dylan's actions.

He frowned. "I am saving her life."

"Nay, you are doing more harm."

"You know a better way? Tell me!"

"Good, a man with brains. 'Twas wise of Rhiannon to choose you." The woman stepped from the shadows of the trees into the firelight. She was a woman in her late forties with hair the color of Rhiannon's, yet her eyes were a soft brown.

"Have we met 'afore? Your voice sounds familiar." Dylan asked as she came over to kneel by Rhiannon.

"Aye, but 'twas not of this form. I was Dela when last we met."

Dylan watched her poke at the wound then nod at her findings. "You are a changeling?" Dylan narrowed his eyes frowning as he raised Rhiannon's head up into his lap.

"Nay, 'tis but an illusion for protection against the Sorcerer." She answered, bringing forth a needle with a thin silvery thread.

"Now watch and learn," she said, bending over, Rhiannon.

Dylan frowned as she pieced Rhiannon's skin with the needle and pulled the threads together, closing the wound by tying a knot. She did the same thing again.

"I knit the wound closed so only a small scar will show. There will be no burns to add to the injured flesh. I will put herbs over the skin to draw out any poisons. Have no worry, Dylan. Your lady will wake soon and all will be right."

He just nodded and held Rhiannon in his arms as Meg tended to the wound at her back.

"Now that Meg has seen to my daughter, tell me how this happened?" Gian demanded. Anger still sparkled in those green eyes, challenging Dylan.

"Rhiannon is your daughter?"

"Aye."

"This explains much." Like the possessiveness Gian showed at their first meeting. He had thought it was man to woman, not father to daughter. Then he remembered Rhiannon's reaction to Gian. "Rhiannon does not know you are her father, does she?"

He caught the quick glance the older man exchanged with Meg before his answer came. "She knows me by name but not by face. Now I have answered your questions, you must answer mine."

Dylan nodded. "'Twas mercenaries. The Sorcerer could not enter the circle, so he paid assassins to see the deed done.

There were nine in all."

"Then you are indeed blessed if you took down nine trained killers."

"I took two." Dylan met Meg's gaze, and she gasped, causing Gian to glance her way.

"You have found your powers." She spoke the statement in awe.

Dylan shrugged, unsure how to answer.

"He awoke a dragon, Gian," she said.

"'Twas he who saved us," Dylan clarified. "Taking the other men with a snap of his jaw."

"Yet left you both unharmed?" Gian's brow lifted in wonder.

"Aye."

Meg smiled, looking at Gian. "I told you he was the chosen, from the beginning. Sometimes not even the high and mighty king of *Tylwyth teg* can be sure of what will happen."

One side of Gian's lips curved up. "You are a challenge, my Love."

"And you are hard headed."

She reached out her hand, palm open, to Gian. "Hand me the faery nectar. I would share some with our daughter."

Dylan watched Gian hand Meg a small vial of liquid. "What is that?"

"A special blend of rowan tree root, wild carrot and five herbs from the faery realm. 'Twill bring her healing about more quickly." She put the vial to Rhiannon's lips. The brown liquid poured in drip by drip.

"My Laird, here is something to give you strength." Dylan glanced to his right to see the young woman who had been stirring something in the big caldron. She handed him a wooden bowl full of stew and a spoon.

He carefully laid Rhiannon back on the mat, then took the bowl and gave the woman a smile. "My thanks."

She returned the friendly gesture, glancing at Meg before turning back to feed the others. As he ate the stew, he watched Rhiannon. Gian and Meg conversed in low whispers, but Dylan concentrated on every breath his woman took; every beat at her throat and every flutter of her concealed eyes.

Weariness ran through his veins, but he was too worried about Rhiannon to take rest. The stew was warm and filling. He was about to take the last spoonful when his vision blurred. He frowned and shook his head to clear it. He lost his hold on the bowl and darkness claimed all thoughts.

Meg watched him topple over to land near Rhiannon.

"How much did you give him?" Gian barked.

"He is not hurt. He was more than weary 'tis all. Move him closer to Rhiannon, and straighten out his legs so he is comfortable," Meg instructed.

"The man is not going to thank you for this mischief."

"He needs rest to build strength for the coming battle, and he would not have taken it with Rhiannon wounded. This way I can see to his head wound and he will not know a thing."

She knelt down and pulled the bandage off, then used her fingers to check his skull. His head was not cracked, so she put an herb pack on the cut before letting the pair sleep.

"You know the Sorcerer will retaliate. He has been defeated too often of late not to be irate and very dangerous," Meg offered.

"So you think he will use the dragons in some way to see to his end?"

"Aye!"

Gian grunted.

* * *

Dylan was the first to stir. The sun burned overhead, telling him the day only half remained. He was surprised he had slept all night and through part of a day. Leaning up, he ran a hand along Rhiannon's jaw. The rosy color of health stood out on her cheeks. The night's rest had done her well.

Her eyelashes fluttered and those bright green eyes opened. They were clear and without pain. She smiled and his heart turned to mush.

"How do you feel?" he asked. Worry still nagged at him. He knew that if something should happen to her, he would follow in death. There would be no living without her. Their hearts beat as one, now and forever.

"Well. Thank you."

"'Twas Meg's doing, with help from your father's faery potion no doubt."

"My father is here?" She sat up slowly, wincing a bit, then glanced about the camp.

Dylan reluctantly sat up. He held his head as a pain shot through it, but it left just as quickly. "Aye, you will know him when you see him," he grumbled.

"You make it sound as if I will not be pleased."

"Do you remember the night of the choosing?"

"Aye."

"Well, he..." Just then, he noticed Gian had been made aware they were awake and headed toward them. Dylan groaned. "Your father comes," he said, pointing in Gian's direction.

Rhiannon turned to see the man who had attacked them in the forest. His golden hair hung long, with a silver streak on one side. Many small braids hung woven with mint leaves in the silver strands of hair. His eyes were bright green like hers.

He stooped down beside her, intently looking her over as

she had done to him. "How do you feel, Lass?"

"Overwhelmed."

"*Och!*" He looked down. "So the lad told you?"

"Aye, he did. Why did you not speak who you were in the forest?"

"So you have not been told the whole of it." He glanced at her and took a deep breath. "I was not in favor of Meg's plan to let this McGregor have you. Nevertheless, it seems to have turned out. Nor was I in favor of her other plan."

"Other plan?"

"Aye, when you where smaller she fostered you off on the McKays. I would have kept you with us in *Tylwyth teg*. You look surprised."

"I am. So why then?"

"You stayed with us until the age of four. Then it became known to her that you would choose a human to mate and fulfill an ancient prophecy. Meg felt you needed to grow up with humans to be happy with the life you were destined for." His eyes narrowed as he glanced at Dylan, yet directed the question to Rhiannon. "Are you happy, lass?"

She ran her hand down his tanned cheek, drawing his gaze back to her. "Aye, most assuredly." Rhiannon bowed her head into his lap. "Thank you for your sacrifice."

Gian ran long tan fingers in a loving caress over her bowed head. "You are my greatest treasure."

A commotion broke out beyond the trees. Yells and curses rode the afternoon wind into the camp, halting the reunion. Gian and Dylan both stood and drew their swords.

Meg joined them. She helped Rhiannon to stand and curved an arm around her waist. All waited until four guards stepped through the trees, dragging a large, struggling man. The cursing pouring from the man's lips made Dylan break out

The Dragon Laird

in laughter. Then Rhiannon giggled.

Gian turned on them. "You find this amusing?"

"Aye. 'Tis my brother, Owain, you hold. And not for long if he has his way."

Gian grinned. "Let him go," he said. The guards turned him loose then ducked out of the way when the large man came up swinging his fist.

"Owain! What brings you here to these woods?"

He turned at the sound of his name, "Dylan?" He hurried over to stand before him. "Thank the gods I have found you."

The smile dropped from Dylan's lips as he saw the concern in his brother's eyes. "Tell me your news."

"Dragons are attacking our village and laying waste to everything."

Chapter Fourteen

Dark clouds moved in from the west, but the distant rumble of thunder could not drown out the screams of the tortured or the roars of the beasts.

The Dragon Laird and his small band had just reached the forest's edge. They stood in horror as two large, black dragons circled the village overhead. Rivers of fire spilled through gaping mouths, consuming man and beast. The earth lay burned; black, smoldering stripes criss-crossing the once green ground. The smell of scorched remains filled the air and Dylan felt a stab of grief deep in his soul.

The dragons roared, baring their talons to lash at each other before parting and blowing fire at someone fleeing toward the woods.

Rhiannon broke the silence, her voice high and strained. "What should we do? We can not let this go on."

Then all but Dylan started speaking at once, throwing out one idea after another. Dylan moved away from everyone and inhaled deeply, then closed his eyes. He reached out with his mind to touch the beasts.

Dylan stiffened as the darkness of their souls filled him. These young rogues were different from the red dragon. Their souls were not yet developed, and he would not be able to speak with them. The Sorcerer had control of their untried minds.

Rhiannon's warm touch upon his arm broke the link. He shivered, but had the information they needed. "Tell us love, what have you found?" Rhiannon asked, running her hand along his neck.

Opening his eyes, Dylan spotted four pairs of eyes seeking his. "The Sorcerer has control of these rogues, and we can not defeat them. But there might still be a way."

"Speak then," Gian demanded.

"The red dragon that saved us yesterday was twice their size and had a fully developed mind, holding to the light of honor. If—"

"I see where you are heading," Gian interrupted. "Aye, use your power, and call upon the beast 'afore all the villagers are dead."

"What power? What is this leaf-man spouting?" Owain broke in, glaring at Gian.

"Later all will be explained," Dylan said. "Now, I ask you all to close your eyes and ask the gods for help. No sound must you make so I might use all my concentration to seek aid."

Rhiannon took the Moonstone from around her neck and slipped it around Dylan's. "May the stone give you protection as your power is tested today."

He wrapped her tightly in his embrace and kissed her with all his pent up fears and hopes. She gave him all her courage, strength, and love. "This day is yours to win. Believe in yourself, my Love, as I believe in you," she whispered.

He walked into the open. His hair swinging in the breeze. He reached up and pushed it back from his face, then pulled his Singing Sword from its sheath and held the handle tight. The blade pointed heavenward and out before him like a shield.

He dropped to his knees, and with eyes closed, called to the red dragon, hoping for an ally. The only concern about his plan was if the rogues came for him instead.

"Come faithful one. I have need of you. Help me save innocent blood." He repeated his request three times before he heard the wheezing growl of a dragon and opened his eyes. Both rogues had turned, heading straight for him.

In a flash of time, he knew if he stayed where he knelt, it would put Rhiannon and the others in danger. Without thought to himself, Dylan jumped up and ran forward to meet the dragons.

He heard a desperate scream come from Rhiannon as she realized what he was doing, but he did not stop. The words he had been saying in his mind now came aloud and clear, giving him courage.

Just as both blacks moved upon him, their jaws opened to burn the flesh off his bones, a powerful wind pushed him to the ground. He rolled over and crouched, his sword back to attack.

Piercing screeches deafened him. Another strong blast of air nearly brought him to his knees. It was then he realized the red dragon's descent and attack brought forth the gusts.

Above, a mighty battle of teeth, wings, and claws ensued. Flashes of crimson scales and black blocked out the clouded sky. Lightning flashed to their right as the storm grew in power.

Dylan knew the red was twice their size, but it was two against one. Stumbling, and then taking off at a run, he rushed toward a small group of villagers cowering by one of the few remaining huts.

"Give me your long bow and arrows," he urged the Highlander, turning back in time to see one of the blacks bite into the red's leg. "Quick, man!"

He took the bow and arrows and moved closer, lying his sword down. He notched an arrow and fitted it into the long bow. His aim must be true or he would hit their ally.

Pulling back on the string, he sighted down the arrow, waiting for a clear shot of a black belly. The strain to hold the bow taut made his muscles burn, but he would not let the arrow fly.

The red gave him the opening, by retreating to find a better attack position. When he did, the blacks turned toward Dylan, their bellies exposed. He let the arrow find its mark. Even before he saw it hit and heard the scream of pain, Dylan had another arrow ready. It hit the identical area on the same black.

The great beast screamed again, trying to reach the arrows with its mighty claws. It belched fire then there was a blast of wind as the dragon exploded in mid air. Sinew and bone hit the earth with a resounding slap and thud. Forks of lightning sliced overhead followed closely by a crack of thunder.

A mighty cheer rose from behind Dylan, but his eyes stayed on the fighting dragons still aloft. The remaining black, now out-matched, continued to retreat, but the larger red advanced his attack until the final snap of the black's neck ended the test of strength.

As the battered red dragon landed some fifty feet away, Dylan caught sight of an archer taking aim on the red dragon.

Adding an arrow to the bow, he turned to the foolish man. "Hold, or forfeit your life!" Dylan yelled. The red was all that stood between them and other dragons, if there were more to come.

The man lowered the bow. "I can take him."

"The red has won this day for us and saved your lives. Would you reward him with an arrow through the heart?" Watching the man turn and leave, Dylan threw down the bow and took up his sword. He walked up to the beast and knelt before him with a bowed head.

The red sat licking the bite wound on one leg but turned to face Dylan. Its large nostrils expanded and contracted. Then a warbling sounded in its throat.

"Again you came," Dylan stated with wonder.

"Again you called." The answer came.

"What must I do to set things right?" he asked, raising his head to face the dragon.

The beast's vertical pupils dilated then focused on him. Its long forked tongue waved above Dylan's head, but he didn't move anything else.

"When it's time for spring, winter must open the door and give way. For each season has its time. However, if winter's doors open too soon, all life as you know it will end. Within lies the key."

The beast turned his large, diamond-shaped head toward the forest then up to the dark clouds. A rumbling sound came from deep within his scaled body. Rain started pouring as he opened his giant wings and leaped into the air.

Dylan covered his eyes with his arm as dirt and ash swirled about him in the beast's wake. Then the dragon was gone.

Dylan stood up on shaky legs. He used the sword's handle for support, the tip planted firmly in the earth. Rain soon plastered his hair to his face and neck and soaked his clothes. He tried to make sense of what the dragon had told him. His name bounced off the wind, making him look up to see Rhiannon with her skirts lifted to her knees, running toward him. Owain, too, exited the woods, then Gian and Meg.

Rhiannon's heart raced. Fear had eaten at her while Gian held her back, forbidding her to follow Dylan.

Now free, her one goal was to reach him. He staggered,

then leaned heavily on his sword.

She grasped him, circling his chest with both arms to give support and to reassure herself of his health. "Are you wounded?"

"Nay, love, just weary. It seems communing with the beast takes much of my strength. I would now go home."

"Go, brother," Owain placed a warm hand on, Dylan's shoulder. "I will see to things here."

Dylan nodded his agreement, wanting nothing more than to find a bed.

Rhiannon noticed the pinch of worry on Owain's brow, and knew she had not been alone in her fear for Dylan.

"Thank you, Owain," she said.

He looked away as if uncomfortable with her thanks. "See him well tended," he added before walking over to a crowd of villagers to yell instructions. Gian had moved over to the dead dragons while Meg followed him slowly.

The trek home was not far but the heavy rain made the way slick with mud. The power of heaven seemed to have opened its gate to flood them. The winds bent the trees and battered Dylan and Rhiannon without mercy. The lights of the castle burned bright in the darkness and were a welcoming sight. Once the hounds and servants had greeted them, a hot bath was sent to his room, and he wasted no time in accepting its warm embrace.

"I think the chill has finely eased from my body," Dylan said, holding Rhiannon close to his chest as the hot water cuddled them both. Her head rested on his shoulder, while her hair fell in a red river to pool on the planked floor. The steam from the bath surrounded their heads and brought life back to his weary bones.

He was too tired to make love, but he still wished to touch

her. He ran one hand over her healing shoulder and down her arm then around one bared breast.

"I would share what was given me to know," he stated, breaking the silence.

Rhiannon opened her eyes, waiting for his words. She knew something was troubling him.

"I was given the key to see things righted, but I have yet to ken the meaning," Dylan explained, resting his chin on her head.

"The Red One gave you this knowledge?" she asked, wonder lacing her words.

"Aye."

"Speak it then."

"He said, 'When its time for spring, winter must open the door and give way, for each season has its time. However, if winter's doors opened too soon, all life as you know it will end. Within lies the key.' If it has to do with the change in season, we will fail. I am no god to change time."

"Nay, I do not think that is what he meant. He speaks in riddles. I believe 'tis the last sentence that tells us where to look," Rhiannon offered. "The key word is door, so mayhap he is speaking of a doorway."

"Aye, you hit it, lass. The door to the dragon's lair." Dylan slapped the edge of the tub in his excitement.

"The Sorcerer must have forced the door open too soon," Rhiannon continued. "That is what the red dragon meant by each season having its time."

"So the answer is to close the door or gateway," Dylan ventured.

"Aye."

"Then where is this gateway?" Dylan asked, narrowing his brow, then his eyes opened wide, and a smile touched his lips.

"The answer has come to you, I see." Rhiannon watched the expressions cross his face. What a wonder he was. She ran her hand over his damp chest. She never knew the bonds of love could grow this deep. It was as if she inhaled and he exhaled. How greatly blessed she felt.

"Aye, my love," Dylan answered, running his fingers along the hollow of her throat. "We leave in the morning to see this finished. I would have this done, so I may spend the rest of my life with you alone."

She knew her smile was weak. Worry about tomorrow's plight took over every thought. "Where do we head?"

Dylan pulled her close to his chest, then stood with her in his arms. He stepped from the bath with a splash, heading for the bed. "The caves."

Rhiannon sat before the window, her gaze watching Dylan's chest raise and fall in easy cadence as he slept, then slid her gaze intimately over his muscled frame.

She rolled the Moonstone pendent between her fingers. He had seen fit to return it after their bath. The glow of the full moon that peeked in and out from behind the residing rain clouds hit the gem, casting sparks of light that danced around the darkened room.

Morning would soon be upon them, yet she could not sleep. What she wanted most was Dylan's arms around her, but she would not be selfish enough to take away the rest he needed.

Destiny would not be denied. They both had been forced into this position. They would set out this morning. Prophecy and fate would be sealed today.

Having stepped through the druid's passage once before and read the ancient words, her mind cleared to find understanding. Dylan was the gatekeeper. He would find and close the dragon's passage, but she was the key. She would lock the gate until another came to protect the gates from evil.

An impression of the dark cloaked Sorcerer invaded her mind and a shiver passed along her skin. Some whispered he was skin pulled over bone. His burning eyes were black and sunken in his skull. They said he wore the devil's pockmarks on his face and hell had burned the hair from his head, but it was all tales. She had no wish to know what he looked like.

A warm unnatural breeze swirled up from the floor stealing her breath away. Fear, like a raging storm, crushed her chest when a vision appeared before her. A swirl of images crowded out the present and filled her view with things to come. Darkness, then the roar of a thousand winds echoed through a rocky tomb. Then suddenly, the floor of the tomb opened into a gaping hole. Clouds of dust and mist twirled and disappeared into the vortex. Cracks of lightning formed jagged arcs within the mighty hole.

Rhiannon watched what the vision meant to show her. A man with dark hair and the red tartan of the McGregors lost his balance, tipping toward the spinning vortex. A death scream twisted his handsome face as he fell into the abyss.

Panic seized her breath, causing her heart to stop beating for a breath of time. His hand reached out for her, his lips forming her name.

Her scream merged with the thundering winds as Dylan was taken into the bowels of hell. Rhiannon screamed again and felt warm arms take her from behind. The vision dissipated, and she found herself clinging to Dylan. They sat holding each other on the bedroom floor.

"What is this, love?" Dylan asked, stroking her back. "You are safe. Was it a bad dream?"

Yes, she told herself, squeezing her eyes tightly shut. "Only a dream."

Her tears poured unheeded to his chest. She could not tell him she had seen his death, nor would she believe it herself. He would not be lost to her.

Dylan ran his fingers through her hair, the gentleness so welcome.

"Tell me, what has troubled you?" he asked.

She slid her fingers over his cheek and along his chin. "I fear to lose you," she whispered against the heartbeat in his throat. The cold dark of terror stood at hand, waiting to devour.

Her whole being seemed to fill with a driving urgency to hold him close and keep fate at bay. She stared, longing to memorize every scar, every line, and every facet of his features.

His gaze roved boldly over her, then came to rest again on her face. His mouth softened. Love, pain, and unquenchable warmth sparkled from his blue eyes.

His manner soothed the dizzying current of panic within, so she could bring it under control and breath easier.

"No matter the outcome of this fight," he whispered. "I would have you know my heart is yours for all time. Even if my body dies and is taken from this world, my spirit will not leave your side. We share one heart, and no force of this realm or the next can divide us. Do you not see this?" His husky voice broke with emotion.

At the small sound, her heart twisted in pain. He also fought the uncertainty of their fate.

Rhiannon knew their love was the rare kind spoken of in the stars, a kind that never died for songs were sung about it.

"Aye."

"We can not stop now, Rhiannon. Think of all the people who count on us. Many lost loved ones last eve. We have the key to stop the suffering. Would I be much of a man if I put my wishes first? And could you love me as you do if I did?"

Her heart sank. "'Tis well I love you, McGregor. You have been my true husband in heart from the time you came for me at the pool. Your hands lay upon my breasts, filling my heart, and your lips drank from my soul."

He groaned, taking her mouth in a soft blending of lips. She wanted this moment, needing him.

The light of dawn peeked through the window, and a knock sounded upon the door. Dylan leaned away with a sigh. He ran a hand down her cheek. "We will finish this task today, so the rest of our years will be peaceful."

He stood and moved to the entrance. She watched him open the door and speak to someone outside. He was a man who had won many battles and was gifted with great skill in blade and bow.

Mayhap it was no vision, only a dream, but she knew deep inside it was foretelling of things to come. She would keep this vision to herself. Telling him would only add another burden to his already heavy load. It would not change his mind.

She prayed the gods would give his feet wings when the time came, so he could fly to the stars. And if the gods were kind, she would soon follow.

Dylan returned to her. "Dress love. All is ready to leave."

Chapter Fifteen

The caves were cool, yet the shiver quivering through Rhiannon's belly had nothing to do with temperature. Dylan and Owain, her only companions, passed with her through the first arched doorway to visit three more passages. Each stood like choices in life. The passage to the left was dark, cold, and ended abruptly. The cavern to their right held light, warmth, love, and their secret pool. The dark passage facing them held adventure, danger, and the unknown. They chose the unknown, which took them to an uncertain end.

The torch's fire warmed the gray stone with light but could not chase the chill of dread from her bones. She had felt this unease since entering the caves. Perhaps, it was the closed in feeling or the oppressive darkness that surrounded them. It could be the combination, but mostly it was the vision she'd had before leaving Dylan's room. The vision could be wrong; mayhap it was only her fears plaguing her thoughts. She glanced again at Dylan. He seemed distant, as if his mind resided elsewhere. He had not spoken since entering these dark halls. He didn't like not knowing what she had seen, but he had enough burdens on his shoulders. She would save him this one and hoped she was strong enough to bear it alone.

Dylan's heart pounded. He could feel the rush of blood through his veins as he continued into the dark-cloaked walls. He needed to reach the dragon's fire to warm his soul. It was near, so near he could smell it and taste it. He knew the way, because his heart led. The Dragons called with a silent hum, pulling him ever forward.

The path turned sharply right, taking them to another doorway etched with ancient script. Dylan frowned, wondering what piece of the puzzle lay here. He scraped away years of spider webs with a stroke of his dagger, then held the torch closer.

"Rhiannon, can you read this?"

She stepped next to him. "When fear is conquered to reach the goal, two loves will join to be one soul." She turned to see the fire in Dylan's eyes. This was the first time since leaving the castle that they had shared a closeness. She would not lose him, even if they only remained connected in spirit. They were bound until the end of time. His glance told her he knew it, too.

"It sounds like the words speak to both of you," Owain commented, a knowing smile lifting one side of his mouth.

Dylan took her hand and kissed her palm. "Aye, it does," he answered. His gaze drove the chill from her bones.

Ducking through the archway, Rhiannon followed Dylan into a large open cavern. Owain came next, protecting the rear.

The dome roof was some forty-foot high. Pictures of dragons, white-robed druids, crystal staffs, waterfalls, and the vortex from her vision covered the walls. The drawing showed a large funnel of wind, disappearing into the floor of a rock bed.

The image startled her, causing her to gasp then stumble. The vision of Dylan falling into the open pit, his arms reaching for her, filled her head, and fear gripped her heart so she couldn't breathe.

Owain grabbed her before she could fall. Worry marred his face with a frown. "Be you all right, lass?"

Nay, nay, she would never be all right if she should lose Dylan. Tears clogged her throat, but instead of sharing the fear she answered, "Aye." She smiled to reassure him. "I stubbed my toe on a jutting rock is all."

Owain glanced back, obviously looking for the rock that didn't exist. As they passed by, she ran her fingers over the cold engraved picture, their edges worn smooth in some places. She remembered the day Fianna sent Sheen off to battle. Rhiannon had told her friend if Sheen were her husband, she would not let him go. Fianna said he had to go. It was a matter of pride, and pride meant everything to a man. Now she understood. If she would stop Dylan from fulfilling his quest, he may live, but his pride would take a mortal wound.

Gazing at the vortex once again, she shook her head. Like Fianna, if the end came, she would be there for Dylan. Life was never sure, only how you lived the hours given made the difference. Somehow, with the decision made, her thoughts became clearer, but her fear remained.

Looking at Dylan's broad back and long legs, she marveled again that he was hers. He carried a coil of rope over one shoulder, a sword in one hand, and a torch in another. His jerkin was sleeveless, showing the muscles of his arms as they tightened and bunched with every move. He was ready for any surprise lurking in the dark. Owain managed a bow and a quill of arrows with extra torches. He continually glanced behind, making sure no one followed. It was no wonder the McKays had yet to win a battle. The McGregors had a strong leadership and were always alert.

As they proceeded, the dark seemed hungry to devour what little light they carried. A twitter of foreboding shook her heart. The gloom stood sinister and secretive, unwilling to share anything within its grip. Unease curled up her spine.

She squeezed her hands into fists, then opened them to let warm blood in, only to squeeze them shut again.

A pale lizard scurried between Dylan and her feet, making her gasp. She covered her mouth to prevent a scream as three more followed before their wiggling tails disappeared through a crack in the wall.

"I could do without creatures popping out at me from the dark," Rhiannon said, her hand falling over her heart.

"I shall let them know, my Lady," Owain offered, a large grin curving his lips. She shook her head and smiled.

The cavern narrowed to a passageway again. Then came a sharp right turn before the floor ended, dropping away.

Dylan held his torch out over the hole. Nothing but darkness greeted them. A deep rumbling worked its way up from the abyss, sending with it a blast of hot air.

Dylan flattened Rhiannon against the wall using his body as a shield. Dirt pelted them and one of their torches blow out.

"The beast stirs," Dylan stated, smiling to give Rhiannon comfort. She was strung so tight, he feared she would snap. Her lips pressed against her teeth, and if her hands were not in fists, they shook. She was holding information from him, and it was killing her to do so. Nevertheless, if she chose that path, he would not press her. Instead, he leaned forward kissing her forehead. There had to be a way to ease her fears.

"Aye! What now?" Owain asked, looking from the dark opening in the floor to Dylan. "If the beasts decide to come up from this hole, we have no place to hide."

"Hand me another torch." Dylan held out his hand, waiting for Owain to comply. Taking the unlit torch, he set it to fire with the lit one, and then dropped the flame into the hole.

The torchlight illuminated the walls as it fell to land some twenty feet below. The light showed another darkened passageway. Pieces of a rotted wood ladder clung to the wall, others were scattered across the floor.

"What are you thinking?" Rhiannon asked.

Dylan backed away from the ledge, scanning the slate walls and floor for something to tie a rope to.

"One moment. Here it is," he answered. A rusty iron loop jutted out from the rock wall about hip high to his left. It must have been used to help support the ladder years ago.

"Owain, hold the rope, while I tie this end."

With skillful ease, Dylan secured one end of the rope to the iron ring and gave several good tugs before taking the rest and throwing the length over the side to hang below.

Turning back to Owain, Dylan snagged his brother's gaze. "I will go first to see if the rope holds. When I reach the bottom, pull the rope up, and tie a loop around Rhiannon's waist. Then I want you to lower her, slowly. You follow her."

"I should go first, Dylan. We do not know what lives below, and you are Laird. Your safety is more important than mine," Owain urged, moving to the edge and planting his feet.

"Nay, 'tis not. Here take this." Dylan handed his brother the torch, then snapped the rope tight and made to step off the ledge when Rhiannon grabbed his arm. He turned toward her and saw fear in her eyes.

"Be careful," she urged.

He smiled. "'Tis not far," he said, disappearing over the edge a foot at a time.

"He will be all right," Owain said. Rhiannon turned to meet a warm gaze so like Dylan's. "What troubles you?" he asked, narrowing his eyes.

"What makes you think I am troubled?" she asked, turning again to watch Dylan's descent.

"Do you think I would not notice the changes, lass." His voice softened. "You are not the daring sprite who dressed like a boy and challenged my steel a few weeks ago. Worry for my brother has you strung tight.

"Have you knowledge of the future, or is it fear of the challenge ahead?"

She sucked in air. How could he have guessed? Owain was perceptive, but she could not share her secret. As for the daring sprite of the past, experiences had changed her life, giving her everything she had ever wished for only to cast a threat that it would all be taken away. She felt a tremor of unease and reached for her Moonstone necklace.

"I am afraid, but I will still meet the challenge," she said, lifting her chin. Rhiannon heard him draw in another breath to speak again, but Dylan's yell from below halted his words.

"I am down. Take up the rope."

Dylan picked up the burning torch from the floor. He wanted to explore the passage a short way, while waiting for the others to join him.

As he moved into the passageway a constant roar echoed along the walls, and he could feel the slight vibrations through his feet. The scent of moisture hung heavy in the air.

"Dylan?"

He turned back. "I am here," he said to Rhiannon as she stood on the ledge.

"All right, Rhiannon, let Owain do all the work. Use your good arm to hold onto the rope. I do not want your wound to reopen. Sit on the edge then push off. Owain hold her tight."

"You need not be so pinched, Dylan. I will not be letting your lady come to harm," Owain grumbled.

"Both of you stop it. I was climbing trees and fighting battles not a sennight ago."

"Aye, but she's spirited." Dylan laughed, moving to help untie her, once she reached the floor.

After he freed her, he pulled on the rope twice. "'Tis all yours, Owain."

"Dylan, I am sending the torch down."

"Aye." Dylan looked up and followed the torch's descent, catching it before it hit the ground.

The rope disappeared into the dark above. The sharp sounds of shuffling fell to their hearing, as if Owain was struggling. A shower of pebbles from above made Dylan pull Rhiannon away so nothing could fall on her, then all was quiet.

"Owain," Dylan called, but received no answer. Had one of the Sorcerer's assassins followed them in?

"Dylan!" Rhiannon said, grabbing his shirt. Her thoughts ran parallel to his.

"Owain, you bloody well better answer me."

Metal scraped against rock followed by Owain's voice drifting down to them. "Give me a minute, Dylan. I have no light to see by, and I nearly got my leg tied up in the rope." Owain slid down the cord, jumped the last few feet, and wiped his palms on his kilt. "I am ready, lead on."

"Let us watch our backs. The Sorcerer may send someone to pick us off, or he could have laid traps. I will not underestimate him again."

"'Tis wise," Owain offered. "I have been watching for such."

"The ground moves." Rhiannon stepped closer to Dylan. "Dragons?" she asked, meeting his gaze.

"Nay, the vibration is too constant and with no change in pitch. But 'tis powerful enough to shake the ground with force."

Dylan reentered the passage, knowing the others would

follow. The further they traveled along the path, the louder the noise became.

"The temperature has risen." Dylan wiped the sweat from his forehead. Turning to Rhiannon, he ran his hand down her arm. "Are you well? Would you like some water?"

"Is it cold?" Rhiannon pushed the hair up off her neck.

Dylan pulled out his water skin, handing it to her. "'Tis warm like me I fear." A lopsided grin pasted on his lips.

"Thank you, my Laird." She smiled, lifting the water to her lips and taking two long swallows before speaking. "You have always seen to my comfort."

He leaned closer to whisper. "As you have seen to mine, wench." His thoughts as carnal as his meaning.

"You are wicked."

Dylan threw back his head and laughed. Her smile grew, then she narrowed her eyes and wrinkled her nose. "The odor of mildew is strong here, and the rock walls have darkened with moisture." She handed Dylan the water skin.

"You are changing the subject." Dylan chuckled.

Heat rushed to her cheeks, and she glanced quickly at Owain. He stood watching them. "You are good for him, Rhiannon. I have never seen my brother smile and tease anyone but me." Owain placed his palm flat on the wall, only to have it come away wet. He wiped his hand across his shirt. "And, she's right about the dampness."

Dylan, still smiling, took her arm and pulled it into the crook of his. The path turned left, growing steeper as they went. "This will make the way slick," Owain yelled to be heard above the thunderous roar ahead. "Watch your footing, woman. 'Tis a long way out for help."

"I have her, Owain."

A great blast of air blew up from the darkness. It covered

them all with a fine mist and made the rock floor slippery and hazardous. The torchlights spit and hissed. The flames flipped and snapped like linen on a windy day.

"There's a gate ahead and more ancient script," Dylan shouted over the roar. Mist and spray rolled toward them in clouds through the iron bars of the gate. The writing stood out against the dark stone.

"Love will lead and trust will follow, to vanquish those of promises hollow." Rhiannon turned to Dylan. "What does it mean?"

His frown as well as Owain's told her they were just as puzzled.

"Mayhap 'twill become clear as we move forward?" Owain said, pushing a wet strand of hair from his eyes.

"There is more writing here." Dylan pointed to vertical words on the right doorpost along the iron lock.

Rhiannon stooped down beside the frame. "Hold the torch closer."

"The flame sputters from the moist air, as if it would extinguish, but I can try. Owain, stand back with your torch so if this one goes out we are not left in total darkness."

She ran her fingers over the deeply cut letters, feeling every point and curve. "To accomplish great things," she started, "one must not only act with strength, but with vision." Rhiannon frowned. "This does not rhyme like the words above, and the script is different, more bold."

"Mayhap 'tis a key to the lock," Owain suggested.

"There is a light beyond the gate, in the other chamber," Rhiannon said, wondering how there could be light so far underground. Then the rattle of the bars drew her gaze to Dylan.

He grabbed hold of the iron bars and pulled. Nothing

happened.

Owain moved past Rhiannon, handing her the torch to lend Dylan a hand. He grabbed the bars right below Dylan. "When you are ready give the word."

Dylan planted his feet then nodded. "Aye." Both men pulled. The strain of their muscles made them groan, but the iron door would not open.

"What now?" Owain asked. Both of them labored to catch a breath and leaned against the damp wall.

Dylan shook his head. "Mayhap 'tis rusted shut?"

Then a loud scraping of metal on rock sounded over the thunderous roar of water. Both men looked at the door, and saw it move.

Dylan narrowed his brow and glanced at a silent Rhiannon. Her eyes were closed and her expression serene as she faced the door. Her hands were raised in front of her, reaching for something unseen. As she moved her hands, so did the door, opening with ease.

"'Tis faery magic," Owain said with awe.

"Aye," Dylan laughed.

With the door now standing wide, Rhiannon opened her eyes to smile in triumph. "Some things only a woman can do."

"How?" Owain asked.

"'Twas the saying on the doorpost." Rhiannon shared. "To accomplish great things, one must not only act with strength but with vision. So I but pictured the door opening in my mind."

"Well, sweet lady of wisdom," Dylan bowed, a smile still curving his lips, "lead on."

She handed each man their torches and walked with an extra swing to her hips.

"You do ken, she will be hard to live with now." Owain

watched Rhiannon disappear into the clouds of mist.

"Aye, she will be riding high for a while, but 'tis well deserved."

A shrill scream pierced his head as it echoed through the cavern walls. "Rhiannon!" Dylan yelled, rushing through the door, Owain close behind.

Chapter Sixteen

The room opened up under a great waterfall that dumped into a fast moving underground river. They stepped out onto a wide ledge that ran along the wall of the room.

"Where is she?" Dylan asked, placing one hand over the sword's hilt, while scanning the area.

"I have yet to spot her. Could she have slipped into the water?"

Dylan's gaze followed Owain's to where the roaring river passed beneath a rock wall at the far end of the chamber. Steam bellowed above the hot turbulent water. If she had been sucked under, she would be lost to them.

"Have you noticed this room has lit torches set in the walls," Owain added.

"Are you thinking 'tis the Sorcerer?" Dylan asked.

"Aye."

Another scream came from the direction they had just come.

"This way." Dylan moved back under the falls.

"You saw something?" Owain pulled his sword free and followed close on Dylan's heels.

"Nay, I heard her."

"I heard naught."

"Then she spoke to my thoughts. Here look at this." Dylan indicated another door off to the right of the one they had entered. The clouds of spray had concealed it until now. Something or someone had Rhiannon, and he feared he knew whom.

A dark fabric covered her head. Both hands were tied in front with a scratchy tweed rope that chaffed the skin around her wrists as she was pulled forward. Mayhap it was a physical sense that told her she was being dragged further from Dylan, but what terrified her most was the heat coming from the Moonstone.

She had no idea who led her, but the Sorcerer was close. Her heart raced, and images of torture filled her thoughts. She was forced some distance before the hood was jerked off with such force it pulled her hair. Blinking from the light of brightly burning torches, she covered her eyes with her bound hands. Then she was lifted from behind and laid out on a stone table.

She kicked out at her assailant, freeing herself to roll for the edge of the table. She was acting in desperation. Adrenaline raced through her veins. Her thoughts whirled.

"Hey now, be a good lass and accept your fate," a male voice coaxed.

Stumbling to her feet, she turned to see Teg. "By the snake, 'tis you. Where is Enid? Has she tired of the game so soon?" Rhiannon took a quick glance around, yet kept the stone table between them. The two of them stood alone. So where was the Sorcerer? When Teg made a move toward her from the left, she moved left as well. They played a deadly game of hawk and dove, but he would find out this dove carried sharp talons and a bitter tongue.

"Nay. The lass chose to tangle with my master and become food for his hound. You should learn from her mistake."

Her stomach knotted with the image his words brought forth. Poor Enid. A foul end no one should have to suffer. But nobody could choose a time or method of death. For some it came as a natural consequence of action, but Rhiannon would not concede without a fight. "Oh, aye. I should lay here and be sacrificed without complaint. Beware, Teg, you have no idea of the forces you are tangled in. Good and evil fight to hold the power and the little people will pay dearly for it. Choose your side wisely or be swallowed up."

He made a quick move to the right and she dashed out of reach.

"Just what has the Sorcerer offered that you play his minion? Women? Wisdom? Or gold?" The widening of his eyes gave him away. "*Och,* so 'tis gold. Are you so valuable that he would pay a fortune for your service? You must be a powerful wizard."

"I tire of the chase, Lass. Be reasonable." He puffed for air and leaned on the table. "Going back and forth makes my head spin."

"Tell me, what makes you think he will not kill you and keep the gold when he has what he wants? Has he dealt honorably with others?"

"Do you ever shut your mouth?" His hands fisted on the table. Anger flashed in his eyes. "And quit looking at me with those hypnotic green eyes. They give me the shivers. I am sure the first thing my master will do is carve the tongue from your head then take the sight from those eyes."

"Be a smart man and return me to the Dragon Laird. Save yourself. Come with me and escape the wrath of the Sorcerer. Live to spend your reward."

He rubbed his chin, a frown marring his brow.

She could tell she was getting through to him. "Would

you not rather live as a hero, or have others spit on your grave?"

While he stood thinking, Rhiannon took note of the room in more detail. The stench of death hung heavy in the air. A bloody corpse dangled by one chained arm on the wall behind her. A cold grate and shelves full of pots and dried plants stood to her left. Her one means of escape opened to the passage behind Teg. This was *his* chamber. A place where the blood of many had soaked the stones from his malevolent rituals. This was a place the pure in heart trembled to go.

"I fear I am as caught in this web as you," Teg said, shaking his head. "No doubt 'twill be as you say." His heavy sigh echoed around them.

"Then let us flee to live another day." Hope flared to life in her breast. "Quickly before 'tis too late."

"Aye, come." Teg stepped back and waved her toward the exit. "I am done with this deed."

For some reason she didn't move. This was what she wanted. He was letting her go, but it was too easy. She feared a trick. Looking deep into the man's eyes before he glanced away, gave her the answer. He lied. He would grab her as she went by. Anger squeezed out the hope. Nevertheless, she had to take the chance.

"Stand yonder." She pointed to a spot away from the door. "Once I pass, you may follow. Then I will know your honor is intact."

His gaze shifted from the exit to her, then to the exit once more before stepping back. "It saddens me, this lack of trust, but I will do as you ask. Hurry! We must be away before my master appears."

Her heart beat like a butterfly tossed by the storm erratic and fast. Her gaze never left him as she inched closer to escape. When she stood half the distance between him and the door, she caught a quick flicker of his eyes and knew he would jump on her, but she was quicker. His fingers barely grazed her as she dashed to the door.

Her sense of freedom was cut short as she ran into a solid wall of flesh and sharp talons cut into her arm. She screamed as a cloak of evil shrouded her, stealing her breath. Demonic pleasure emanated from him in waves, drowning the purity of her soul and stealing her life's essence.

"You are mine, at long last." The Sorcerer laughed a deep-throated growl of victory.

"Turn loose. You are killing me." Rhiannon whispered. The Sorcerer dropped her arm, and she fell to the floor. Her strength gone, she bowed her head, and her shoulders sagged. *Dylan hear me. I need you.*

"Do you think he can defeat me?" He asked from under his hood.

For a moment, Rhiannon wondered if he could read minds. Then decided he only sensed the link between her and Dylan.

"How am I so weak?"

"Meg should have known better than to keep you uninformed. Darkness swallows light. It feeds and grows powerful as the light diminishes. You will make me invincible."

Her mind raced. If darkness could swallow light than couldn't light burn away darkness? There had to be away to turn the tables.

The Sorcerer turned his back on her and walked over to the stone table. She sat knowing she did not have the strength to escape. He had sucked it out of her. She raised her gaze to him, but he had turned toward Teg "You are a careless man.

You play with what is not yours and almost lost her. I will deal with your failure."

Teg's eyes grew large as they darted from the Sorcerer to Rhiannon. "'Twas I who brought her here for you, master. I always follow your orders and have been faithful."

Rhiannon could see the man shaking in fear. His fate had been sealed from the beginning, because he was blinded by greed.

"Aye, and here is your reward." The Sorcerer raised his hand and pointed at Teg as words fell from his lips.

"Please!" Teg begged, before he screamed and bent over, holding his gut. He fell to the floor, twisting and crying in pain.

She could not watch and not try to help. She turned to look again out the door. A large black hound trotted in past Rhiannon to sit at the feet of the Sorcerer, giving no notice to the moans coming from the corner.

Without warning, a vision passed before her gaze and strength seeped slowly back to her limbs. Dylan drew closer. He was reaching out to share himself. She could feel the beat of his heart. She closed her eyes and drew in a deep calming breath.

The screams stopped abruptly, and she glanced in Teg's direction.

"He lives." The sinister voice answered from behind her. She jerked around to face the enemy. "You will come now. I have need of you."

He grabbed her arm and dragged her over to the table before picking her up and laying her on top of it. She tried to raise her head. It felt heavy, but she succeeded. "Your doom is sure," she spit out.

When he grabbed her wrist, she tried to pull away, but her

arm shook with fatigue. She watched in growing panic as he took rope and tied her wrist to an iron ring at the corner of the table.

The fabric of his robes swished as he moved to the other side to do the same with her other wrist. Then he flipped back his hood and revealed his face.

She could not help the gasp that escaped. He was not the monster everyone had guessed. His hair lay in golden waves around a handsome face. He looked more like the light's messenger, but his eyes were icy, no warm thoughts played in his mind. Evil had rotted away their depths, so now they mirrored the wickedness festering in his soul. The contrast between beauty and beast was unsettling.

"You can see why I hide my face. 'Twould be hard to instill fear and respect while seeing it."

"Why show it to me?" Each moment that passed brought her more strength. A sinister twist curled his lips, causing her to shudder. He flattened his palm on her belly then lower. She jerked away.

"Unhand me!"

"So, Enid spoke truth. The Dragon Laird breeched your maidenhead." He frowned, then slapped her across the face. The throbbing pain brought tears to her eyes and she tasted blood, but she turned back and smiled at him. He would not defeat her.

"Aye, 'twas given to him gladly."

"Your mother cheated me out of first blood, by giving herself to Gian, but now I will have my due. 'Twill be my face sweating over your body that your eyes will last see. And 'twill be my rod between your legs that you will last feel before I pull the blade across your neck."

He walked over to the shelves and picked up a ritual

dagger, twisting the four-inch blade smoothly within his hand. Walking back to her, he spoke one word, and a fire burst to flame in the grate. Rhiannon jumped and the bindings dug cruelly into her wrists. This feeling of helplessness fed her fear. Not being able to struggle was beyond cruel.

As he leaned over her, the flash of the light on the blade caught her attention. Her breathing quickened, and the sour taste of terror filled her mouth.

"In begetting children, Gian and Meg combined their powers in you. In taking the life force from you, I shall be more powerful than all creation."

He pulled up her skirt to the waist exposing her lower half. An insane gleam sparkled in his eyes. She could not let this man rule. This was what Dela had seen. A scream built up inside to swell in her throat.

Then a whisper crossed her thoughts. Dylan stood just outside the door. She had nothing to fear, but could she keep the Sorcerer distracted. Mayhap she could by making him angry. Strong emotions clouded the senses, and consumed all else. Powerful he may be, but he was mortal like other men and could be killed. She needed to be careful not to make him too angry, else he would kill her outright.

"What of the dragons?"

"What?" He shook his head, as if coming out of a trance.

"The dragons carry more magic than any human can."

"I have them within my power." The Sorcerer seemed to swell with his boast. "They are weak of mind." He ran a finger along her leg and up her thigh. She tried to move away from his touch but his claws dug into her flesh, holding her in place.

"Only the young are. The adults can not be turned so easily. They will devour you just like they would any man."

Anger marked his brow as he leaned close, his breath fanning her cheek. "Mayhap at present, but now I will have your power as well." He brought the blade to rest along her neck, making a small cut before there was a whoosh and a thump. The Sorcerer cried out and stumbled back. An arrow had sliced through his elbow to pierce his side, pining his arm to his body.

Rhiannon looked up to see Dylan in the doorway. A look of black rage twisted his face, yet he was wonderful to behold. With his jaw tight and his fists clenched around the bow, he looked like her avenging angel. Her heart raced with excitement. She wanted to run to him and be wrapped in his strong arms. Together they could defeat evil.

"Beware the hound," she yelled just as the Sorcerer spoke, and the animal passed around the table to attack. Dylan dropped the bow and pulled out the Singing Sword. As the hound leaped for his throat, he sidestepped and swung the blade, taking the head from the beast. The body hit the earthen floor with a thunk, but Dylan had his gaze locked on the Sorcerer.

"She is mine!" The evil man bellowed.

"Nay!" Dylan countered still advancing. "She's mine." Dylan felt the power of the dragons pour through his veins. He would tear the man apart for touching her. Her fear and pain had twisted in his gut until he promised revenge, but first he would see to her safety.

The Sorcerer raised his good hand palm up and spoke a few words. A wicked smile curved his lips.

Unease wormed its way into Dylan's stomach, just as he walked into something solid. He staggered backward unsure what had happened. He saw nothing in front of him, yet the way was blocked. Reaching out he found the surface hard and cold but invisible. A Sorcerer's trick, a way to keep him from Rhiannon. Panic poured like a river into his heart. He pounded on the invisible wall with his fist, but it didn't give. With growing desperation, he slid his hands over the shield from right to left, up and down, looking for any way through.

"She belongs to me," the Sorcerer said, a note of victory in his voice. He sliced through Rhiannon's blouse baring her breast and moved the dagger slowly along her bare legs inch by inch without a mark to reach what lay between. "I wonder, Dragon Laird, will you watch as I reap the rewards from between her legs, or mayhap I shall carve my symbol in her breasts."

"Nay!" Dylan screamed, pounding on the wall. "Touch her and I will kill you." His gaze focused on Rhiannon, wanting to be as close as he could. Her eyes were small and sunken with bruising underneath. The cut at her throat slowly oozed blood to pool in the scoop of her neck. Her breathing came sharp and rapid with fear. He could do nothing to help her while trapped behind this invisible shield.

Then as the Sorcerer brought the tip of the dagger down toward her heart, a blinding light radiated out from her necklace. The Moonstone.

The Sorcerer cried and threw the dagger down to rub at his eyes with his remaining working hand. "You have blinded me, bitch."

"I have found your weakness," she said.

As, Dylan turned away from the light, his gaze fell on the Singing Sword in his hand. Gian had said it would cut through anything. Would it cut through a magic shield wall?

Stepping back, he raised the sword overhead and sliced it through the air diagonally. There was a pull on the blade as it moved through the wall. Then he brought it slicing through the opposite way and felt a release.

Unsure of what he had done, he stepped forward with his hand out and found the wall gone. As he stepped past where the barrier had stood, the blinding light from the Moonstone died.

Dylan met the Sorcerer's watery gaze and knew the moment the man realized the spell was broken. The Sorcerer gabbed for the dagger intending to hurl it at Dylan, but another arrow flew through the air pass Dylan's head to pierce the bone in the mage's shoulder, rendering the arm useless. The scream was one of fury, as if the Sorcerer could see his defeat coming.

After a quick glance to see where the arrow had come from, and a quick nod to his brother, Dylan raced to Rhiannon and sliced through her bonds.

"I knew you would make it," she whispered. "I feared only to face him alone."

"Love, you were never alone. I was with you. And you have far too much spirit to be defeated"

Dylan lifted her over his shoulder and noticed Owain notching another arrow. Holding her legs to his chest, Dylan backed from the room to shield her with his body.

The Sorcerer's eyes turned red. He shook with the force of his anger and screamed again. Then a chant fell from his lips as he charged them.

"Dylan, he is casting a spell. Hurry!" Rhiannon warned.

As Dylan stepped trough the door, he swung the sword up to crack the doorframe, slicing through wood and stone, causing it to collapse. The rocks fell like rain, slowly filling the exit and cutting the Sorcerer off.

"You will die!" The Sorcerer yelled over the clatter of rock. "I have seen to it. You will die."

Through the falling debris, Dylan saw a man from the

corner of the chamber stand and stumble up behind the Sorcerer. A dagger caught the firelight before he sank it into the evil man's back. The Sorcerer arched, his mouth open in a silent scream, as the rocks and dirt from above sealed the door closed like the lid on a coffin.

Dylan hurried away, followed closely by Owain. They ran back to where they had left their torches, then Dylan sat Rhiannon on her feet and pushed her against the wall to kiss her. His mouth, hungry for the taste of her, drank from her lips. His hands dove into her hair on both sides of her head and his hard body pressed close. That such evil could have touched his lady was more than he could bear. He wanted to erase the fear and anger with the stroke of his hand and the kiss of his lips. She was his and no one else would dare touch her

"By the gods, I feared to lose you."

"Aye," she whispered. Her hands were busy running over his shoulders and into his hair, while her lips joined his.

Dylan stepped back and lifted her chin. "The cut in your neck is gone," he said, looking from one side to the other.

"'Twas the Moonstone. I felt the heat burn away the wound and restore my strength."

"Aye. I see the beautiful sparkle in your eyes once more."

A throat cleared close by, and they both turned to see Owain leaning against the wall, watching with a frown. "If you do not mind, I would like to finish this quest and be away home."

"Aye," Dylan said, turning back to Rhiannon. He smoothed her hair behind her ear. "I would have you alone this night in my bed."

Owain groaned and Rhiannon's cheeks turned a bright pink. Dylan decided he liked the color. "Let us be away then," he said, taking up one of the torches.

"I hate grumpy Sorcerers and hungry dragons," Owain stated, taking the last torch.

Rhiannon laughed, and Dylan squeezed her hand. Now that he had reclaimed her, he was not going to be separated again. They reached the waterfall within minutes. As they moved along the wall, the light from the torches cast dancing rainbows in the spray. The thunder of the water shook the ground beneath them. Here was a power of nature in its most wondrous form.

"This path leads to another opening ahead. We are close to the dragon's lair." Dylan said.

"How do you know this?" Rhiannon asked, frowning.

"I feel it."

Reaching the opening, they had to bend at the waist to enter the next chamber. They stumbled through only to face the open jaws of a snarling dragon.

Chapter Seventeen

Carved into the wall of granite in front of them was a gaping dragon's mouth. Cautiously, Owain stepped forward, moving the lit torch closer.

The flickering flame was swallowed up in a black opening no bigger than the width of a man's shoulders. Air was sucked into the mouth, as if the dragon devoured all that entered. A whining sound moaned from the dark depths like a banshee singing someone's death chant. They would have to squeeze to make it through.

"Do we go on?" Owain asked, looking to Dylan.

Rhiannon took Dylan's silence for consent. "There has to be another way." Her trepidation made her voice high with strain. Each step they took brought Dylan closer to danger, and fear of the foreboding event made a shiver of dread slither down her back.

Dylan took her chin between his fingers, bringing her full attention to him. "The hole looks small but 'tis the way in."

"How can you be so sure?" She wanted to believe that he could conquer the beasts, but the knowledge of his fate made her question his decision.

"The beast calls to me." He gently kissed her forehead. "I must go. I have no other choice."

"Dylan, my skirt will hamper me. Cut it above my knees so I can move."

Dylan glanced from Rhiannon to Owain and back to her.

"He has seen my knees 'afore. Be quick, and have it done," she said, frowning.

Dylan grunted, then knelt down in front of her, slicing through the fabric and throwing the scrap to the ground.

Owain pulled a dagger from his belt. "Shall I take the lead or will you?"

"Hand me the torch. I will lead. Rhiannon will follow, and you will protect our rear as 'afore." Dylan gave her a meaningful look that spoke of love and his faith in her. Putting the blade of his dagger between his teeth, he entered the hole.

The tunnel was a rough-edged tube that pressed against them from all sides. As she pushed further into the dragon's jaw, Rhiannon tried to concentrate on the torchlight shining ahead of Dylan, but at times his body blocked it from view, leaving only the confining darkness. The ceiling hung a mere few inches above her head, so she could not relieve the twisted muscles in her neck and back. Each time Dylan pushed forward dust and dirt clouded the air. She felt as if someone was covering her face with a cloth, closing off her air supply.

Fear invaded her mind like a serpent, coming closer to sink its powerful fangs into her heart. Panic skittered along the edge of her thoughts, taunting her. They were in a tomb of rock, buried alive. She did not want to die trapped under mountains of earth and rock. With every shallow breath, she felt like the rock was, pressing in on her.

From somewhere beyond Dylan, she heard a roar. The ground trembled, loosening a shower of dirt. She shook her head and fought to control another surge of panic. A desire to scream broke free in a moan. She gritted her teeth and desperately searched for the torchlight beyond Dylan.

"Rhiannon?" When she didn't answer, Dylan cursed. He

had heard her moan, but had no way to turn and help her if she faltered in the cramped space. "I'm almost through. I see the opening." The tightness of the tunnel had tested his nerves. He had to use his arms to drag his body forward. In a short time, they had become scrapped and raw. A protruding rock sliced into his shoulder, and warm blood dampened his arm, but nothing would keep him from his goal.

The powerful gusts of wind announced the end of their struggles. With one last mighty push to the rim, Dylan tumbled out into a large cavern. He reached back, pulling Rhiannon free and into his arms.

"Rhiannon, 'tis over. Take a deep breath." He smoothed the hair from her face. She gave a nod but continued to grasp his shirt. With her trembling body held tightly to him, he removed the blade from his teeth and awaited Owain.

As the other man stepped forth, he glanced around. "What is this place?"

Gusts of wind pulled at them, making it difficult to stand upright. As Dylan held up the torch, Rhiannon gasped. She had seen this place before. "'Tis the vortex of my dream." Here was where she had seen Dylan's death. Her grip became stronger around his waist. If he felt her tightly clinging hands, he gave no notice of it. Her heart ran with the speed of a frightened bird. The test had come.

"This path only leads to our left," Dylan observed. "It seems the river from the waterfall runs under the tunnel we have just exited and passes to our right around this great black hole in the floor."

"You dreamed of this place, Rhiannon?"

"Aye, Owain." She gave a shiver.

Lightning cracked inside the large funnel of spinning wind then disappeared into the black hole below them. "By the blade! Watch yourself. Stay to the wall. Those gusts may pull us into hell," Dylan warned.

Owain led as they moved along the path. "Dylan, I see another opening ahead."

Awestruck, they came to a stop when they saw what Owain had indicated. This new entrance stood some thirty feet high and twenty feet wide. Inside the room, a large green-scaled body passed in front of the opening to disappear deeper within a room beyond.

"'Tis the dragon lair," Dylan whispered, his face alight with wonder, his breathing ramped.

"We have found the eternal gate," Rhiannon said. "'Tis here we will see prophecy fulfilled."

"I see no gate," Owain said, his brow narrowing.

"Nay, you would not. 'Tis of another realm, another plane. Yet I see the gate's beauty with my heart." She turned to Dylan. "Can you see the crystal gate, Dylan?" He must see it if they were to close it.

"I see only the nesting beast within."

Taking a good look into the dragon's lair beyond the opening, she felt the blood rush from her body. "We must close the gate before the beasts see us, or we are all dead. That large green female is nesting and will attack to protect her eggs." She turned to Dylan, the dragon's power had him enthralled. "Please look at me, Dylan."

His jaw hardened, and his brow narrowed. His neck muscles strained, as if he pulled his gaze from the reclining beasts with great effort.

When his gaze finally settled on hers, She took his face between her hands. She saw him relax with her touch. "I know the pull of their power is great, even more so for you who carry their mark, but you must resist. We must become as one, using our love and the beat of our joined hearts."

She took his hand and placed it over her heart. "Close your eyes, my Love and feel my heart. Think of nothing else, but my love for you."

She put her hand over his heart. Seeking out of her body and into his, she found the ring of his heartbeats sang a different tune from hers. She had to make them ring the same. Listening and meditating, the two rhythms became louder, stronger. She inserted a reminder of the night of choosing. The power of it ran through their veins, and it was as if their souls recognized the other, uniting their heartbeats to sing in unison. They moved onto a realm all their own.

"Dylan, open your eyes and see me," Rhiannon asked.

Slowly at first, he blinked then met her gaze. His eyes carried a fire, burning hotter than anything she had ever seen. Dragon's fire. He held it within, with strength beyond mortal men. She worried what it was costing him and if it would burn him from the inside out.

Rhiannon slid her hand from his chest then down his arm to take his hand, never losing contact with his body. She would not lose their bond, for to do so would break the union of their hearts and all would be lost.

"Look at the gate, Dylan. Do you see it now?"

He pulled his burning gaze from hers and glanced toward the dragon's lair. "Aye, 'tis as bright as the sun."

"Tell me what you see." She had to know if he really saw the gate, or if he was delusional.

"Two large doors made of crystal shards that glow in a rainbow of colors. 'Tis like looking at the gates of heaven. Gold hinges hold it to the rock walls."

"They stand open Dylan, and you, the Dragon Laird, are the one chosen to see the breech closed until the beast's season comes once more."

"Aye, I see the truth of it."

"'Tis your strength that is needed, but know this, I must be touching you at all times to keep our powers as one."

"How are the doors sealed?"

"I will see to that. Now quickly, before we have to work against the dragons."

As they moved toward the large opening, Owain shouted, "What are you doing? Stay back."

"Do not interfere!" Rhiannon yelled, yet never took her eyes off Dylan.

When Dylan reached to close the first gate, a large female turned in their direction. Her prominent nostrils widened as she tested the air.

"We have not much time I fear. She will attack, be you friend or foe. Now, Dylan."

"This gate is not light in weight." The muscles in his arms tightened and bunched with strain as he pulled one side closed and latched it at the bottom in a gold bracket. "One more."

The other gate stood wider and would take more work to close. To reach it meant stepping into the dragon's line of vision. They knew the danger they faced should they be spotted but they would have to enter the lair.

Dylan glanced toward Rhiannon at his side, his chest heaving from exertion. The need for caution upper-most in his mind. Her gaze held all the love she carried, nodding her encouragement.

He would not let her down. Taking a deep breath, Dylan grabbed the final gate and pulled. His muscles stretched and swelled. His thighs rippled as he leaned backward using his weight, as well as his strength, to move the gate.

The green-scaled serpent raised her head to the ceiling and

gave out a deafening roar. It vibrated through the walls, shaking the very bones within their bodies. She lowered her head and pulled her massive body up to face them.

"Dylan, she's going to charge. Hurry!"

He pulled from a deep reservoir of strength and the door moved by inches. He feared he would not make it.

Smoked curled from the dragon's nose as she snorted. Then she raised her horned head and roared again weaving her head back and forth until it appeared that no air remained in her lungs. Her sides expanded as she sucked in air with a hiss.

She lowered her horns and lumbered toward them with more speed than her large form would seem to permit. The ground trembled as she charged the gate where they stood.

Dylan had three foot to go before the gate would latch when the dragon's massive scaled head swung. Rhiannon screamed. Dylan added a yell to his strength and closed the gate just as the dragon hit.

The force of the charge against the closed gate, threw Dylan and Rhiannon away. Out of the corner of her eye, she saw Dylan hit the far wall. The force threw her toward the vortex and the bottomless black hole.

Rhiannon screamed and dug her nails and feet into the rock floor, trying to slow her momentum, but the dark pit came closer, a yawning chasm that held only death.

Owain passed her line of vision as he threw himself between her and the circling column of air. He pushed her to one side but he could not stop himself from falling. One moment the security of rock was under him then emptiness.

He looked up to see Rhiannon leaning over the ledge with her hand, reaching down for him, but he couldn't grasp it. He felt the wind toss him and snatch the whisper of her name from his lips before the darkness sucked him down.

He had the sensation of flying, then lightning crackled around and through him. Heat warmed his cold fingers and ran along his arms and legs. Any thought of lost love, sadness, happiness, and pain left him, as the heat burned into his brain and heart, encasing him in brilliant fire. Then he felt nothing at all.

A cry of such pain came from behind Rhiannon before Dylan's hands seized her, pulling her back from the abyss. She was shaking all over.

"The dream. The dream." A shudder ran through her. "'Twas not your death I saw. 'Twas Owain's," she cried.

The loud roar and thrashing of the dragon brought her pain-clouded mind to the gate. She raised a shaking hand, palm open toward the gate and sang. Her voice wavered a little with the emotions she held back, yet she sang all notes loud and clear. She would seal the gate before she gave in to her sorrow.

When she sang the last high note, fire appeared in colors of blue, green, and yellow along the seam of the gate. It started at the top in bright sparks and danced its way to the stone floor to disappear.

Then an image of a rock wall fell like sand over the opening, concealing the entrance once more from human eyes. Rhiannon wrapped both arms around Dylan's stiff shoulders and let the tears come in a low, tortured sob. All the pain and fear poured from her heart.

Dylan sat holding Rhiannon, reliving that horrible scene of Owain slipping over the edge of the vortex. Gone! His brother sucked from this life with no chance to bid farewell.

Such oppressing loneliness sat on his shoulders. A suffocating sensation tightened over his throat. A deep agonizing groan slipped past his lips. The pressure of tears pushed at the back of his eyes, but he could not cry. The pain ran too deep and raw, burning like acid in his stomach. Instead, he let Rhiannon weep for him.

Holding her tightly, he found the silence wide and yawning. A parallel to his mourning. Rocking slowly back and forth, Dylan allowed himself memories of his childhood with his brother. He saw them racing on horseback along the moors, testing their skills at swords, laughing together in victory, and consoling each other in loss.

"Finally to each faithful warrior comes his rest," Dylan whispered. Her soft hand moved along his jaw and down his throat to rest over his heart.

Light filled the cavern by slow degrees, as they huddled together on the cold hard ground. A single sunbeam fell to circle them in warmth.

Dylan looked up. Night had fallen away to reveal a large opening in the cavern ceiling above them. That was how the dragons had entered their world. He and Rhiannon would use it to make their way out. Dylan raised Rhiannon's tear reddened face to his and placed a gentle kiss on her lips.

"The quest is over, and I have my treasure." He ran a finger over her cheek. "Let us head home."

She nodded. "Aye, my Love. Home."

Epilogue

Dylan and Rhiannon stood inside the sacred ring of stones, her hands clasped in his as they faced one another. Meg, Giver of Life stood over them speaking words of devotion, love, faithfulness, but he heard little of it. His heart beat too loudly in his ears, and the wonder of the ceremony clouded his thoughts. She was to be his wife, but all he could think of was kissing those lips and tasting the flesh below her ear.

"Dylan?" Rhiannon prompted.

"Aye?"

She smiled and nodded as if he had done something right. Meg wrapped a golden ribbon around their wrists.

"With his consent I give you Laird McGregor and his wife, Lady Rhiannon," Meg announced.

A mighty roar filled the air as the villagers cheered. "You can kiss me now," Rhiannon whispered.

A deep smile curved his lips as he stepped forward, grabbing her around the waist and bringing his lips down to fed hungrily on hers. He was a man of little patience these days. He wanted to fill his life with all he had missed.

The cheers soon waned, and he stepped back with a promise to have her alone as soon as possible. It was not until the first villager stepped forward that a change hung in the air. One after another, people came to lay flowers at his feet. When he glanced toward Rhiannon, there were tears in her eyes.

"They pay homage to you. They honor the Dragon Laird for putting his life in danger to save theirs. No longer do they see the curse, only the man I have always known."

Warmth wrapped around him like a blanket as each clan member came to bow before him. This day he was handed all he desired, and the power of it stood overwhelming.

The celebration ran all day with dancing, races, eating, and drinking. Now the pink sky told of the night's birth and his chance to be alone with Rhiannon.

Dylan walked up to one of the giant stones in the sacred ring and ran his fingers tenderly over a name engraved there. A sad smile traced his lips. "I fear you would have beat me this day at swords." There was a long pause as he tried to control the pain. "I took Rhiannon as wife this day. Something you would have agreed with. You should have been standing by my side." His words caught in his full throat. "I miss you, brother."

Dylan turned to seek out Rhiannon, needing her. As if sensing him, she turned from instructing a lad on swordplay to look at him. She smiled and held out her hand beckoning to him. He passed his hand over the name once more before following his heart. On the stone the words read.

>"Owain McGregor
>*When your quest is done,*
>*May the gods lead you home."*

About the Author

Deborah Lynne has a love for all things romantic and magical. It is the heartbeat of all humans. She first started writing stories in first grade with a friend drawing the pictures. She held on to her secret passion through high school and won various writing awards. After graduation, she met her soul mate, David, and they married in 1982.

Ms. Lynne studied commercial art in college, developing several commercials for channel 6, as well as menus for some top restaurants in Florida, but her love of the written word held fast.

Along with her husband, she has two young daughters to share life with. Deborah has completed four novels and one short story with many others in the works. Her published works have appeared in health magazines, newsletters, and other short story publications. She is the founder of Taylor's Writing Guild and several other independent writers groups. She also works as an Editor for Echelon Press helping other young authors attain their dreams.

Visit Deborah Lynne at
www.Deborah-Lynne.com

Wild Montana Hearts

Sarah Storme

Working as the lead horse wrangler for the Green Ridge Ranch and clinging to the only family she has left, Meg holds tight to her dreams.

Ian Drake has big plans for his new property. By breaking the Green Ridge into cabin sites he plans to make a bundle. But when happiness with an unlikely spitfire becomes more important than business, can he save his fortune and his heart?

ISBN 1-59080-127-X

To order, visit our web catalog at
http://www.echelonpress.com/catalog/

Or ask your local bookseller!

Dana Elian
Music of my Heart

2003 EPPIE Finalist
"Four stars!" –Romantic Times

    Adrianna Whitaker has a lot of thinking to do. Staying behind at the hotel while the rest of the band and crew flies home for Thanksgiving sounds like a great idea. Luke Preston needs a break after five months on the road, and a week of uninterrupted peace and quiet is just too good to pass up. So much for solitude.

    Without the band and crew around for distraction, Luke and Adrianna find that mutual admiration and respect is only the tip of the iceberg. A wonderful sonata of passion and compassion sizzles just below the surface. Soon the unexpected symphony has Adrianna wishing for things that can never be, and Luke entertaining thoughts of fatherhood.

    With the help of one very sassy angel, perhaps these old friends will finally see what's been right in front of them for years.

ISBN 1-59080-035-4

To order, visit our web catalog at
http://www.echelonpress.com/catalog/

Or ask your local bookseller!

SECOND CHANCE at FOREVER
NATALIE J. DAMSCHRODER

"Highly recommended." --WordWeaving

Having just moved to a new city, Angie Detmer is determined to get on with her life. After being left widowed and penniless by her cheating husband, she has nothing but the unborn child she carries and a scant few possessions she has managed to save. She will never again be owned by a man, and that includes the sexy superintendent for her new apartment.

Michael Ripley can't seem to get on with his life. Left to his own grief by the death of his wife and their unborn baby, he's bent on working himself through his debts and his despair. In order to do that, he holds down four jobs, the most lucrative as a male dancer. Even still, he feels compelled to take care of his new tenant, whether she want him to or not.

Neither expects the gentle bond that grows between them as Michael fights against his growing attraction to Angie and as Angie fights to maintain her independence.

ISBN 1-59080-005-2

To order, visit our web catalog at
http://www.echelonpress.com/catalog/

Or ask your local bookseller!

BLAIR WING
HOUSE of CARDS

"4 ½ Roses! Sensual, steamy and passionate."
--A Romance Review

    Sydney Rawlins is on the run with nowhere to go and no one to trust. Her brother is accused of murder and presumed dead, and a priceless piece of 200 year old art is missing. Refusing to give up hope, Sydney will do whatever it takes to find the truth even if it means losing her heart--and possibly her life--to a man with too many faces.

    Graham Montgomery is not who he appears to be and the fewer people who know this, the better. Betrayal leads him on a dangerous journey to find peace with his life and past. With ties to both sides of the law, he has no time to waste protecting a headstrong woman determined to get herself killed in the name of justice.

    The bright lights of the Vegas set a backdrop for intrigue and betrayal in a world of politics and art where no one will come out unscathed.

ISBN 1-59080-187-3

        To order, visit our web catalog at
        http://www.echelonpress.com/catalog/

        Or ask your local bookseller!

Secrets of the Sea
Leslie Burbank

Lord Nerus
When an assignment leads Theodora "Red" Redmon, a skeptical reporter to Scotland, her main goal is to debunk a myth. But then she finds herself in a place that time forgot and attracted to Lord Nerus, a legend destined to steal her heart. Can this merman prove that love is real, no matter what?

Lady Syren
Seeking a prize more valuable than anything, Lady Syren makes a bargain with a notorious pirate. How bad could marriage to Keirnan "The Black" Macleod be, he is after all human, and that is what she wants more than anything. Will the treasure of love make a woman of this mermaid?

ISBN 1-59080-193-8

To order, visit our web catalog at
http://www.echelonpress.com/catalog/
Or ask your local bookseller!

Cursed Comes Christmas

Alexis Hart, Pamela Johnson, Blair Wing

"A magically woven tale!"
--Kathleen de la Lama, author of *The Fool's Journey*

It began in 1799 with the love of Ian MacLachlan and Elizabeth Sinclair. Two lovers whom fate cast into a curse that would test their love through time.

The Sinclairs and the MacLachlans will see their clans joined in peace on Christmas Day, but when Elizabeth bursts into her intended's chambers, she is shocked to find him in the arms of another. In a moment of blinding jealousy, her doubt sets the star-crossed lovers on a journey through time with a mission. They must correct the errors of fate by bringing three lost couples back together. Only when the quest is completed can Ian and Elizabeth be together again.

Join Ian MacLachlan and Elizabeth Sinclair as, through the centuries, they help Lucinda and Flynn, Maggie and Ryan, Chandra and Duncan, find the love they lost and thus right the wrongs of the past.

ISBN 1-59080-025-7

To order, visit our web catalog at
http://www.echelonpress.com/catalog/

Or ask your local bookseller!

Crumbs in the Keyboard

Stories From Courageous Women Who Juggle Life & Writing

"This is wonderful!"
--Fern Michaels, New York Times best selling author

Eighty authors come together with words of wisdom, encouragement, humor, and true-life stories of what it is like to juggle the demands of a career and maintaining relationships with those around them. Each author is donating 100% of her royalties from the sale of Crumbs to The Center for Women and Families in Louisville, Kentucky. Echelon Press is matching those monies dollar for dollar. By purchasing Crumbs, you will help in the fight against domestic violence.

ISBN 1-59080-096-6

To order, visit our web catalog at
http://www.echelonpress.com/catalog/

Or ask your local bookseller!

Printed in the United States
1301100002B/55-96